For Art's Sake

OTHER BOOKS BY W.O. MITCHELL

Who Has Seen the Wind
Jake and the Kid
The Kite
The Vanishing Point
How I Spent My Summer Holidays
Dramatic W.O. Mitchell
Since Daisy Creek
Ladybug, Ladybug ...
According to Jake and the Kid
Roses Are Difficult Here

For Art's Sake

A Novel by

W.O. MITCHELL

A DOUGLAS GIBSON BOOK

M&S

All of the characters in this book are fictitious, and any resemblance to actual persons living or dead is purely coincidental.

Canadian Cataloguing in Publication Data

Mitchell, W.O. (William Ormond), 1914–
For art's sake

ISBN 0-7710-6050-5

PS8526.I53F67 1992 C813'.54 C92-094744-1 PR9199.3.M47F67 1992

Printed and bound in Canada by Trigraphic
The paper used in this book is acid-free

A Douglas Gibson Book
McClelland & Stewart Inc.
The Canadian Publishers
481 University Avenue
Toronto, Ontario
M5G 2E9

For Merna,
as always my creative partner

With gratitude to
The Faculty of Social Work
The University of Calgary
and
Louis Muhlstock

Part One

Globe and Mail, Monday, July 2
Priceless Artworks Stolen At Livingstone University

Thirty-one priceless art treasures by world-class artists disappeared from Livingstone University Art Gallery sometime during the weekend in Western Canada's largest-ever art robbery. Missing are 16 woodcuts, one etching, and three engravings by Albrecht Dürer, which formed a large part of the private collection of Maxwell Lampert, the well-known Texas oilman. The stolen artworks, on loan for a 20-day showing, are given a tentative estimated value of $1,500,000, though experts admit the works are irreplaceable. The best of the Dürer prints making up this stolen collection are worth well over $50,000 each, according to the vice-president of a major international art auction firm in New York.

The stolen pictures date back 450 years, a span of time that most westerners are scarcely able to comprehend, their interest in the distant past being confined to pre-glacial times when dinosaurs roamed the prairies and foothills, dropping the deposits that countless millennia later would turn into coal and oil and gas, the provinces' major commodities.

According to art experts, Dürer was the main channel through which the Italian Renaissance style was introduced into northern Germany. One local art dealer has said that Dürer is as important to German art as Michelangelo or da Vinci to Italian.

Police say thieves gained entrance to the library block of Livingstone University campus, where the gallery is located, by breaking a basement window which provided access to a locked hallway in the building.

By smashing through a thick glass window reinforced with wire, the thieves are believed to have been able to unlock the door from the hallway that leads into the gallery.

See PRICELESS ART page A2

As well as the Dürer prints, a lily pond painting by Monet and several by artists of the Group of Seven were stolen.

A police spokesman described the raid as "very daring" and "obviously the work of professionals."

Thomas Parsons, Livingstone University vice-president in charge of security, was not available for comment.

I

Chirped awake by those robins out there; next there'd be the sparrows and their noisy young in that nest tucked up under the roof peak. He looked at his watch: 5:13. Must have been well after midnight when he'd dropped off; five hours' sleep at the most, and that was all he was going to get, because now it was about time for the magpies to flutter and squawk, then the poet's turn on the other side of the bedroom partition to sneeze again and again and again.

Five years of lonely nights without Irene beside him. "Sleep no more," quoth the magpie. "Never more."

What a bird junkie she had been – probably the main reason she'd talked him into getting the place out here. Hated sparrows and butcher birds, nest-robbing starlings most of all. Unlike most people she'd loved magpies. "Bishop birds" she called them. "They have such avian dignity in their surplice and cassock."

What a creative partner she had been. How often she had broken art blocks for him, pushing and shoving him out into the studio to go flat on his ass again. "Come on, Art, you're always telling your students to keep on trying every day – every week – every month – every year. Same goes for you too, doesn't it?"

As always right again, Irene.

At the bottom of the stairs, his tail pluming a morning

welcome, the Professor greeted him with his plastic toy, small and quite indestructible, like a miniature black pineapple in his jaws. Until the coffee percolator was bubbling, the dog carried on his usual five-minute conversation, grunting and growling, whining and muttering and repeating, always with a scold note because Art still was not listening carefully to him or was too stupid to understand what he was trying his best to tell him.

Erich Fromm had been all wrong in *The Art of Loving* with his thesis that humans were the only animals possessing an interior lighted up by consciousness. This golden retriever did have an illuminated self. Otherwise, why would he hate the very sight of Mr. Rogers putting on or taking off his goddam boots for the hundredth goddam time? A canine television watcher, why would he growl and bark with his nose an inch away from those ugly puppets on "Sesame Street," follow with a metronome head a tennis ball going back and forth over the net, or Hank Aaron knocking out another grand slam? Why else would he growl at a new piece of the sculptor's that had suddenly appeared on the kitchen table?

The Professor had one high I.Q. Indeed that was why he had named him Professor: it was such a beautiful contradiction in terms.

It had been Irene's suggestion that out here they could have the dog companion that apartment residence in the city had denied them. He couldn't have agreed with her more.

What a blond and stubby darling he had been! There were four left in a litter of nine as he and Irene had stood and looked and looked and looked, just as they always did in art shows, waiting for their hearts to be won, then keeping their silence contract till final rapport. One blond tail-wagger had stood up against the kennel fence again and again, switched back and forth to him to Irene – to him to Irene. Love at first sight, but he had kept his mouth shut then looked questioningly to Irene.

She swallowed. She pointed. Double Bingo!

And what a puppy prodigy he had been: housebroken in record time, no more shoe or purse destruction after Irene had daubed them with Tabasco sauce just once. Holes dug in flower beds and climbing up on couches, beds, or chairs had ended thanks to mousetraps set under newspaper or leaf cover. Just one perhaps two snaps under his nose did it for Professor.

Poor guy. For weeks after they'd lost her he never emptied a dish, went again and again to the windows, whimpered at the door. When was she coming back? Why had she rejected them?

Just five years they'd shared out here, Irene and Art and Professor. Each spring and summer their day would begin with the robin wake-up call, or in the fall the honk of Canada geese or the dawn howl of a coyote, then out to the shed studio for a couple of paintbrush hours. Or onto Tongue Creek with rod and creel, but only if Irene didn't spot him goofing off again. Then it would be into town for a nine- or a ten-o'clock at Livingstone University.

They had established a noon ritual, and each teaching day he would phone her on the dot. Never ever would he forget that May day near the end of the spring semester. He had tried to reach her five times. How often since then he had heard the echo of the unanswered phone within himself. *Buzz – pause – buzz – pause*. Why wasn't she answering? One and two and three ... Out in the garden? ... four and five and six ... On the deck sunning herself? ... and seven and eight ... Taking Professor out for a run? Into town with Frances for a hair-do?

Buzz – wait – buzz – wait.

He canceled the lunch tutorial, knocked it off early.

As he passed the General Office door, Bev called after him, "Banker's hours again, eh!"

His apprehension grew and grew as he waited for the elevator. Silly worry, he told himself over and over. Quit it! He couldn't.

He ran to his car, made it in record time out to the farm.

Professor had not come to meet him at the gate, was nowhere in the yard either. He was in the kitchen, whimpering and slobber kissing her as she lay on the kitchen floor in front of the stove; he probably hadn't touched one morsel of that beef stew spilled from the broken bowl beside her.

Never to answer the phone again! Ever again! Again – again – again – again ...!

"... or ever the golden bowl be broken ...!"

Come on, Ireland, summon the happy times. Remember the two years you had your T.A. getting your master's at Digby College of Art and Design and she showed up in your freshman class and you fell for her at first sight. Dark hair. Dark eyes. Arthur Ireland never did prefer blondes.

He had behaved for a whole year: teachers do not date their students, especially if they happen to be six years younger. She had made the first move, invited him to her sorority spring formal. She had been so lovely in that floor-length gown of black velvet when she answered the Gamma house door chimes. He had never seen a dress like that before. Look, Ma, no shoulder straps. She sure as hell had plenty to hold it up!

First time he had ever seen her with her hair done up in a Victorian crown. When she walked ahead of him into the living room, where sisters waited for their dates to pick them up, she was the queen of them all. He waited till she got her evening wrap and they were out in the hall to give her the florist box.

"Oh, Art, they're lovely!" She took the gardenias from their nest of transparent green paper, held them against the black velvet shoulder. Well, actually *under* a shoulder, given the gown that defied gravity so beautifully. "Pin it on for me."

Where?! "Aaaaah … the pin."

"My waist. This side."

He was able to manage that location. Very, very carefully.

She stood back. "Well?"

"You look – lovely."

"You too, Mr. Ireland, trim and handsome in your smoking." She looked down at her gardenia corsage. "*Three* of them."

Both of them knew what *three* gardenias said: "I – love – you."

She had been taking design at Digby; indeed she had done the evening gown herself, would have created many more if she had not run around to the head of the Gamma table when it was her turn at the graduation supper to announce that she too would be marrying her one and only in the coming year. Indeed it had happened that fall when he won his first sessional at Digby.

Winston showed up in the kitchen just as the ham and eggs were done, which showed one thing about him as an actor: fine sense of timing. Professor didn't make much fuss over him. He did like ham in his dish but not on or off stage.

They'd just sat down when Darryl came in, dressed as usual in three-piece suit with ascot. He would don his roll-brim homburg when he left for work in Sears Men's Wear.

"All hail to the Prince," Win said. Darryl was indeed a royal ringer, from ear to ear.

"Up yours, Winnie."

"*Win*, damn it."

"Sorry, Win. In case you've forgotten – my given name is Darryl."

"Of course. Darryl Duckworth, the celebrated poet."

"And you of course must be Winston Forsythe, stage and screen star, well remembered as Uncle Ben with Aunt Martha on the Nellie-winning series 'Kiddie Garten of the Air.' Also as the shill for countless beer, real estate, car ..."

"Up yours."

"– as well as those unforgettable hemorrhoid suppository commercials."

"All right, you guys. Knock it off," Art said.

"What is it this morning?" Darryl said. "Try-out at the Suck and Buckskin?"

"*Sock* and *Buskin*."

"Great. 'Break a leg.'"

"Pass the butter."

"Or 'May your hemorrhoids expand.' That one works a lot better, I've been told."

"You made up your mind yet whether you're the Prince of Wales or Darryl Duckworth?"

"Both. They're analogous."

"Well – well – hail to thee, blithe asshole. Bard thou never wert."

"Come on – come on, you guys ..."

"Pass the butter, please, Darryl."

"For just one morning as soon as your bare feet hit the floor, I wish you two would not pick up the verbal battle you cut off the night before!"

"Sorry, Art," Darryl said.

"Okay," Win said.

"That's better. Pleasant conversation –"

"– aids the digestion," they both said.

"Thanks," Art said.

"And the catsup," Win said.

"With pleasure," Darryl said.

Breakfast continued more smoothly, though the odds were they'd pick up their wrangling on their way into town in the van. Win's van. Aw, well. Little enough price to pay for their comfort and companionship here in the rural art colony. Win had been the second one to join him out here.

Three years ago, he'd found Win living in his van. He'd noticed that it had been in the same spot on the campus parking lot for over a month. It had been a bitter January day and the parking lot attendant had wakened Win to tell him for the last time that permanent residence here was against Livingstone University regulations. Win was looking so forlorn beside the van when Art came out to his car that morning that he had to ask the kid what the problem was.

"I just been told to get out of here or get hauled out. It's a real problem when you're out of gas and your battery's dead and you're stone broke and haven't eaten in three days!"

"Get in my car."

"Huh?"

"We'll go get a can of gas. I've got starter cables. After we get you moved out, we'll have lunch in the student cafeteria. On me."

Over lunch he got the whole sad story from Win.

"All I ever wanted to do was act – direct – maybe be a playwright. That's why I majored in drama here at Livingstone. I used to dream about making it on Broadway or the West End. The real stuff. Not doing another Dame Twankey in *Aladdin* or *Dick Whittington and His Cat* or *Ali Baba and* ... Certainly not Uncle Ben in cowboy hat and chaps and fringed jacket with Aunt Martha in pinafore and bonnet one hour live every

Saturday morning from nine to ten – the gerbils and the kittens and puppies and goldfish – and the kids sitting lotus position all around her. Me up on a fucking pinto rocking horse! No – it was the rabbit did *that*."

"Did what?"

"Fucked on camera. Aunt Martha had got me to find a pair of rabbits for her. We didn't know one was a doe, the other one a stud – or whatever they call the male rabbit."

"Buck."

"Whatever. He quit hopping and nibbling the carrots and lettuce the little kids had brought him and started humping the girl rabbit – in close-up. Live!"

"Oh no!"

"Oh yeah! Camera man had stepped aside to refill his coffee cup. When he came back he slid off the rabbits and zoomed to close-up so he could capture the shocked disgust on Aunt Martha's face.

"That made up my mind for me. I'd been waiting for just the right show to kiss 'Kiddie Garten of the Air' goodbye and this was it. Educational. Kids loved it and gave it an all-time record poll rating. Also, three days before, I'd got a call to try out for Willy Loman at the Tyrone Guthrie in Minneapolis. Didn't make it."

After he'd cleaned out most of the long counter in the cafeteria, Win pushed his plate aside, sat back and sighed.

"You sure you've had enough?"

"Uh-huh. Thanks. Saved my life."

"So. What now?"

"I don't know. I don't know. Actors don't get unemployment insurance."

"No artist does."

"No chance in January for car washing. It's term break, so

it'll be at least ten days before they'll want my crown jewels on display in Visual Arts ..."

"What?"

"With or without a jockstrap. Life class model. Fifty bucks a session." He sighed again. "No-Win Win. Had a birthday last week. Twenty-four."

"Not quite senior citizen yet, Winston. Let's go."

"Sure. Thanks again, Professor. See you later."

"No."

"Huh?"

"Now. You follow me in your van – out to my place. You can stay there till you get back on your feet."

Three years now since Win had moved in. A year later they were joined by the poet, Darryl.

One evening in midwinter Art had sensed that Win had something gnawing at him. He had said little all through supper, which was unusual for him. Afterwards when Charlie had gone up to bed they sat in front of the fireplace.

"Something bothering you, Win?"

"Yeah."

"What?"

"Met an old friend of mine today. Ran across him in Sears Men's Wear, where he works. Hadn't seen him for over a year. We knew each other ever since we were in Chinook College together. After we finished there we shared a basement suite till I made it as Uncle Ben with Aunt Martha and moved out to shack up with another companion. Opposite sex. She ditched me when I left 'Kiddie Garten of the Air' ..."

He sighed, stared into the fireplace flame.

"Go on, Win."

"I had enough trouble of my own so I lost track of him. Till today. We talked over old times together. He's still writing poetry, been doing it ever since he was a kid in England. He said he was into a new style called sprung rhythm invented by some Jesuit guy named – uh …"

"Gerard Manley Hopkins," Art said.

"Yeah. Brit, like him. That's his problem."

"What do you mean?"

"He's pretty typical. It's why he always dresses like royalty the way a lot of them do when they migrate and they're sure they're going to make it big outside the main ring of the circus. When they don't, it hurts. When I ran across him today I could tell Darryl was hurting. He said he'd quit sending his stuff out. Tired of rejection slips. I know just how he feels."

"We all do, Win."

"He's feeling pretty low. Always has been an up and down guy. When we were sharing that basement suite, one time I found him …"

"Yes?"

"Never mind. His young years were just as bad as mine. His mother made it through the bombing of London, but she died when he was five and he got passed from relative to relative until his father brought him over to Canada. The old man wasn't exactly royalty. He was a plumber, named his Canadian shop The Royal Flush."

"That's pretty witty."

"Only good thing about him; he was a match for my dad. Poor Darryl, never saw his mother or his beloved granny again. He loved her a lot too."

"All right, Win. What's the point of all–?"

"When you saved my bacon on the campus that day I wasn't

worried just about myself. Him too. I should have – when you took me in and I saw the set-up out here I should have known it was just the sanctuary and friendship he could use."

"Okay."

"You mean it?"

"Of course I do."

The sculptor hadn't surfaced yet by the time they had finished breakfast.

"He worked till daybreak," Darryl explained, "trying to make the deadline on his show. Just ten days away."

Charlie, the sculptor, was the only one of them who managed to live by art alone. Art had come to know and respect and like him well during the years they'd taught together at Livingstone. Five years ago, just months apart, both of them had lost their life companions, and Charlie had been the first to join him out here. A year later he had done what Art had promised Irene he would do – and had not done: devote all the rest of his life to his art.

Sorry, Irene, sorry again – I know – you don't have to remind me it's years since I've had a show. Eight years since we paid off the mortgage on the place and I went back on my promise to devote the rest of my life to brush and palette. But we had no children of our own, and teaching is a pipeline to the young, and I've got the poet and the sculptor and the actor with me on our place now.

When Darryl and Win had cleared the table and started on the dishes he went outside, stepped down off the back stoop, and headed for the car and another day in Academe.

As he rounded the corner of the barn he noticed the vanilla

smell of milk lingering still, so long after he'd sold Sara and Bernadette to the Hutterites in their nearby colony. Irene had named them, milked them, pastured them. When she was gone, it had been time for them to go too.

He heard grunting behind himself: Florence. Descendant of Yorkshire ancestors, she should long ago have joined Weight Watchers. Irene had found and saved the runt piglet before that bastard Ottowell on the next ranch could hammer it. She'd made a nest for Florence behind the kitchen stove, bottle-fed and housebroken her. More and more as she matured, Professor resented her trespassing on his inside territory; she made no effort to behave the way he did in here. Look how she took up three-quarters of the living room couch!

In the end Irene had agreed that the house must be off limits for Florence. That had been all right with Florence. She loved to go angling with him, came with him every time he headed out to flog Tongue Creek.

It had been Irene's suggestion that he get Florence to pose for him so that he could do a porcine madonna. That had started him on a lovely run: chickens, calves, colts, geese, pigeons, goats. Hadn't been all that different from his early Paris days, when he was learning human form. He had never decided which flesh – animal or human – he had found more challenging or more satisfying.

"No, Florence – not doing any nudes of you this morning. Headed for Livingstone University – not the creek for rainbow or cutthroat. Maybe this evening when I get back."

The May Day tree was in full blossom, almost as though it had accomplished it overnight, though there must have been bud signals before now. And today was May Day. How she used to curse that tree if it hadn't burst into bloom on daylight saving time by May first.

Florence had oinked off by the time he reached the tool shed, where he'd parked the car yesterday. This was where Irene had picked up the chunk of metal plate leaning against that rock that had nearly tripped her.

"You all right?"

"Sure. Look at this."

"Yeah? What about it?"

"All rusted."

"So what?"

"The way it's shaded and colored. The lovely patterning."

God! Had she ever been right: what a creative accident! Surf rust. Cloud rust. Shadow rust. And there and there not-yet-rust so that metal glints could punctuate with silver. It had been the morning that his rust period was born. End of another artist block for him; she didn't have to shove him into the studio for the next two years. What a creative partner she had been, moving him on from figurative to impressionist, to expressionist and to abstract. End of the line. Surrealism could wait till he was no longer on this planet.

The twenty minutes it generally took him to drive from home to campus was a pretty nice gangplank, during which he could put a final mental polish on that day's lecture. He went five times a week to teach in the Livingstone Fine Arts Faculty. Or *not* so Fine Arts Faculty ever since Hopper showed up at Livingstone. Every single year for five years now as dean, he's made you appeal unsuccessfully for tenure – even got one of your own students to betray you by writing that two-page damaging critique, saying that Professor Ireland takes a distractingly personal and much too casual approach to teaching his courses.

At least the bastard hasn't managed to shove you out of Fine Arts and into Continuing Education, a euphemism for the former Department of Extension. Not yet, he hasn't. But it's been five tough years ever since he showed up at Livingstone with his Harvard doctorate in his hip pocket. In Business Administration. How fitting a degree for a dean of Fine Arts. Five long years without Irene to comfort this academic Eliza trying to make it across the river, jumping from sessional ice cake to sessional ice cake, with Simon Degree in hot pursuit.

Come on! Knock off the self-pity, Art. You're in good company with the poet and the sculptor and the actor on these lovely eighty acres in the soft swell of the foothills, well away from the city's concrete phalluses. Correction, Art: phalli. And you have got the Professor and Florence.

Hey! That was a meadowlark! There! That telephone pole. Second one – no – the third, announcing spring. Look at that faint green showing along the barbed-wire fence, and you did spot some crocuses – croci – Sunday afternoon when you and Florence tried Tongue Creek for the first time this year. But best of all, Hopper's still got a good two months left on his sabbatical. In Dallas now, isn't he? After he'd done Australia, then Italy, Germany, then France, and finally Texas. Who cares!

What an arrogant one-man show he was! Drama had to clear with him every bloody play they wanted to do. He had to have final say on every University Art Show. He did leave Music alone, though, a considerate and wise restraint, since he was tone deaf.

He entered the South-West outskirts, managed the industrial district, then hit slow, bumper-to-bumper traffic and a detour. Since his trip in last week, the city had begun its usual springtime road repair. Now for the campus parking lot. As he got out of the car he realized he'd be one of the minority wearing full-length pants or skirts: Bermuda Shorts Day. Not for the teachers. Unless they were spending their hard-working sabbatical in the Caribbean or on a Texas golf course.

He entered the Arts building where carrels were occupied either by studying students or, in every third one, a sleeper with head truly buried in a book. Then through the overpass to Wapta Tower. He didn't trip on any of the bare extended legs belonging to students sitting on the floor with backs against the walls. For a change, one of the four elevators wasn't frozen in the basement or on the top floor.

Three hallway greetings, then into the Fine Arts General Office to pick up any departmental junk that had got caught in his slot of the mail trap line. One memo.

"Shee-yit!"

Behind the counter, Beverly looked up from her word processor. She did not seem startled.

"Bev."

"Yes, Professor."

"The dean! He's back!"

"Middle of last week."

"What the … but his sabbatical – it isn't over for another –"

"He wants to see you, Professor. Soon as possible."

"I know. This memo …"

"He said it was urgent."

"So does this memo. You got any idea what it's …?"

"Not really … I don't think he …"

"Okay. Okay, Bev, after my nine-o'clock."

"He said *before* your nine-o'clock."

"Did he now. It'll have to be *after*. It's the last one! I've got to say goodbye to my –"

"There won't be one, Professor. He canceled it."

"Whaat!"

"Thursday morning. I posted it for him. You."

"Shee …!"

"You're repeating yourself, Professor."

"Huh! Oh, Bev, you're right again. I guess I do repeat myself."

"Me too. 'Specially that word – ever since last week. But mainly to myself. Whenever I'm here."

"I love you, Bev."

"Take your place in line, Professor."

"I will." He headed for the door.

After he'd gone back to the General Office for the attaché case he'd forgotten in front of the counter, then into his office, he tried to get a grip on himself. What the hell was so important to Hopper that he'd lop two months off his sabbatical? Aw well, brace yourself, Art. You'll know soon enough.

Maybe – just maybe this time you'll tell him to stuff it. Quit telling yourself the art of teaching is as important as the art of art. Almost true. Sorry, Irene, sorry again. I know – I know – don't have to remind me …

This is it! Canceled my goodbye class! Maybe I will tell him to go piss up a rope! Maybe I will. Don't bank on it though, darling. You see – since I lost you I seem to have also lost faith in impulse. Second-thought contradiction always follows. Better take a leak … nope … better turn in for the night … nope … catch the late night news … get the stuff to the dry cleaners … nope … do it in the morning, Art – or the beginning of the week … you need a haircut … ah … not really … income tax returns …

Let's just see what the bastard wants. Then. Maybe …

He leaned back in his chair. No time off his sentence for five years of good behavior in this twelve-by-fourteen, windowless office, gray with filing cases. Same desk. Same chair. Same coat rack. Same tired broadloom. Same dean behind the back wall they shared; at least *all* of his wall and probably a *fourth* of the dean's. And now he's come all the way back from Texas two months early, to plock his balls in there again at least twice a day. *Golf* balls.

All right. Move it, Art. Brace yourself.

"Assistant dean's in there with him, Professor, but they're – I think they're almost finished. Have a seat."

"Thanks, Lottie."

"*Charlotte*, Professor."

"Yes, Charlotte. Sorry."

Now why had he called her Lottie? She was one fine single mother of two, responsible for anything right that Hopper had ever done. He knew very well that she didn't like to be called Lottie. Behave yourself, Art. God knows, she's got enough on her plate as the dean's secretary.

"All right, Ireland. Let's get to the heart of the matter at hand."

"May I sit down?"

"Do."

Hopper was consistent in his style with office visitors. He never rose behind the curving sweep of that long and black-veined desk to greet them, nor did he ever invite anyone below the rung of department head to sit. At all. Certainly no student. He had designed the desk himself; twelve to fourteen feet long, it arced around his high-back armchair, which he had also designed. Squatting now behind the inner curve of the rosewood desk, with his low, bald forehead, his pouched and protruding eyes, it was inevitable that he should be known, behind his back, as Frog Hopper. Rosewood lily pad.

"I've had to cut my sabbatical short for several very important reasons we haven't got time to go into right now. When I was down under – before I went to New York, where I managed to persuade the International Snuff Bottle Collectors to hold their annual conference the year after next in our city, with a snuff bottle show in our art gallery ... ah ... during my absence our faculty has gotten a very bad press. I speak of the lawn ornament incident, of course."

Frog was referring to the gang of art students who had stolen scores of plastic Bambis and fluorescent flamingos, bear cubs climbing trees, and dwarfs lurking under toadstools from lawns throughout the city. After a six-month search, police tracked them down – *well* down – under one of the city's garbage landfill sites. The culprits had yet to be identified and brought to plastic justice.

Art and others had thought it wasn't all that bad a public art statement.

"Wasn't all that bad a public –"

"More importantly and to the point I succeeded while in Dallas in persuading Maxwell Lampert, owner of the world's finest collection of Albrecht Dürer engravings and prints, to let us have a twenty-day show of his art in Livingstone Art Gallery. Opening June twenty-eighth."

"Mmmmh."

"*This* year. Just two months from now. The chancellor couldn't believe it when I phoned him from Dallas. Within two days he got back to me to tell me he'd already nailed down transportation and insurance costs with contributions from the Chancellor's Five Hundred Club. Five figures – not including promotion costs. Now – here's where you come in."

There they were in the corner by the filing cabinet. Hadn't forgotten to bring his golf clubs back with him from Texas. Or from Australia. Or Italy. Or France. Or Germany.

"This is a difficult time of the academic year for me, Ireland. Right in the middle of spring hiring ..."

And firing.

"... preliminary arrangements for this show are going to be considerably challenging ..."

That grass-green plastic putting dish, at least three feet in diameter, was leaning up against the wall over there. Just waiting.

"... a lot to do to be ready for the opening June 28th, same time as the North-west Stampede. Max just loved that ..."

Quite fitting. In his day, Albrecht Dürer had been such a great rodeo fan. Pity he'd never done any engravings of bareback or saddle bronc riding or chuck-wagon races or steer wrestling, though.

"... indeed he told me he had always wanted to attend our North-west Stampede. I've been in touch with P.T. Brockington, chairman of the Stampede Board. Just possible he can set it up for Max to lead the parade this year. If he does, Max will bring up his own Appaloosa quarter horse. Silver-mounted saddle –"

"That's nice."

"It's a brutal deadline. End of June." He reached into a drawer and pulled a foolscap-length sheet onto the desk. "I've made out a detailed agenda. Number one: art gallery to be repainted. Number two: a whole new system of track lighting to be installed." He looked up from the sheet. "Something I've wanted done for over two years now. Number two – no – three: two separating walls that trisect the gallery must come down so that they do not interrupt the show flow."

Why the hell was he telling him all this stuff!

"I've already delegated a draftsman from Engineering to blueprint these organic changes."

"What's this got to do with –?"

"I wasn't successful with Finance to get the burglar alarms and electronic device system installed. Something I've tried to get done for over *three* years now –"

"Why –?"

"Here." He shoved the sheet to the edge of the desk. "I've just mentioned a few of the more important items. There are many more."

"I don't understand. What has this got to do with –?"

"I'm putting you in charge, Ireland."

"Shee-yit!"

"I would appreciate it if – while you are in my office, Ireland – you would try to clean up your language!"

"With difficulty. It's term end and I have plans for the next four months. Without trip-ups ... interruptions – I want to be in my studio –"

"And I have to be in this office. Two months off my sabbatical. We all have to make sacrifices –"

"Get somebody else to –"

"I am needed here. Or hadn't you heard about the savage budget cut we're all facing? In every single Fine Arts department ..."

"Get somebody –"

"– every single department of every single faculty, cuts have to be made. It is the most painful –"

"Get somebody else."

"You're my choice."

"Well *un*choose me. I'll be painting, all right, but not in with the fellows redecorating the art gallery."

"I see." He leaned forward and drew the work list toward himself. "Thank you for the blunt candor of your refusal."

"And thank you for canceling my nine-o'clock for me. Damn it! Last one with my students."

"This is more important to the department – as I think should be clear to any employee who has the best interests of the department at heart."

"I like to say goodbye to my protégés."

"Your decision is final?"

"Yes."

Frog reached over, took the phone off the hook.

"Is that all?"

"It is all."

"May I have your permission to leave now?"

He stopped in the middle of dialing, put the receiver back.

"You have it. And Ireland – I have an important meeting now with the associate dean, and the heads of drama, visual arts, music department. Very tough. Suggestions on how best to handle the budget cuts – early retirement – sessionals to be or not to be. Not good news for some people."

"Good luck. And in regard to your budget problems, I have a suggestion for you, Froggie boy – stuff *my* sessional up your administrative arse!"

Euphoria time, Irene. I did it! I did it! Finally kept a promise to you. I can hardly wait to tell the boys I've made the break. Especially Charlie, who did it five years ago. When I should have. Freelance time! Paint, palette, and canvas time out in that studio as soon as it's daylight in the swamp. Every morning! Every day. Every week. Every month. Every year, for the rest of my life!

Oh, you should have seen his face when I told him what to do with my sessional!

You say God agrees with my decision? That was His

intention for me right from birth? Well – who am I to argue with Him. Or you.

Just one thing bothering me, though. Frog's wanted to get rid of me ever since he showed up in Livingstone. Maybe I've played right into his hands, by resigning. Maybe that's what the bastard had in mind when he tried to dump all that gallery …

God would disagree with me, you say. Well, what would He think if I were to teach just a couple of evening Art Appreciation and Art History classes a week? Department of Continuing Education. Oh, He's left, has He? To paint an evening sunset in the Eastern Hemisphere. I see.

Oh, my darling, how I miss you with me down here!

2

He'd told Bev first, as soon as he'd stormed out of the dean's office.

"Oh no, Professor!"

"'Fraid so. I'm going to miss your dear red head over your word processor every morning."

"Auburn, and I'm going to miss you too. We'll all miss you. When are you ...?"

"Week or so. I'll be coming in to get all my finals' marking done. Probably take me two, three days to clear out my office. I'll need enough cartons to hold a lot of years."

"Sure."

"At least half a dozen."

"I'm really sorry, Professor."

"Should have done it five years ago, Bev."

"Glad you didn't. I'd never have known you if you had."

"You've been a nice way to start my teaching day, Bev. I'm going to my office now to write my resignation."

"Just rough it out and I'll do a clean copy for you, take it in to the dean."

"I'd like to do that personally."

"Of course."

He turned from the counter.

"Just one more word, Professor. Sums up how I feel about your resignation."

"Yes?"

"Shee-yit!"

As usual Professor was waiting for him at the gate and joined him in the car to sit on the front seat. When Art told him in detail of how he'd let Frog have it, he seemed to feel that his master had made a good decision. As they crossed the wooden bridge over Tongue Creek, then up to the house, he went on at great length about how the goddam magpie had cursed and teased him the whole goddam day long. Almost got Maggie this time. Sure as hell would the next time she flew down to entice him with hop, strut, and flutter. Just wait and see. Sooner or later her time would come.

Win's van wasn't in the yard yet; be a good hour till he and Darryl showed up, but Charlie was by the barbecue. He had a special treat for them tonight: a new pork tenderloin recipe.

"I marinaded them over last night and today."

"Don't tell Florence."

"Of course not. Lemon juice, brown sugar, ginger, cumin, coriander, garlic, chopped onions, melted butter, Kikkoman soy sauce. They go on spits. Shish-kabob style."

"Sounds great, Charlie. You sure you didn't miss your true calling when you started sculpting?"

"I sure as hell didn't. This supper is a celebration, Art. I worked all last night, finished up the last piece for my show, and it's going to be a doozer!"

"Hold up. Remember Art and Charlie's first art law: 'Never ever say anything optimistic or positive or by next Thursday it'll be all friz to rat shit.'"

"Not this time. Last thing I did, I set them up all around the shop to get an idea how they'd – come on, come on. I want you to see them. Get your response."

No wonder Charlie was on such a high. Here was a whole year of work set out over the shop floor, much as it would be displayed in the Queen's Gallery show. There were fifteen new pieces; four of them that Art had never seen before, since by mutual agreement he had never entered Charlie's half of the building during the past two months. It had once been an abandoned Nazarene church a couple of miles down the road to the city. Now born again here as a twin studio with a ceiling-high dividing wall.

If ever there was an artist who did his art simply for the joy of doing, it had to be Charlie. On the other side of that wall for the past five years he had worked in all media: leather, wood, stone – finally metal. Never had he stood in one art spot to dribble commercially down the inside of his own leg.

For long moments after they entered the shop, they walked and they stopped and walked and stopped in silence. Large, medium, small abstracts of black metal, the sculptures were like air drawings that delighted and surprised often as the viewer circled about each piece. About and about and about.

"Oh, Charlie – Charlie, you've really done it again! And you were right! Forget our art law. This *is* one doozer!"

He was so taken by the work that he didn't right away tell Charlie his own great news. He was about to when he realized there were a number of Charlie's old ceramic pieces set out there as well, all from his frog period. At the foot of the large and arcing abstract that hinted flying dolphin, there was the ceramic bismark with lettuce and sliced tomatoes between the long bun halves, and little green frogs peeking out from under. There was the frog bishop, miter and all, and there the teacher frog with her tadpole pupils. And that one was the tureen with the floating frogs, their bump eyes and snouts showing just above the frog soup surface.

"Those ceramics going to be in the show too, Charlie?"

"Yep. I thought they'd be a nice sort of punctuation."

"Great touch." Now he was looking at the bullfrog wearing a mortar board, its academic robe spreading out and down over the kidney lily pad.

"That one's my favorite, Charlie."

"Mine, too. A lot of takers for it, but I've kept it for myself. For sentimental reasons. It's not for sale in the show. They're pasting a red sticker on it."

"It's about five years ago you moved out here and into ceramics, isn't it?"

"That's right."

"You say – said – for sentimental reasons?"

"Uh-huh."

"I don't think I ever asked you before. What led you – how come you moved into ceramics? Did all these frog sculptures?"

"Hell. Same reason I finished the fall term back then and took early retirement after the new dean took … "

"I guess I guessed. Had a pretty good hunch." He picked up the academic bullfrog, stared down at it for several moments. "Sentimental reasons?"

"Mmmh."

"May I have it?"

"For sentimental reasons?"

"Not exactly." He set the bullfrog down. "I have something to tell you. I handed in my resignation today."

"Oh, Art! That's great! I've been hoping you'd –"

"Should have done it way back when you did. Kept my promise to Irene way you did with Doris. Now – about this piece …"

"Say no more. It's yours to keep, Art."

"I haven't leveled with you on it, Charlie. I don't want it to keep for myself. I want to give it to someone."

"Oh now – I don't know about that. Hey – wait a minute. I think I know who you want to give ..."

"Whom."

"Whom. Oh God, how I'd like to see his face when you hand it to him."

"As a parting gift," Art said.

"Yeah!"

"I can arrange that. When I've wound up at Livingstone next week, you come into town with me and you come into Froggie's office with me. We *both* give it to him."

"Thanks, Art. Now I really know why I hung on to this one."

"As you said. Sentimental reasons."

It was a great celebration dinner for all of them. Charlie's new marinade recipe for the barbecued pork tenderloin was a winner, especially when washed down with chokecherry wine.

"How did you come by it, Charlie?" Darryl said. "I thought we'd used up the last ...?"

"Thank Peter."

"Saint Peter? Was he fishing Tongue Creek today?"

Darryl always called Peter, the goose boss, *Saint* Peter, though he was not a resident of the New Testament but of the Hutterite colony three miles west up Wild Horse Road.

"He dropped by. Sold me the pork and a jug – left over from their last year's vintage."

"Damn good year," Win said.

"I agree," Art said.

Probably no other neighbors had as much intercourse with the Hutterian Brotherhood colony as their art colony had. He'd first come to know them when he and Irene had gotten the bone-setter to witch their new well. It had been Hutterites who had restored all the fencing for him in return for two years' grazing and hay crop rights. Later, when he had bought the abandoned Nazarene church, young Hutterite boys had dug and cribbed the basement foundation, then converted the building into Charlie's shop and his own studio. The devil did find work for young and idle hands.

So in a way now there were two colonies side by side: the hook-and-eye and the equally devout one of the painter, the sculptor, the poet, and the actor.

Over dinner, Win had good news to tell; he'd won his try-out at the Sock and Buskin.

"Two parter. *Happy Journey from Trenton to Camden* and *The Devil and Daniel Webster*. Whole summer run and – I got the lead in *The Devil and* –"

"Playing Daniel . . . ?"

"No, Darryl. The devil."

"Great! You'll make one hell of a good one."

"Cool it, Prince."

"I mean it, Win. Congratulations."

"Six-week run. Three-week rehearsal. Equity rates."

"You want, I'll read lines for you."

"Thanks, Darryl. Appreciate that."

Win meant it. In spite of contradiction and argument, controversy and dispute, theirs was a warm rivalry, an ironic but deep friendship. At first when Darryl had moved out here, it had taken a while for Art and Charlie to get used to his sneezing, which peaked in fall (goldenrod and ragweed), in spring (cottonwood fluff), and all summer long whenever they held their weekly ritual meetings up in the hayloft cathedral.

Darryl had finally confessed that he loved to sneeze, except for paroxysms of more than seven successive sneezes.

"There's an orgasmic quality to them and nothing is more disappointing to me than sneezus interruptus – ambrosia interruptus – solidago interruptus."

He could often be seen surreptitiously twisting the corner of a kleenex and inserting it into a nostril of his regal nose to initiate a sneeze.

"Matter of fact, you could say that love of sneezing runs genetically in my family. The maternal British side. Never forget how my Tottenham grandmother used to sneeze. Until I was seven, when we migrated to Canada. Did she ever let them go! Always the same sneeze melody with the same arranged single tones. She was a fine singer. Contralto. She must have composed her sneezes very early in her life.

"She always sneezed with an opening quite similar to the overture of Beethoven's Fifth – you know the way it goes: 'Haugh-ha-ha-haaaaaugh!' She didn't sneeze just contralto; she also had a soprano screech that could rattle and clink every Bohemian crystal on our dining room chandelier."

"Sounds like Brit bullshit to me, Darryl, but somehow I do believe you," Win said.

Matter of fact, Darryl had explained to them, if it hadn't been for his sinusitis attacks he wouldn't have had the marvelous breakthrough that had led him from concrete poetry into sound poetry.

"After your prick poetry period," Win said. "'Song of the Penis Vendor'?"

"'*Peanut* Vendor.'"

"Whatever."

"I realized then that my favorite sound was zed."

"Zee."

"Look, Win. I was born in England, live in Canada. Get back over the forty-ninth. The English invented the English language. Last letter of the English alphabet is properly pronounced zed. Not zee. May I continue?"

"Of course."

"I have just received good news. I hope you fellows are going to miss me the last two weeks of August."

"Oh," Art said. "What's –?"

"I'll be away two weeks. San Francisco."

"San Francisco!" Win said. "Summer vacation time?"

"Yes and no. Breaking the Forty-ninth Sound Barrier."

"What the hell is that?"

"Just the sound poetry conference of the year. International, with poets from north and south of the border – British Columbia, Alberta, Saskatchewan, Manitoba, Montana, California, Oregon, Washington, even from New Mexico, North and South Dakota."

"How nice!" Art said.

"Letter was waiting for me this morning at Men's Wear – my business address, you might say. Soon as I saw the return address on that envelope: Stanford University, Palo Alto, I just knew what it was. Had to be Breaking the Forty-ninth Sound Barrier. I'm to do a reading and workshop there."

"Good for you!" Charlie said.

"Wow!" Win said. "But what's – Breaking the Forty –?"

"Exactly what it says. It says the border was drawn wrong – East–West. Should have been North–South. Conference of sound poets from the western half of the North American continent will make that geographic statement when they read their sound poetry and break the forty-ninth sound barrier. Get it?"

"Almost," Charlie said.

"Interesting," Art said.

"It's an emotional theme," Darryl said. "What better than sound poetry to realize it. The voice music of sound poetry."

"Good going!"

"Hurray for you!"

"Congratulations!"

He'd left his own good news to the last. What happy coincidence; all four of them scoring together! Win and Darryl both felt that the planned presentation of the academic bullfrog was a perfect finishing touch to his resignation.

It hadn't worked out quite the way he had promised Charlie: presenting Hopper with the academic bullfrog in his office as a parting gift from himself and a delayed one from Charlie. Worked out much better actually, for the Fine Arts support staff and his colleagues had arranged a surprise coffee, wine, and cheese farewell party for him with the dean, the associate dean, and department heads in attendance. It was supposed to be a surprise party, but Bev had intentionally unintentionally alerted him.

Charlie was delighted when he told him they would *really* croak Hopper in front of everybody in the Faculty Club Lounge.

"I thought of something else, Charlie. You know that coffee mug piece of yours? The one to be handed to someone – full, so they don't know till after they've drunk it empty that there are two little green frogs fornicating on the bottom of the mug. Did you do an edition of it?"

"Mmh-hmh."

"How many you got left?"

"One."

"Too bad."

"Why?"

"Well, besides dean froggie on his lily pad, I thought it would be nice to supply those mugs for the ones at the party that won't be drinking wine. If there'd been any left ..."

"When did you say this party was?"

"Tuesday."

"That's three days from now. I can fire up the oven and – how many?"

"Oh, half a dozen."

"Easy."

"I guess we're a couple of naughty boys, aren't we, Charlie?"

"You certainly are, Art. Way naughtier than I am."

"Yeah. I'll have to buy that."

Public insult! He stared at the sculpture squatting there on his rosewood desk. Planned and deliberate humiliation!

The lily pad was long and curving. Tinted pink as well.

Not just snickers; there had been several outbursts of laughter both at the presentation and again and again as people drained their coffee mugs.

Was it just the two of them? Had there been others in on it? Must have been. No way of knowing who else. No way of punishing.

That frog face with the mortar board, its gold tassel hanging down past the bulging left eye, verged on human. Those weren't webbed flippers: one of them was holding a rolled parchment. They were hands. And crimson! Harvard School of Business Administration colors!

Oh God, how it hurt! He looked away from it and toward the window, got up and went over to it. As soon as he had taken over as dean here, he'd replaced the mean little four-by-four window with this high and wide beauty. Designed it himself with two hinged, clear halves that would swing open.

Breathing deeply, trying to get a grip on himself, he leaned over the ledge to look down on the campus. Twelve stories. Two-way concrete walk headed for the Social Sciences building.

Hey! Hey!

He went back to the desk, picked up the sculpture, and returned to the open window. What a fitting end to this china insult.

Just as he was about to let it drop to the concrete below, he had a second thought: *insure it first*, then ... A thousand ... fifteen ... sixteen hundred. He went back to the desk, set the sculpture down. Maybe *two* thousand.

After he'd taken out an art insurance policy and paid the premium, he'd just wait a couple of months then ... my, my, what a sad happening. Came into my office this morning and there it lay shattered on the floor. Broken beyond all repair. No amount of claim payment can begin to make up for this loss. Not the slightest idea of how it could have happened. Unlikely to be another piece of student vandalism, which, I am sorry to say, is not all that unusual here in Livingstone University. No student is allowed to set foot in this office unattended. Had to be a most unfortunate accident, perhaps the fault of some clumsy clean-up person from Maintenance on night shift or weekend duty. Couldn't have been Security, for Livingstone has the finest patrol officers of any university.

Make it *three* thousand with written estimates from a couple of people in Visual Arts and a gallery or two. Maybe wait a year.

He didn't have to look at the damn thing; stick it back inside the gift box and hide it over behind the putting dish and the golf club bag. Yeah!

Probably go at it with a nine iron just before the next year's premium payment was due. Hole in one!

3

He knew now that it wasn't going to be all that easy. His initial euphoria had dimmed within his first few successive whole days alone in the studio. Again and again he'd had to resist putting down palette and paintbrush for creel and fishing rod to go out on Tongue Creek with Florence. In the five years since he'd lost Irene to love him and to push him, he'd lost one hell of a lot of creative momentum. Going to take a while to get it back again. Only one way to do that, Art: get your ass out and into that studio every day – every week, every month. That was Louis Simard's law. Remember?

How often over the years, almost half a century of them, Louis came back to him from that Sorbonne summer. How he would owe that man for the rest of his life. What was left of it. Sixty-second birthday last Monday. Thank God the boys hadn't known about it; birthday cakes were a royal pain in the ass! Just how many did he have left to him? Fifteen? Ten? No way – not after they found that abdominal aneurism three years ago. No way!

Yeah, Louis Simard was the reason he had become a teacher and a painter. And now, Louis, you better be the reason I spend the rest of my years – five maybe – as a complete artist. Forget being a complete angler.

The middle of his first university year he had decided he must do what Fred Petersen had done the summer before: go by cattle boat to Europe. Not simply like Freddy for adventure's sake, but also to take a summer art course at the Sorbonne. Professor Argue in Agriculture was able to get him a free trip by caboose to Montreal. The cattle he would be responsible for would be in their boxcars ahead, Argue had explained, but he would never have to even set eyes upon them all the way to Montreal or on the cattle boat to England.

The more difficult hurdle would be his mother.

Home for reading break, he brought the matter up with her. She did not like this *Wanderjahr* idea at all. He had just turned eighteen a month ago, she reminded him, and most people took him for fourteen. She didn't have to say *she* still had him pegged at ten! He was all she had now that his father was gone forever. She didn't want to lose him too. She wouldn't lose him! Oh yes, she *would*, if he didn't grow up and quit coming up with wild and senseless and hare-brained …

She cooled down some when he explained that he wanted to take a summer art course at the Sorbonne. All right, then; if he could get accepted she would consider possible approval. He applied. He was accepted. She gave in. Indeed, she staked him to five hundred in travelers' cheques after he had promised to write her at least twice a week.

The journey east was unforgettable. At the first divisional point stop, an old hobo climbed off a flatcar and showed up in the caboose, introducing himself as Mr. MacFee. The freight conductor permitted him to stay. Mr. MacFee explained that he was headed for Ottawa in order to patent a gate lock he'd invented. Mr. MacFee spent most of his time in the caboose, sandpapering lengths of hay-wire to a sterling shine, then spiraling and kinking them into egg boilers. At their next divisional point stop, Mr. MacFee talked him into selling them for him. "They don't buy it when I tell 'em I'm a wounded and homeless and starvin' war veteran. Kid like you could move one hell of a lot of 'em. They sell for fifty cents. I'll split the take with you."

Mr. MacFee had been right. He'd made three dollars and a quarter, but when he returned to the freight yards, the cattle train had pulled out! But Mr. MacFee was still there and had a fire going and the coffee pot on. The rest of the way he rode another freight with Mr. MacFee to Montreal. By tender on a bed of coal. Not very goddam tender!

His cattle boat had already sailed for England!

It had taken him a whole week to sign on another ship, since he had no A.B. or union papers and could not be granted membership without having shipped out before, which he couldn't have done unless he had union papers that would enable him to do so …

He haunted the docks, learning that the ship's bos'n was the fellow to get to. Finally, he made it with a little Cockney in the *Onassis Penelope*, which would take on her paper cargo in Quebec City to be carried to Purfleet on the Thames. He must have been the last one of the crew to sign on. All of them had been preceded by eleven sheep in chicken wire quarters in the fo'c'sle peak. Probably without union papers. None of them would make it alive to Purfleet, where the cargo of paper rolls for the *London Daily Mail* would be unloaded.

When he boarded the ship that night, the bos'n told him to go aft to deckhand quarters portside under the poop deck and pick out a bunk there. He put his pack on a lower one only to have a fellow come up behind him, reach round and hump it up onto the upper bunk.

"Didn't you see the pillah?"

He did then, a large plump thing of blue ticking.

"My bunk. My pillah. Goose down. I'm Slim. Quartermaster. What's your name?"

"Arthur."

"Okay, Artie. You're up. I'm down. Don't touch that pillah."

"I won't."

"First time?"

"Yes."

Slim shook his head. "Poor choice, kid. Both of us. She's one hard time packet."

As deckhand, he would spend the next three weeks in this seaborne league of nations, Canadian, American, Turkish, Greek, Italian, Portuguese. Eight hours a day he would soogey decks, push a holy stone back and forth to skin them down. The stone was well named, for it did look a lot like a large concrete Bible with a long and swiveled handle. There was brass everywhere to be polished, and acres of red lead to be chipped off all walls. He was on lookout duty, up with the sheep in the fo'c'sle peak, in fog all through the Strait of Belle Isle, where they damn near ran aground off Saint Pierre and Miquelon. He should never have let Mr. MacFee talk him into selling those egg boilers. Not likely they would have fed you sheep stew and bread and molasses all the way to England in a cattle boat.

Slim helped him get the awful fodder down, for he'd brought on board with him a whole drum of Roquefort and a dozen cakes of maple sugar. Second supper out Slim gave him a generous chunk of the cheese and four cakes of maple sugar.

During the voyage he came to know Slim very well. He told him he was skipping ship in Purfleet to head for Paris, where he would take an art course at the Sorbonne.

Slim's mouth came ajar. "Art?"

"Mmmh."

"Paintin' pitchers?"

"Uh-huh."

Sitting on his bunk, Slim laid down the sock he was darning. "Don't sound sensible to me. Understand most artists starves up in them attics a' theirs."

"I guess they do."

"Well, you're sure gonna get in good practice at it this voyage." He had picked up his ditty bag and tucked scissors, thimble, darning needle, and yarn inside. "Tell you somethin'. That pack sack a' yours. You get some red lead. Paint on her in big letters."

"Paint what?"

"Canada. You see, wherever you go over there – 'specially Paris – they'll take you for American, an' ever since the Yanks discovered Europe after the war they been flashin' their money all over the place, an' they ain't too popular. Always let 'em know you're Canadian – *not* American."

"I will."

"Make it one hell of a lot easier for you. An' stay away from skatin' rinks."

"What for?"

"Don't even know whether there is any in Paris, but there sure as hell was in Rio when I was a kid like you."

"They got no ice in Argentina, have they?"

"*Roller* skatin' rink. 'Bout your age first year I shipped out as peggy."

"Peggy?"

"Yeah. Haulin' grub from the galley to the a.b.'s an' the black gang – waitin' table on the firsts an' pettys. I made her to able bodied inside three years. Then 1916 the navy. Halifax."

"What happened in the Argentine roller skating ..."

"Oh, yeah. That's where I picked up my dose. First one. Off

a' this girl. See, all 'round that rink in Rio they had these cubicles alongside for puttin' on your skates an' … for … well, she was a pro-stand-up job behind the cubicle curtain. Never took off her roller skates." There was a thoughtful pause. "Reminds me a' somethin'."

"What?"

"Reason I'm in this goddam packet. I was beached in Norfolk, Virginia, three weeks. Now if that ever happens to you, just head for the nearest Canadian Consul. Tell 'em all about them awful headaches you been gettin' reg'lar again."

"Huh!"

"Ask 'em to give you a Wassermann test. When she shows up positive they'll write you down syph sick right away an' ship you right back to the land your birth. Free! That's how I got out a' Norfolk. You get beached, use that wrinkle, kid."

"If I did I wouldn't likely test positive."

"Don't bank on it, kid."

"Slim – would you do something for me?"

"Sure."

"Quit calling me kid."

"Okay, Artie."

"*Art*."

"Uh-huh." He slid the ditty bag under the pillow, stood up. "Gotta do my turn now. Wanna come along?"

"Oh – I'm not supposed to go up there."

"Most the time you ain't, but not when I'm in the wheel house – 'ppreciate your company, Art."

Up on the bridge Slim explained the pillow. His mother had given it to him when he joined the navy.

"Saved my life in '17. Couldn't swim a stroke, torpedoed just off of Boulogne. No life jacket but that pillah kep' me afloat till they got to me an' hauled me in."

Slim was a prairie gopher.

"Maybe I ain't got salt in my blood, but I sure got horizon there, and she don't make much difference to me whether she's wet or she's dry."

When he had wondered about the ship's name, Slim had explained that to him.

"Young Greek fellah down in Argentina or Brazil, bought two ships off of the Trimmer Line. All wore out, I guess. This is the first one. *Onassis*, that's *his* name. *Penelope* – his ma maybe or his wife or his sister or his girlfriend. Likely the latter. Whichever, I'm skippin' her in Purfleet."

"Me too."

"Yeah – but I ain't plannin' to paint pitchers in Paris."

When Slim did his turn at the wheel, he often invited Art onto the bridge, even let him take over a couple of times. Wasn't all that exciting.

Crew quarters under the poop deck in the stern were divided by a half partition, deckhands portside, black gang starboard. There always seemed to be a battle going on the other side of the partition, between one of the coal passers and a trimmer. It seemed that the passer was not shoveling enough coal up to the trimmer so that he was getting hell from the second engineer for not keeping his fire up. This let pressure go down, and when that was corrected it went too high and they had to let off steam so that pressure went down again. It looked like they were going to teeter-totter all the way across the broad Atlantic.

The trimmer, better known as the Liverpool Rat, never shut up. He was a sea lawyer. If he wasn't bitching at the passer he was going on and on about such important articles of the seas as: "We're supposed to get fruit once a week!" The first Sunday the cook himself brought in a dessert of virgin white plum duff he'd steamed – probably in his underwear.

"There you are," he announced as he set it down on the black gang table. "Plum duff with raisins which are grapes – dried, but still fruit."

Every third morning the cook's helper would slash the jugular of a sheep, skin and disembowel it on the deck between the galley and the rail. Blood and guts were very resistant to soogey and holy stone. The cook's helper was a portly gentleman named Mr. Gulliver. He had no intention of making it to Lilliput or Brobdingnag, Laputa or the land of the Houyhnhnms; another first-timer, all he wanted to do was get back to Birmingham for the rest of his life.

As the youngest in the floating all-male family, Art had not anticipated he would become a fun target for the others. Especially the Liverpool Rat.

"She's a Greek packet, sonsy boy. Keep your eye peeled and your arsehole covered at all times."

One night he sang to him over the partition: "Rocked in the Cradle of the Deep," but with changed lyrics.

"Which would you prefer, lad? Rocked in the cradle of the deep or locked in the hold with Johnny the Greek?"

The black gang and the sailors laughed, but not Slim. "All right. That's enough! Knock it off!"

Most of them did. Till the next time. A couple reassured him by saying that the captain and the mate and first engineer and the donkeyman each had a favorite curl friend up there in the fo'c'sle peak, so he didn't have to worry all that much. At least till slaughter time.

His mother's concern just might have been valid.

They hit fog when they left the Gulf of St. Lawrence. Next came waves nine feet high. A lot of sheep stew and bread and molasses got tossed up and over the rail. Strangely he hadn't a touch of seasickness, because a considerate bos'n sent him up on the fo'c'sle peak on lookout. The cold wind driving much of the Atlantic Ocean into his face was probably what saved him. Thank God he hadn't been up there when they missed Saint Pierre by inches.

The war between the passer and the trimmer from Liverpool intensified with the boiler pressure gauge kiting up and down even after they had passed the chin of Newfoundland. The Liverpool Rat waited till the enemy slept, then sat at the black gang table with a loaf of bread and a butcher knife, alternately taking a swipe at the loaf, a glare at the sleeping passer, another slash at the bread … Then, practice over, he went for the *real* sonovabitching target!

Just before the knife could plunge, the fellow in the bunk above, who had been awake and watching, dropped down on him, and with the help of others pinned the Liverpool Rat to the deck. He ended up in irons under the fo'c'sle peak, screaming all the rest of the way to Purfleet. Then Bedlam.

Of all people, Mr. Gulliver took his place below. Not a smart decision, because down there seasickness was at its most intense. Mr. Gulliver was just making it by the skin of his dentures, but he hung on until peggy put down sheep stew and bread and molasses and tea then quite unnecessarily told them of when he'd been a waiter on the *Empress of Britain*. It seemed he had been going up the stairway with a bowl of boiled potatoes for tourist class, when a seasick passenger coming down met him midway, inhaled the steam, and puked right into the potatoes.

"Goddamit! Now I'll have to go back below and mash these fuckers before I can serve 'em!"

Too much for Mr. Gulliver, who jumped up, made it to the deck and out to the rail, where he vomited sheep stew and bread and molasses overboard. Along with his false teeth. For him it would be oatmeal mush the rest of the way to Purfleet.

On May Day they sighted England with cheers from everyone, he and Slim and the donkeyman doing a maypole dance round a fat ventilator tube on the foredeck. English Channel next, then the Thames, then Purfleet. He'd made it!

As they stepped ashore after the bos'n had paid them off, Slim said, "Know how she got her name, Art?"

"Nope."

"Queen 'Lizabeth. After the Spanish ships gave 'em a shit kickin' an' they made it back to port, she looked at 'em an' she bust into tears an' cried, 'Oh – my poor fleet!'"

With Slim and the bos'n and the donkeyman he had his first decent meal in almost a month at the King's Head Inn. He asked the waiter where he could get lodging for a couple of nights, and was told that a Mrs. Sage was in a white house just around the corner down the lane. Took in brief boarders, she did.

He shook hands with Slim, the bos'n, and the donkeyman, said goodbye and picked up his gear. He left the King's Head, found the lane, then went through a hawthorn hedge to Mrs. Sage's house. As he knocked, he heard a dog bark inside, and long moments later the door opened.

She was stooped with age. At least in her midseventies, he guessed, with white hair, a prune face, and rheumy old eyes that traveled up then down then up again to fix on his face.

"I'm looking for a room for a couple of nights, Mrs. Sage."

"Are you naow."

"Waiter at the King's Head – recommended – said you took in … "

"I do that. Where you from?"

"Canada. I just came over – *Onassis Penelope* – docked this afternoon."

For several more calculating moments, she stared at him. "Look right enough to me, you do." She stepped back, pulled the door wider. "Come in, lad."

Inside she said, "Just me 'ere, naow – me an' me dog an' me cat. Old 'uns likes of me, we can't be too careful, can we then?" She pursed her mouth, ran a fingertip along her thin lower lip. "You was to stay 'ere wiv me, you wouldn't do me no 'arm, would you?"

"Oh no, Mrs. Sage."

"An' I wouldn't do you no 'arm, neither. Florin a night."

"Pardon?"

"Ten shillin' – 'alf a quid."

"Fine with me."

"'Ad supper 'ave you naow?"

"Oh yes."

"Shillin' extra. Would be."

It was an upstairs room. She pointed out the loo halfway down the hall, a chamber pot under the bed, then headed back downstairs.

It was a double bed with a log cabin quilt. Oh, how lovely it was going to be after the springless bunk he'd endured for over three weeks. He took off his shoes and jacket, lay back against the pillow. Yeah! Yeah!

He heard her on the stairs. She came through the door, then to the night table by the bed to set down a tray with a bottle and a pewter mug.

"Thought you could do wiv a night cap, lad."

"Oh. Thank you. No thanks, Mrs. Sage. I don't . . ."

"No charge – before you turn in."

"Very nice – but – I don't drink," he said. "Yet."

"Oh – well then – cuppa. Compliments the 'aouse, too."

"Thanks."

She picked up the tray and as she turned, tilted her head toward the wall where a clock seemed to be hanging upside down.

"That fryin' pan clock – me daughter's. Was. All I got left of 'er. 'Ad it for nigh on twenty years naow. Up there. 'Er room this was. That fryin' pan clock was give to 'er by a down-under lad she loved – an' 'e loved 'er right back till 'e got it in the leg in the Somme. Then gangrene." She sighed. "Just me an' me dog an' me cat an' me daughter's fryin' pan clock. That's all."

When she returned with the tray she said, "Just tea, luv, but sleep tight all the sime."

At the door she turned back to him. "Just me an' me cat an' me dog an' me daughter's fryin' pan clock." Then once more, the refrain: "Mind. You don't do me no 'arm – I don't do you no 'arm."

... sure liked their tea strong ... half a cup ... all he could ... sit back a minute ... lean back against the pill ...

The dog barking somewhere downstairs and the headache stabbing both temples had finally wakened him. He was lying on top of the log cabin quilt in shirt, tie and pants, and socks, jacket on the chair back, where he'd hung it last night. He might puke at any moment!

Could a person get *land*sick as well as seasick? Maybe Mr. Gulliver was busy vomiting this morning.

Morning! The frying pan clock was contradicting that! Two-fifteen!

He sat up. So did his stomach. He managed to hang on till

he had dropped to his knees and pulled out the chamber pot. Bull's eye! By the time he got into his jacket, his stomach had steadied some, but the headache still pulsed.

The dog and the cat were, but Mrs. Sage wasn't, anywhere downstairs. He headed for the King's Head.

Same waiter as last night. He managed to choke and keep down a couple of slices of toast and marmalade and tea. Bitter again. When he'd finished he reached into his breast pocket for his wallet.

Gone! Nineteen pounds! Gone! All his money! Gone! His passport, the travelers' cheques were still there but ... Then he remembered that last night when he'd paid off the waiter he'd taken all the notes out, laid them on the table corner.

"Did I – I've mislaid nineteen pounds somehow ... Did I ... you ... did I forget and leave ..."

"No, sir," the waiter said. "Nineteen quid. That's a lot. You didn't leave it here. I'd of seen it. I didn't."

He cashed one of the travelers' cheques to pay for the toast and marmalade. As he did, the waiter said, "Too bad, lad. Tell you what, though. Just you step over to the post office round the corner. Somebody ran across it, that's where they'd turn it in."

"Really! You mean people here would turn in money they'd found –"

"Most Purfleet folks would do. Check it out."

There had not been nineteen pounds turned in at the post office, the clerk behind the wicket told him. If it did show up, where could they get in touch with him? He told him he was at Mrs. Sage's and as he turned away from the wicket he found himself facing a policeman.

"Did I hear you say you were at Mrs. Sage's place?"

"Yes."

"Who sent you to her?"

"I just paid off the *Onassis Penelope*. King's Head waiter told me she took in boarders."

The helmet nodded. "That's right. In her time, she's taken in a lot of people. You come with me and we'll just have a word with Mrs. Sage."

As they walked to Mrs. Sage's, the bobby said, "You're a Canadian."

"Yes."

"Came over in that Greek freighter, did you?"

"Yes. Do you really think Mrs. Sage could have ..."

"Is it customary in Canada for parents to turn children loose all over the world without any –"

"I'm seventeen. Do you think Mrs. Sage might have ..."

"We'll just see. I'll do the talking."

Through the hawthorn hedge and up the three steps. The policeman knocked.

"Tell me. Last night – was there anyone else here in the house?"

"I didn't see anyone."

"Middle-age chap – size of me – full mustache and brown – Ah, good morning to you, Mrs. Sage."

The old eyes swiveled from the constable to him then back again.

"This young man stayed over with you last night. This morning he found there was nineteen quid went missin' from his wallet." He paused, scratched one ear. "He's checked out the King's Head – the post office – and I was wondering –"

"What!"

"Just a possibility, Mrs. Sage."

"Possibility of what!"

"Well ..." He scratched briefly at the other ear. "He just – it just might have dropped out – perhaps got picked up, got carried off by your dog or your cat somewheres, and if you were to take a good look round the house you might find it for him."

"Not very fuckin' likely!"

"Mrs. Sage –"

"And the sooner that little shitfice gets his gear outa me fuckin' 'aouse –"

"Now just you look here, Mrs. Sage. A house can get a bad name when –"

"An' you get that prick helmet an' your lard arse off me front steps –"

"Mrs. Sage –"

"Both of you – piss off!"

The constable turned to him. "Before we do that, lad, you get upstairs an' get your stuff!"

"An' pay me the florin you owe me for your room an' your tea I brought you."

"Oh, did you now? Very interesting. No charge at all for those chloral hydrate drops made the lad pass out – give him his headache an' nausea –"

"Fuck you!"

"Thank you but no thanks. Move it, boy! Right now!"

She was not at the front door when he came down with his pack. As they went through the hawthorn hedge, the constable muttered, "West Ham."

"Pardon?"

"Not Purfleet. Not from around here. Showed up here with her daughter year after war broke out. I've got to carry on now, but I have a few words of advice for you. Smarten up and watch out!"

He was hearing anger in the constable's voice. Not at Mrs. Sage now but at him!

"You could have ended up as a Thames water baby. You're

lucky Charlie wasn't there. If he had been, you'd be the fourth sailor in the past eight months stayed with her an' never been seen since. No body, no proof, nothing to be done."

"Oh no!"

"Oh yes! The world's a dangerous place to be in, boy, and it's high time you learnt that before it's too late! How's your headache – your guts?"

"Better. Some."

"Okay – looks like she slipped you the *child* dose of knock-out drops. Christ! How I'd like to nail her!" He stopped, took him by the elbow. "You heard me well, didn't you?"

"Yes, sir."

"Look, son. I'm a father. And if you were mine I wouldn't let you out of me sight for the next five years. Not till you could smell danger off a bitch like her. Last two years o' the war her house was off limits to every soldier an' sailor in every nation of the Allied Forces. Just her an' her daughter doin' their bits day or night for the war effort. Either one of 'em had as many pricks stickin' *outa* them as they had stuck *into* them they'd of looked like a couple fuckin' porcupines! Mind what I've just told you now."

"Pretty hard to forget, sir."

"That's better. You'd be one hell of a lot safer with those grizzly bears an' red savages back in Canada."

"Unless I got scalped, sir."

"You damn near did last night, boy. Happy Whitsuntide."

Whatever the hell that was.

He'd managed Purfleet to Paris without any more disturbing incidents. The first night he pitched his pup tent and cooked bacon and eggs in a sheep field at Camber-by-the-Sea. Early in the morning, he struck camp and made it to Dover to catch the Calais ferry, getting through customs and immigration with no great difficulty. He liked to think that he had introduced hitch-hiking to Europe, certainly the thumb signal instead of an arm held aloft. Several times a car passed him and stopped and he ran to catch up, only to find a spread-legged driver stopped by a call of nature. In one instance it was a woman who had lifted her skirts and dropped her knickers to squat right by the road-side for all to see. The French national slogan, he decided, must be: "Quand il faut pisser, on pisse."

His first-year university French seemed to be working all right until the night just before Soissons, when he stopped at a farmhouse and used his memorized pitch on his first farmer: "Bon soir, Monsieur. Je suis un étudiant canadien qui fait la tour de monde pour étudier et je porte à dos ma petite tente. Je veux permission d'employer un de vos champs pour monter ma tente."

"Eloise – Eloise! Viens vite! Nous y avons un fou canadien!"

The farmer's wife came running.

It seemed that he had pronounced "champs" as "chambre," "tente" as "tante," so that the farmer thought he'd said: "I carry my little *aunt* on my back, and I would like permission to use one of your *rooms* to mount my aunt."

With some difficulty they managed to clarify his request and he *was* granted permission to mount his *pup tent* in one of their *fields*. They were quite interested in Canada and invited him in to have supper with them.

The whole way to Paris the next day was curtained with long rows of Lombardy poplars, and again and again he saw war scars on buildings restored with wood or stucco instead of stone. A friendly priest picked him up, and let him out in the center of Paris with best wishes and a last pat on the knee.

He reminded himself that Fred Petersen had warned

him not to drink tap water, which was pretty generally polluted in Europe, and had told him that wine was cheaper than bottled water, so that the French probably used it in their car radiators. He had also told him that lodging in Paris was dirt cheap: a room for the night, twenty francs. A dollar twenty *was* cheap. He had to price a dozen before he found l'Hôtel du Nord on rue d'Opéra: seventy-five francs, not twenty.

In spite of his short stature, the doorman cum porter was almost impressive in his tricorn hat, his fierce Guards mustache winging wide. Art let him carry the pack up the four flights to his room. The walls were pink. The bed was pink. The carpet was pink. The lace curtains were pink. The pink toilet puzzled him. It had no lid, and the scupper was blocked with a perforated disc that could let nothing solid flush through. Who needed hot and cold water taps on a toilet? Must be a foot bath. Before his Paris summer was over he knew it was not for foot bathing.

The porter took him down the hall and showed him another surprise – the fourth-floor toilet, a standup cubicle with two foot pedestals that could have served in a shoe-shine parlor. It was called a Turkish toilet. He had already seen the street pissoires with spread-legged males aiming their urine streams at the trenched circle below. Urination and defecation style, he decided, must be important cultural signals.

With five days to spend before classes opened, he was able to visit the Louvre, to see for the first time actual paintings by Monet, Gauguin, Van Gogh, Matisse, the Dutch Masters. Till this marble sight of her he had not realized that Rodin's reclining Danaïde was so small and so adolescently beautiful. She could never have murdered her husband, to be condemned to Hades to pour water forever into a bottomless vessel. Her older sisters, perhaps, but not this sweetheart!

He discovered the Latin Quarter his second evening in l'Hôtel du Nord, though to get there from the hotel he had to run a gauntlet of importunate *poules*, who fell into step with male passersby, frequently grabbing an arm or coat tails or worse. Didn't keep him out of the Latin Quarter for three nights, though. On his return each night the same woman would be waiting for him on the rue d'Opéra corner near the hotel, always in the dusk outside the streetlamp. She had good reason for staying out of revealing light, for she was no Danaïde and seemed to have dunked her face in a flour barrel just before going out on her trap line. She had a contralto croak that coaxed and insisted. No soft sell for her.

"Une tranche, p'tit!"

"Non. Merci, ma'm'selle."

Every single goddam night!

"Ma chambre, cher p'tit singe."

"Non, merci –"

"Viens! Viens! Une belle tranche de cou –"

"Non. Mille fois merci, mais non!"

"– belle belle tranche – beaucoup des tranches ..."

He registered at the Sorbonne his second day in Paris, and found that he was sharing studio space with a Roger Penne from Anglet. Roger's English was probably about as good as his own French. Roger shared his lodging with a girlfriend; as did several other students, it seemed. Roger's companion helped him with the rent by working as a life model, and through the summer course Roger would paint her often, alternating between her and the Roche de la Vièrge as his subjects. It was Roger who got him the basement room in the same building where he lodged. Thank God!

His last night at l'Hôtel du Nord, the cartoon ghost face waited for him, luminous in the lamplight shadow.

"Bon soir, chéri." She had him by the elbow. He pulled loose and made a move to go around her, but she grabbed his shoulder. "Si longtemps que je t'attendais –"

"Va t'en, sale cochon!"

"Viens avec –"

"Va t'en –"

"– à ma chambre –"

"– sale coch –"

"Merde!"

"Va –"

"Tu – p'tit trou de cou de singe!"

"J'irai aux flics si tu continue m'arrêt –"

Her finger claws raked down his eyes. "Écume de pissoire!" They blurred. With blood! Both cheeks were suddenly on fire. He couldn't see a goddam thing, but he felt night chill kiss his bare shoulders, then his back and his waist as she ripped off his shirt.

He staggered back, trying to clear blood from his eyes. Her kneecap caught him twice in the crotch before he went down. He did manage to get to his feet before she could land a kick at his jaw, but not before she had him by the belt and took him in the solar plexus with her head. He hadn't got his breath back when he felt his belt burst apart, then his pants being dragged down to his ankles. He managed to get them back up to half mast while she pounded and pounded him in the stomach with both fists, and then managed to shuffle and stagger away from her back to the hotel.

He checked out the next morning, did *not* tip the porter. Oh, how he wished he could be up in that room when the guy ushered in the next guest and saw what had been left in the pink bidet. All the same – in spite of Mrs. Sage, who had broken her promise to do him no harm; in spite of the lady by the lamp; and in spite of spending three nights in l'Hôtel du Nord without knowing it was a four-story whorehouse, he owed them all for his necessary loss of innocence. As well, for years afterwards he would get good laughter mileage out of those experiences.

Even now he looked back upon his Paris summer as the most delighting and exciting of his life. How often he would sit in memory at a sidewalk table of the Café de la Paix, seeing the same fat old gourmands with napkins tucked under their triple chins. On the street he remembered the gowned and red-fezzed Moroccans with for-sale rugs draped over an arm. He remembered his first licorice taste of Pernod Fils, the Folies-Bergère, and the Folies de Paris – no! Only once! That had been the true end of all innocence: the priest and his religious-rite copulation with the nun – dog fashion!

But most important of all, Louis. Dear old Louis! He had not been his teacher that summer, officially. But he was a mentor whom he would owe for the rest of his life. However hard he tried, he knew he would never be able to discharge his debt to Louis Simard. Louis's place, a top-floor apartment, was a drop-in center for young artists, a place to bring your own wine and your own art, both to be shared.

The most important quality of art, Louis told them, was that it must be unique, never normal. "Your work must surprise. Both your viewer and yourself."

Louis shared with them his own paintings, many of them done before the turn of the century, for Louis had not parted company with a great deal of his own art. And what a superb draftsman he was!

"You must know that the practice of art is the most difficult thing humans attempt. I tell you this now and you all nod agreement." He pointed to his head. "You are agreeing up here.

A few hard years down the road you will come to truly understand the truth of that." He pointed to his stomach. "Down here. In your heart. This will be the most difficult time of your apprenticeship. This is when most young artists stop trying. Don't you do that. Do *not* quit. I almost did. Perhaps I should have. Some might say I should have. I shall probably never know.

"You see, the most constant inner state of an artist is uncertainty. You must face confusion, self-questioning, dilemma. Only amateurs are confident. Why shouldn't they be? All their friends and lovers and blood relatives tell them their work is masterly – will one day win the Nobel prize for art.

"God hates amateurs. Their motivation is vanity – usually – and when acclaim is denied, the pain of disappointment is therefore much more acute. God has seen to that because He detests them. God Himself is no amateur, though He has made mistakes. Many consider the human race to be one of them.

"If He intended you to be an artist and you do not stop trying, be prepared to live with fear of failure all your art life. There will be days when you will wince at the very sight of canvas, palette, brush. Artist's block. There is only one answer to that: get into that studio every day, every week, every month, every year. Never let a gap happen. The greater it is, the harder it will be to regain your creative momentum.

"Do *not* quit."

So often he had been tolled back to Louis. Unique Louis, with his goatee and beret, who early in his career had decided not to put his work in commercial galleries for sale to private buyers. Just in public galleries. Louis showed them his own work. Again and again he would see in memory that triptych of a pregnant nude, probably in her third trimester, feel Louis at his shoulder, hear him say, "Pregnant – she is no longer naked – is she."

How often over the decades the voice of Louis Simard would come back to him. Throughout his own teaching life he had plagiarized Louis again and again and again. Bless you, Louis, wherever you may be. You gave me back my innocence. I have never stopped trying to discharge my debt to you!

4

All of them, one after the other just like four dominoes, and he had been the first to go down. He had played right into Frog's webbed flippers when he'd handed in his resignation. With this year's income and property taxes two months overdue, and the wooden bridge over Tongue Creek washed downstream in the spring flood, there was no way he could possibly survive on the thin trickle of early retirement pension. No choice for him but to arrange with Val in Continuing Education to teach Art Appreciation and Art History. Yet another broken promise to you, Irene. But don't worry, I'll put in whatever time I can in the studio.

Darryl had been the next casualty, tipped out of the international poetry conference in San Francisco when the National Arts Council had turned him down for honorarium and travel expense grants. Except for red tape collage work, the average run of bureaucrats were not avant-gardists, had never even heard of sound poetry before.

A week later Win had come home glum. He was not to have a devil of a time in a long summer run at the Sock and Buskin; the artistic director had caved in to the board and the financial director and made a last-minute change.

"What are they doing instead?" Art said.

"*Here Comes Charlie*. Hokum time again. I got it."

"Charlie?" Charlie said.

"That's right."

"Drag time again," Darryl said.

"Shut up, Prince."

"Could have been worse, Win. What if it was *Anne of Green Gables*? Aw – I'm sorry, Win."

"You sure got one funny way of showing it."

"Sorry. I really mean it, Win."

"Apology accepted."

"Gresham's law," Art said.

"Never heard of him," Win said. "Representational – landscape –?"

"Sixteenth-century English merchant, Thomas Gresham."

"What's his law?" Win said.

"Oh – that there's a tendency of the inferior of two forms of currency to circulate more freely than, or to the exclusion of, the superior, because of hoarding of the latter. Bad money drives out good. Art's just as vulnerable to Gresham's law as coinage."

"You can say that again, Art," Darryl said.

With his usual generosity Charlie had offered a helping hand.

"Look, Art – this show of mine is shaping up great. Looks like a record breaker. I can let you have enough to tide you over. Forget those courses at Livingstone and do what you're supposed to be doing on the other side of that wall between us."

Aw – bless Charlie!

Ten days later Charlie's gallery filed for bankruptcy. Last of the dominoes to go down. The art colony gloom was contagious, settling even on the Professor. For the first time ever since puppy housebreaking, he left three brown sculptures on the living room braided rug. When he came downstairs in the morning, Darryl stepped in only one of them.

For each of them in his own art, the sorry state of all art today had just been brutally clarified, and something had to be done about it. But what, damn it! Centuries ago Martin Luther had found an answer to his religious problem: no price tags on forgiveness. So had the descendant followers of Jacob Hutter, three miles west up Wild Horse Road. In Paraguay, the Grand Chaco of Mexico, on the prairies and in the foothills of Canada and the United States, communal societies of the Hutterian Brotherhood preserved their faith and simple lifestyle. They had survived a grand massacre in Russia, which reduced them to fifteen souls, from whom all of today's Hutterites were descended. Wherever they were, all of them dressed as they had centuries ago, sang the same Gregorian hymns, emulated Christ's apostles, resisted worldliness, and obeyed the stern old men called "bosses" in their patriarchal societies. From colony to colony little was different beyond individual preference for black jacket fasteners: dome or button or, up Wild Horse Road, hook-and-eye.

So why did he keep coming back to their way of life again and again? Possibly because art was his religion, and Charlie's and Win's and Darryl's. Yeah – that was the reason why: after the atomic holocaust God would still be holding Hutterites and artists as His two hole cards to win the human game again. Shelley would agree to that. Poets *were* the unacknowledged legislators of the world.

He was onto something here, some hidden beginning to the answer they wanted. Just possibly he might have it by their hayloft meeting next week.

Now, back to this painting you've been struggling with, Ireland. It might even paint itself for you.

It hadn't. Painter's block again.

For the past three years now, as soon as another spring had colored land and sky, they would begin each week with a Sunday get-together up in the hayloft. The ritual seeds must have been sown the year he'd been at the Sorbonne, when he had left Paris for a couple of weeks in London and discovered the Oxford Group. Well, not so much Buchman's fellowship as dear Louis Simard's wine and art sharing. Now, years later, they were poet and actor and sculptor and painter in a society of caring friends. No confessions to be made but confidences by each of what he was trying to do in his own art. Yeah – just like the Louis gatherings, for they too had celebrated love and unselfishness. Oxford Group purity or divine guidance were not ingredients in their meeting recipe, though, so that would let him off the hook for what he was going to suggest to them tonight. Maybe.

The hayloft was such a perfect place to hold a creative gathering. The one small diamond window, high in the barn's cathedral peak, released a slant banner pulsing with dust motes, to scrawl the warped board walls with light. Always their meetings would begin with a slapping explosion of pigeons' wings as humans yet again trespassed upon their gothic territory. Then it would be quiet, time to lie back against hay drifts with eyes upward, open or closed, to breathe deeply the incense of sage and sweetgrass and the faint, lingering shit ghosts of horse or cow or goat long gone to that great green pasture in the sky.

Just lie back now. Relax. Let it happen. Let it happen. Let it happen.

If he'd forgotten to take his antihistamines, Darryl would be sneezing again and again and again, but it would simply punctuate the hiccup and mourn choir of pigeons soon reassembled outside along the barn ridge.

"Ticket-ah-roo. Ticket-ah-tah-rooooo."

"Ah-huh-hah-choooo. Huh-huh-hah-chooooo!"

Let it happen. Let it happen. Let it happen now.

"... The practice of art is the only thing done by the human race that does not involve an adversarial relationship. I am plagiarizing Dr. Colin Dobbs, whom you may know, a teacher of creative writing in Livingstone English Department. In his fine convocation address last year, he said there are no victors and no vanquished in the art experience, nor is the artist concerned with win or lose. He must do it for its own sake – for the sake of doing. This is not true, of course, of war, or of sport, which is simply a parody of war. More importantly: commerce is not an art.

"We are all of us – as are most artists – victims of a materialist, commercial, money-motivated society. This has been so ever since the industrial revolution, and has carried on, thanks to the robber barons, into this century. The art robber barons thrive today as they never have before. You'll find them south of the border, in Europe, in Hong Kong, in Tokyo. They have turned art into a commodity – aided by international art auction firms in London, Paris, New York. They have turned art into capital gain art.

"Art is no longer for all; it is for the private consumption of the individual, wealthy and commercially elite. Were they here with us, I am sure that Adam Smith and John Stuart Mill would agree with me that this is not right, in the light of their belief that the goal of free enterprise is the greatest good for the greatest number. All the same, Adam and John had trouble with art, and copped out by labeling its value 'unearned increment.'

"In his *Republic*, Plato had difficulty with poets. For him the poet meant maker, or artist. The poet's low role in a just society shows it wasn't all that important to Plato – ironically, since he was not simply a philosopher king but a great poet as well. In the Middle Ages, the time of city states, and the Renaissance and beyond, the patrons of art were princes and kings and emperors and members of the aristocracy helping painters and sculptors and composers to survive by art alone. Or else the church, where art could be seen and heard by everyone who came to worship. Art then was for all. And it should be for all, not just for one rich old miser gloating over a wonderful painting in the privacy of his dining room."

"What's your point, Art?"

"I'm getting to it, Win. In the light of what has happened to each of us recently – you, Win, having to do another hokum role at the Sock and Buskin – Darryl denied travel and honorarium funding to attend the San Francisco poetry festival – two years of Charlie's work down the drain with his show cancellation because the gallery has gone into bankruptcy. I include myself, for I am going to have to rob time from painting by going back to teaching Art Appreciation and Art History at Livingstone. In the light of all that, the time has come for us to do something about it."

"Like what?" Win said.

"Ha-hu-hah-hah-chooooo!" Darryl said.

"Well, brace yourselves. I have a suggestion you may find shocking."

"Go ahead and shock us, Art," Win said.

"Hah-huh-haaaah –"

"For God's sake – turn your head –"

"– chooooo!"

"As you know, the Livingstone Art Gallery is holding a

twenty-day show of the world's finest collection of Albrecht Dürer engravings and prints. They belong to Maxwell Lampert, Texas oil billionaire ..."

"Go on, Art," Charlie said.

"Well – I'm finding it difficult. The thought occurred to me that something dramatically public should be done about what I've just been talking about."

"I get it, I get it – we organize artists and art students to picket – protest at the open –"

"No, Win. I did think of that possibility at first, but it has to be something – ah – more ..."

"Well, what?"

"– much more dramatic than that, Win."

"What – what is more dramatic?" Charlie said.

"What if we were to take the Albrecht Dürer collection from Livingstone Art Gallery and from Maxwell Lampert?"

"Tick-ah-tah-roooo – ticket – aaah-rooo," the pigeons above said.

"Ah-huh-huh-holy sheeee-yit – ah-chooooo!" Darryl said.

"Jeeeezus Murphy!" Win said.

"Just a minute, Art," Charlie said. "You aren't suggesting we break into the gallery – steal the Dürers? You're not really serious about this – are you?"

"I am, Charlie."

"I think it's one hell of an idea," Win said.

"Hold on – hold on," Charlie said. "We're not talking here about a student theft of plastic lawn ornaments, but it sure smells like an adolescent prank to me!"

"No, Charlie."

"Just what bloody relevance has it to your lecture and its thesis that art is for all? We steal the Dürer collection, we'd just transfer it from Lampert's hands and into ours. That isn't art for all."

"No, it isn't."

"So forget your feeble rationalization for doing such an outrageous –"

"I still think it's a hell of an idea –"

"Grow up, Winston. You too, Art."

"Charlie, it isn't a rationalization. I haven't explained – ah, the plan – fully. We take the art but not for ourselves – not for crass profit, which is the reason of many wealthy collectors looking for capital gain and selfish possession. We take it for *all*."

"And how's that?"

"We return it to where it belongs – the public galleries."

"I repeat. *How?*"

"We'll work that out."

"Well, when and if you do, you can count me out!"

He reached over and took his watch from the bedside table. Five-twelve! With poet sneezes the other side of the partition and magpie squawks just outside the bedroom window, sleep was impossible. Aw hell, he'd hoped to put a finish on that painting before he had to show up at Livingstone by eleven. Wait a minute. Get out there now. Turn on the fluorescent track lighting and get going, Ireland.

The Professor greeted him in the kitchen. His tail was not wagging welcome. He had more important matters on his mind over there by the window. She was at it again! Let him at her! Whole goddam family of them going at it out there: Mama Maggie Magpie and Papa Pete and all their squawking bastard young!

"No, Professor. I'm going out to the studio. You stay in here. Leave them alone."

"Aaaaw-rrrh-aaaah-uh-uh!"

"All right. You can come with me."

Now the tail was wagging.

He *would* have it finished before he took off for town. The Professor seemed to like it.

He'd just started mixing when Win showed up.

"How can anybody get any sleep with all that sneeze sound poetry going on!" Win said. "Even without Darryl sneezing his ass off – I wasn't able to sleep so good. Tell me something. I think I know what your answer will be, but anyway. Have you ever done any break-and-enter?"

"No, Win. I haven't."

"Has Charlie?"

"Not to my knowledge."

"Uh-huh. Which leaves Darryl, who has difficulty breaking open a pill bottle or a box of snap, crackle, and pop."

"Just what are you driving at, Win?"

"What I'm driving at is this. Theft is an art and it ain't for amateurs. Like you guys. After what you suggested last night – what we might try to pull off – that Livingstone art caper – let's sit down a minute. Art, there's something I got to tell you about myself. I said you guys were amateurs. I'm not. Besides being an actor, I'm – was … once …"

"Go on, Win."

"Look, Art – when you saved my ass that day in the campus parking lot, fed me, took me in here – I should have told you something about myself. You see … well, I been on the point of doing it several times, but – uh – I haven't. After my mother died. I was nine. I didn't lead a sheltered life."

"Look, Win, you don't have to –"

"Yes. I do. Now – after last night I do."

"Okay."

"I guess you know – my mother was an actress. If she hadn't

had both of her legs she'd been another Sarah Bernhardt. Matter of fact, in our front hallway we had a chair once belonged to Sarah – Queen Anne."

Win had told him before about the Queen Anne chair in the front hallway. Several times.

"After Mother died I used to go over and over her reviews and notices. Rave ones. I guess in the moor love scene, in *Love on the Dole*, she had Wendy Hiller skinned a mile. She's why I'm an actor today.

"She taught me pantomime. How to sew my fingers together with imaginary needle and thread. Look."

He took a phantom needle from his jacket lapel, spool from his pocket. After several times, squinting and aiming, he ran the thread successfully through the needle eye, bit it off, knotted the end, lifted his left hand, separated out the little finger, shoved the needle point through the finger tip, took it out the other side and with short pulls that jerked the little finger, pulled the thread all the way through. Next finger, next, then the forefinger.

He braced himself to do the thumb, lifted his needle and thread arm high and wide. Stabbed. His silent mouth said "Ouch!" His face contorted with acute pain. He shoved the thumb up his crotch, lifted his knee to squeeze and squeeze out the hurt. Finally stuck the injured thumb in his mouth and sucked.

When he'd stopped laughing, Art said, "Never saw you do that one before, Win."

"Oh, she taught me lots of them. How to catch my toe on a heel so I'd trip and sprawl out flat on my face – do pratfalls – open up and climb a shaky stepladder, then teeter and lose my balance on top to fall off of it. How we must have pissed off my old man."

When was he ever going to get to what he wanted to tell him? Or did *not* want to tell.

"She taught me all I've ever known about timing. Got me to read from Genesis, Song of Solomon, Ecclesiastes, till I could capture biblical strophe."

Poor Win. Whatever it was, it must have been hurting him a long time.

"She taught me to project without seeming to be shoving up from the diaphragm in order to reach the very last seat in the house –"

"All right, Win, what is it –"

"Did her damnedest to teach me restraint ... She gave me my first stage role – when I was six, I think. She directed our elementary school play. Know what I played in that?"

"No."

"Coffee pot. It was a health play and I was lead villain: coffee, along with the other villains, cigarette and coca cola and candy, always arguing with the good guys, milk and tapioca and oatmeal porridge –"

"Win, what is it you want to tell me – about amateur –?"

"Oh, yeah. She was always on. Like me. Well, I better get to the point. As well as acting I have another talent – the gift of theft. Probably got it from my old man. He was a big time developer, knew all the right people on town councils, in the legislature, which ones were on the take. When mother died, she left me in his tender hands. I can show you dramatic scars, Art, on my back, my arse."

"I believe I have seen them, Win."

"About Grade Eight I ended up in the Rose Buddies. Not really a gang – just four of us. At first it was crossing starter wires on cars in lots that didn't have high fences or Dobermans or German shepherds. Just for the danger fun of it, you understand.

"By Grade Nine we were into break-and-enter for jewelry, cash, that sort of stuff. We were good at it, knew every pawn shop in the city. Only a short matter of time, of course, till we got busted. Lucky for us we were juveniles, first offenders, so we got suspended sentences with no time in the reform bucket.

"One good thing about it though. Dear old Daddy kicked me out. Quite a change – big Rosedale house to Cabbagetown alleys. Thank God it was summertime. I survived, washing dishes, waiting on tables. Early September I headed West – to get as far away from him and that part of my life as I could. Hitch-hiked all the way out to the foothills, had a good run on harvest crews, steady job waiting table through winter. Aw, shit, cut it short. Took me three years to get my high school matriculation in Chinook Community College, then five more for my BFA in Livingstone, working weekends and night shift waiting table during the school year and construction jobs and oil field rigging during summer break."

"Good for you, Win."

"So, now I've filled you in on the – ah – criminal part of my curriculum vitae, which should come in damn handy for us. I was pretty good at it. That's why I had to tell you."

"I appreciate it, Win."

He stood up. "Guess I've screwed up enough of your working time –"

"Not at all, Win. I have to confess something to you, too. I welcome the slightest excuse to knock it off. It's called fear of failure."

"Yeah. I know what you mean – art fright. For painting, for acting. But I'll tell you something – you're going to find it's a hell of a lot worse when we go on stage in that Livingstone gallery."

"Somehow that doesn't surprise me, Win."

"About this art caper of yours – ours. You do agree with me that you wouldn't know diddly-squat how to pull it off?"

"Yes."

"You need me for it."

"Of course I do."

"Doesn't mean I've fallen off the wagon. Whole different matter, and we're not the Rose Buddies. I buy what you said tonight. Art for all. Back when you rescued me in the campus parking lot I was that close to going back to my artful dodger days." He swallowed a couple of times, took a kleenex from his jacket pocket. "You – uh – saved my life then, Art. I'll owe you for the rest of it." He wiped at his eyes. "Shit! Must have got some of your goddam paint in my eye!"

5

Charlie had meant it when he'd said to count him out, and had done his best to persuade them not to go through with it. He'd focused mainly on Art.

"Come on! You've got to drop it. Art! Let's have a little common sense! No way you can go through with this outrageous –"

"We'll see."

"You know why you're really wanting to do ..."

"Yes."

"– just a criminal act of selfish revenge."

"No it isn't."

"Yes it is! To get even with Frog, and you've already done that. In spades. With my help."

"You're wrong. I have a much more important target than Hopper. I've given it a lot of thought and I'm deadly serious about it."

For long moments Charlie stared at him, then shook his head. Sadly. "I'm afraid you are, Art. Which makes it all that much more disturbing. I just wish I could make you see –"

"You do agree with me that art is for all."

"Of course I do. And do you agree with me that theft is a deadly sin?"

"Not in this case. We are simply transferring this collection from Lampert –"

"Save it for your cult faithful, guru! Aw, Art, please don't go through with it. Don't drag Winston and Darryl into this half-cocked, dangerous silliness! Don't put them both at grave risk!"

"That's for them to –"

"The hell it is! For those boys you call all the shots because they respect and love you." He turned away. "Almost as much as I did. Once."

Win certainly did have twin talents. He began his strategy planning right away.

"I'm the skip."

"What does that mean?"

"Curling term, Darryl. I call all the shots right from the casing. If we do the job right to the ninth end, we win the MacDonald Art Brier."

"What the hell does that –?"

"It means I'm the skip – the boss. Now. There's an inside and there's an outside. You and I inside, Art. Outside, Darryl, as lookout in the van."

"Where's Charlie?" Darryl said.

"He's busy right now."

"I mean when we – where is he when –?"

"I understand, Art, that there's other stuff besides this great German art in the show?"

"That's right."

"That's not so hot – valuable?"

"Yes."

"Why isn't Charlie here?"

"Which is why Art and Charlie have got to be insiders with me so we clip only what's worth taking."

"Yes. Also these are precious, internationally celebrated paintings. One of a kind, which have to be handled with experienced care."

"Uh-huh. So I'll need you and Charlie in there with me."

"I don't think so," Art said. "I'm afraid Charlie's out. No way he wants any part in it."

"Okay. Just you and me and Darryl then. That answers the first question: Who? Now about when. After the opening of the art show? Before the opening?"

"After," Art said. "So the general public has seen it and through press reviews knows the value of what's gone missing."

"Uh-huh. When is the opening date?"

"Thursday – twenty-eighth."

"Great – four days before the first day of the Great North-west Stampede, which is Sunday, July first, so that means reviews will be in the weekend papers. Couldn't be better timing. We'll do it over the weekend – the long holiday weekend, Dominion Day. If people aren't out at their summer cottages, they'll be downtown for the stampede opening day parade.

"You fellows sure about Charlie not wanting –?"

"Yes, Darryl," Art said. "He made it quite clear to me."

"I mean – maybe – maybe he might just change his mind if he was only out in the van and I went inside with you fell –"

"No, Darryl. You're our lookout."

"I'd still –"

"That's it, Darryl. Lookout's important. Believe me. Also – there's another good reason ..."

"What other good reason?"

"Never mind."

"Come on, Win!"

"Well – there's a hell of a lot of campus cottonwood fluff drifting out there, and we're not doing a sneeze and enter."

"That's what I like about you, Winnie. You put everything so nicely."

"I try. Now, next item: break-in tools. We are going to need the following: gooseneck bar, at least two flashlights, large screwdriver, skeleton key, tape rolls, glass cutter, peen ball engineer's hammer ..."

Meanwhile, *away* from the ranch, other plans were being laid for Dominion Day. These were for the opening of the Great North-west Stampede, and the discussions were taking place in the boardroom of Magna Meat Packers Inc. P.T. Brockington as always occupied the chair – or saddle. As well as being president of Magna Meat Packers Inc., Brockington was past president of the Foothills Quarter Horse Association, owner of the Northern Blades of the Patrick Division of the NHL and the Western Broncos in the CFL, and chairman of the Great North-west Stampede board. In his audience were other members of the city's elite.

As usual the mayor, Harry Blakely, a.k.a. Harry Come-Lately, was late for the briefing, so he was missing P.T. Brockington's preamble to the planning of this year's Great North-west Stampede.

This was truly a banner year for the event, he explained, its fiftieth birthday. The opening parade would take off at City Hall, then horseshoe for thirty blocks throughout the business district, ending up at the rodeo grounds. Maxwell Lampert, the Texas oil magnate, whose Albrecht Dürer art collection showing would have opened in Livingstone University Art Gallery to great press acclaim several days before, would lead the parade on the Appaloosa quarter horse he would be bringing up with him from Houston. A quiet and elderly palomino mount had been found for the winner of the Great North-west Beauty Contest, Queen Wild Rose, who would ride beside him. She had already begun instruction at Cottonwood Meadows Riding Academy.

At this point Mayor Blakely showed up with a brief apology. Brockington accepted it and back-tracked on his preamble.

"We have quite a prestigious list of guests showing up this anniversary year," Brockington went on. "Buckingham Palace has sent the Queen's royal regrets; seems She and Philip are tied up at Wimbledon, but the Duchess of Kent is coming in Her place. Because of an important meeting in Camp David with President Ford, Prime Minister Trudeau can't make it either, but he's sending us the federal minister of agriculture. We already have the president of the Western Stock Growers Association and Dr. Aaron Hopper, dean of the Livingstone University Faculty of Fine Arts and a close friend of Maxwell Lampert.

"Now here's where you come in, Hank."

"Make it quick," the mayor said. "I have another important meeting –"

"Okay. It would be nice if there could be a formal ten-gallon white hat presentation in City Hall made to these people –"

"I'm afraid I really have to –"

"– with special attention to the one for the Duchess of Kent. Back during the Centennial year they left it too late to get one big enough for her head size."

"Sure. Sorry I have to leave ..."

"Hold up just a minute, Hank. The best news of all is yet to come."

"Make it brief."

"I will. Hot-air balloons."

"What?"

"With the warm updraft of our chinook winds, our foothills is – are probably the finest hot-air ballooning part of the earth's skin. IAHAB, the International Association of Hot Air Balloonists, has decided to hold its annual rally and race here – taking off on opening day of the Great North-west Stampede."

"What the hell has –?"

"From the rodeo grounds."

"Look, I'm late for ..."

"This means we have another prestigious guest, named Monsignor Bourget."

"Fine," the mayor said, "so we have a distinguished guest from Quebec."

"Paris. He is a church dignitary, Monsignor Bourget, but he is also the world's leading hot-air balloon pilot and he's bringing his bubble and basket over with him and he will take off –"

The mayor had already made it halfway to the conference room door.

"– from the rodeo grounds. Others will be taking off from other locations, of course. In the basket with him will be: the minister of agriculture, the president of the Western Stock Growers, Maxwell Lampert, Dr. Hopper, Queen Wild Rose, you –"

The mayor stopped with his hand on the door knob. "Me?"

"Of course. As mayor of our city –"

"I'll talk with you about that later."

"All right," Win said. "I've cased it and it's looking good. I think I've found our point of entry, a good-sized basement window in the Library Block. Usually it's a window you're looking for – easiest way to get in – and this one's a dandy. It's away from any main campus traffic route either by car or on foot. Completely obscured by lilac bushes, pussy willow, and cottonwood trees. Unfortunately it's frozen right into the concrete foundation wall, so we can't do a quick and easy take-out. Have to smash it. No problem.

"Another piece of luck: this window lets us inside just down from the stairs leading up to the Library Block main hallway, maybe a hundred paces from the entrance door to the display room of the gallery itself. So far, so good. Up to this point only. The window in the door is thick plate glass reinforced with wire, and the door has an inside iron bar. We're going to need a sledge to smash the window in the door and a cutting torch to handle that reinforcing wire to make a hole big enough to get the gooseneck through to hook up the inside bar. That'll open the door, and bingo!"

The mayor had been less than enthusiastic about joining Monsignor Bourget, Queen Wild Rose, the president of the Western Stock Growers, Maxwell Lampert, and Dr. Aaron Hopper in the basket.

"Look, I have to tell you something. I have a peptic ulcer. I guess it goes with the job. Actually before that – back to when I was just a kid and I never went on a roller coaster or a merry-go-round, even a swing. Wherever I have to go it's never by air. You got to count me –"

"We can't, Hank. Too late for that. We can't have it without the mayor. It's been announced again and again that you –"

"No way. I'd throw up –"

"It's just a ceremonial lift-off – a gentle five minutes aloft till we land in a field on the city edge. There'll be a limousine waiting there –"

"I can't."

"You better, Hank. There's a municipal election coming up next spring, isn't there?"

"Yes. But –"

"No buts, Hank. Have you forgotten how much Magna Meat Packers has contributed to your two campaigns so far?"

"No. And I appreciate –"

"No chicken shitting at this late point in time. You be there. You climb into that basket or else. We'll supply an airsick bag for you!"

"At first I thought Darryl would let us out on the road nearest to the basement window side of the Library Block, then wait for us on lookout there, but I changed my mind. Soon as he's let us out, I want him to take the van around to the *back* of the building, where the loading and unloading ramp is. I will, I hope, a day or two before the heist, have gotten hold of one of the maintenance dolly carts and hidden it outside and well under cover.

"I go inside with Art. He points out the stuff we want. No. Art – what do you think – you and I go to the show opening and *that's* when you show me which ones to take."

"You're the skip, Win."

"And you're my third, Art. It'll save us time, and quicker is always better. As soon as we do get inside, you go right back out while I'm taking down the pictures. You go get the cart and bring it in. We load it, wheel it out and down the ramp and straight to Darryl and the van and away we go.

"One other good thing – I couldn't believe it – there are no burglar alarms or any electronic systems for us to worry about.

"Sometime before the opening of the show we'll go out there and I'll take you around – sort of a rehearsal. For now here's a map to give you a rough idea of the layout."

It had been such a beautiful coincidence, P.T. Brockington, chairman of the Great North-west Stampede board, explained. In all the promotional radio and television and press interviews he waxed enthusiastic about the natural twinning of the fiftieth anniversary year opening of the stampede and the International Association of Hot Air Balloonists' annual race. The Goodyear blimp would hang high over the rodeo grounds for the entire two weeks of saddle and bare-back bucking, steer wrestling, calf roping, and chuck-wagon racing, and each night would conclude with a brilliant fireworks climax. Both the IAHAB race and the Great North-west Stampede would be featured on TSN, the CBC, the BBC, the ABC, and a Tokyo network.

"Now then. The Monsignor Bourget balloon will take off after the opening parade and from the rodeo grounds infield right after the 'Oh, Canada.' But timing is of the essence. So all the basket occupants must be there in time for the national anthem, including the mayor, who has graciously finally agreed to be a most prestigious basket case in this opening ceremony."

"Not funny, P.T.!"

"Sorry, Hank. Just in fun."

"Not funny! At all!"

"Where was I? Oh yes – there is to be a briefing given to each and everyone well before lift-off. The Monsignor does not speak English but we have a fine interpreter to relay his instructions, which must be followed to the letter. Any questions?"

"I have one," the mayor said. "Why the hell aren't you going up in that basket with us?"

"Because, Hank, I will be in the Magna Meat Packers' grandstand box – having tea with the Duchess of Kent."

Metropolitan Tribune, Friday, June 29

Livingstone University Dürer Art Show

The display of Albrecht Dürer's 450-year-old Renaissance masterpieces in the Livingstone University Art Gallery showing that opened with an enthusiastic crowd of two hundred in attendance yesterday, illustrated dramatically that the work of Dürer has en-Düring charm.

The artworks are on loan for 20 days from the private collection of Maxwell Lampert, the well-known Texas oilman. This collection of the world's best prints and engravings "took me 12 years to assemble," Lampert said.

The Dürer woodcuts combine masterly draftsmanship, technical refinement, vivid imagery, and inventive design in sometimes grim and grotesque depictions.

"It's hard to pick a favorite," Lampert said, "but his 'Samson Rending the Lion' sure turns me on."

Because Dürer's work is so portable, Lampert explained, "I've sent them on tour all over Europe and America."

So near to the fiftieth anniversary opening of our Great North-west Stampede, it was quite fitting that Lampert attended the show in Western dress of ten-gallon hat, chaps, and fringed white doeskin jacket touched off by a stars and stripes bandana.

"Way I see it, judging from what I notice folks up here wearing, looks like there isn't all that much difference between Texas cowboys and you Canadian ones," he said.

Lampert will be leading the opening day parade Monday on his Appaloosa quarter horse he brought up with him.

He and Albrecht Dürer certainly had a fine art opening day with the Livingstone University show.

In his opening speech welcoming "the most influential and most cultivated people in the city," Dean of Fine Arts Aaron Hopper modestly discounted the story that this show represented a personal triumph for him. After joking about the persistence and persuasion he had employed with Mr Lampert, he went on to predict that the show would put Livingstone University Art Gallery on the map of the world of art.

6

Today was the day! He had not slept well, nor, he suspected, had Darryl or Win. Charlie either, for that matter. All night long he had kept asking himself the same question over and over again: how come he had gotten himself into this. It was not simply a selfish and long-delayed act of revenge – though God knew, Hopper certainly had it coming to him!

Eight years ago, when he'd gone along with Irene and cut loose from teaching to concentrate on his painting for the rest of his life, he'd managed for just two years to pay taxes and grocery bills. They'd been good but apprehensive years for both of them. No steady-job years! He'd kept on trying for a year after Good Night, Irene, then had gone back to Academe. Things had looked good, then there was talk of a new dean, and then no tenure granted thanks to Froggie boy.

But that wasn't the heart of the matter, so why? Why? Why pull Darryl and Win into it? More importantly, why didn't he now feel the slightest twinge of regret?

He was the first up and downstairs. The Professor had news for him. This was the fifth day in a row that Mama Maggie and Papa Pete hadn't showed up to tease and annoy him. Neither hide nor feather of them to be found anywhere on the place. Searched high and low for them. Kind of miss them. Goddamit!

Darryl showed up. One look at his anxious Prince of Wales

face, all nose and ears, and he felt a surge of concern for him. What a vulnerable young fellow he was.

"You all right, Darryl?"

"I – I will be."

He put his arm around Darryl's shoulders. "You know – it's up to you. Your decision. If you don't want to take part I'll understand. Win will, too."

"No, Art. I want to help. I really do."

"You sure?"

"I'm just a little bit uptight, but I'll be all right once I get breakfast down."

His breakfast seemed to do that for him.

They were just finishing when Win made a dramatic entrance into the kitchen.

"Good God, Win, what are you doing in that outfit?!" Darryl said.

"Touch of insurance," Win said.

"Where the hell did you get –?"

"Sock and Buskin costumes. Borrowed just for the occasion."

"Wow!"

"It's not a Livingstone patrol uniform but if a university guard did show up, I'd just explain I'd been hired for special watch duty for the art collection."

"Aaargh – aaaw – grrrh – aarh – ou – ou – oo – ou!" the Professor said.

"It's all right, Professor," Art said. "It's just Win."

The Professor wasn't so sure of that.

Besides the dark-blue uniform Win had a duffel bag. He went through it with care, making a last check of the break-in tools after breakfast. By the time they left, Charlie still had not made an appearance.

The Professor was not happy to see them leave. When the

others were in the van, Art said, "Just a minute. I have to have a word with the Professor."

"Now, listen carefully, licorice lips. I'm perfectly aware that it's Saturday and we're supposed to be in the studio together, but this Saturday is different. Win and Darryl and I have an urgent and very dangerous task to perform in the city. We'll be back well before supper. Till then I want you to stay close to home. I should probably put you in the run, but I know how much you hate that. Just in case you've forgotten, there's that sonovabitching neighbor to the east of us who doesn't know it's closed season on golden retrievers."

He was referring to Jeff Ottowell next door with his purebred herd of ugly Charolais cattle. Two years ago the Professor had gone close to – but not through – the fence to play tag with bulls, cows, and calves, but that had not stopped Ottowell from trying to score his first canine baker's dozen for the year. With his thirty-ought-thirty he'd drilled the dog high and just ahead of the hindquarters. If he hadn't just missed the spine it would have been so long, Professor. Unlike the Hutterites, Jeff Ottowell did not have any use for gentle persuasion.

Well before the van reached the city outskirts they began to spot the hot-air balloons. As well as the Goodyear blimp, others drifted up there: Mickey Mouse, a Labatt's beer bottle, a Re/Max ranch-style house, a Whopper hamburger, a Shell gasoline pump, a Dairy Maid triple-decker vanilla soft ice-cream cone, even a Great North-west Stampede ten-gallon stetson.

Monsignor Bourget's balloon with its blossoming fleur-de-lis had not joined them up there yet but was being readied on the infield of the rodeo grounds.

A good half-hour before rodeo buck-off time, Queen Wild Rose, Dr. Hopper, the minister of agriculture (and four aides), the president of the Western Stock Growers, and Maxwell Lampert had arrived beside the balloon for briefing, all of them (except the aides) in cowboy dress, including Queen Wild Rose in frilly white skirt.

"Where's the Duchess of Kent?" Lampert said. "And the mayor?"

It was explained to him that the Duchess was not flying with them today but that the mayor would show up at any minute now. By the time balloon inflation had begun, there was still no sign of Harry Come-Lately, so the briefing had to start without him.

They ran into an interpreting problem, for the translator, a nice young man from Quebec, had no difficulty with *l'accent pointu de* Monsignor Bourget's *français de Paris*, but the distinguished churchman had great trouble understanding Quebec French, and did not seem to try very hard. His gestures of explanation became wilder, then stopped abruptly. The passengers looked at one another and shrugged. What could go wrong?

It was supposed to be the first of July, but once they had entered the city limits it was more like a blizzard day in January, for the air was bewildered with gust-driven clouds of cottonwood fluff settling into drifts against curbs and buildings, then lifting to float and fly and swirl and fall again. The Livingstone campus seemed to be at the heart of the arboreal storm. By the time the van had reached the Library Block, Darryl had started sneezing.

"Did you take your antihistamine pills this morning?" Win said.

"I – hah-hah – think I did."

"Here." Win was holding out a pill bottle. "Just in case you didn't, I brought them for you ..."

"So that's why I couldn't find –!"

"Take them and shut up! Okay, Art, if you'll get over behind the pussy willows, I'll bring the duffel bag."

Darryl sneezed down his aristocratic noise and blew out the pill he'd just put in his mouth. He tipped another one out of the bottle.

"Now, Darryl, you know where I showed you. Take the van to the north side – near the ramp service entrance side of the building. Understand?"

"Uh-huh. Hah-hah – huh – high-doooo!"

"I take that to be affirmative. Park the van not *on* Poundmaker Drive but just off of it. When Art and I show up with the cart full of pictures you head straight for the ramp. Understand?"

"Huh-high – high'm trying tooooo!"

"You all right?"

"I'm scared shitless!"

"Good."

The interpreter had managed to explain for Monsignor Bourget that air balloon lift-off was a delicate and precise operation since it involved controlling the rise and fall of a two-ton weight. Queen Wild Rose, the federal minister of agriculture, Dr. Hopper, and Maxwell Lampert each had a duty to perform. As did Mayor Blakely, who had not showed up yet.

Through the interpreter and through the sullen gestures of Monsignor Bourget they gathered that the lift-off crew would be holding the basket rim of the inflated balloon. The federal minister of agriculture would grasp the red cord hanging from the balloon mouth and, upon signal from the pilot captain, Monsignor Bourget, would give a couple of tugs to open the valve and release hot air into the balloon.

Upon another command from the pilot captain, Queen Wild Rose, in charge of sand bags hung around the basket rim, would drop the first one. For greater lift Bourget would then signal the federal minister of agriculture to give two more tugs for another shot of hot air. Only two. The crew on the ground would then release their hold. This sequence of sand bag drop, exhaust, hands-off, hands-on would carry on till the basket lifted a couple of inches then settled back to earth, indicating that the balloon was precisely on balance.

At this point Queen Wild Rose must drop three or four bags. Hands off! Lift-off to thunderous cheers from the grandstand!

One final and crucial caution from the nice young man from Quebec: "At the end of descent when basket has touched earth, do *not* exit basket until pilot captain has given exit signal."

Just as Win had predicted, entrance by the Library Block basement window was no problem. Win smashed it, cleared away the shards, and crawled through. Art handed him the duffel bag of tools; then Win helped him through the hole, catching him as he dropped to the basement floor.

Nobody in sight.

Up the stairs.

Nobody in the long hallway.

Halfway to the gallery entrance Win took him by the elbow and pulled him into a doorway alcove. "Just me from here on, Art. You stay here, out of easy sight. Soon as I make it inside, you join me. Together we take down pictures, lean them against the walls. Then while I stack them near the door, you head out for the cart, bring it in, and we load it."

He went down to his knees over the duffel bag, opened it and took out the short-handled peen-ball sledge, the cutting torch, and the gooseneck.

He stood up. "Okay. Here we go."

"Break a leg, Win."

"No, Art. May our hemorrhoids expand."

"I think mine already have."

"Good sign."

The city limousine had raced into the rodeo grounds infield just in time. The mayor jumped out and, after what seemed to observers to be a moment's hesitation, made it up and over and into the basket with Queen Wild Rose, the minister of agriculture, the president of the Western Stock Growers Association, Dr. Aaron Hopper, Maxwell Lampert, and pilot captain Monsignor Bourget.

On signal, one after the other, Queen Wild Rose dumped four sand bags.

The ground crew, in unison, let go the basket rim.

Bon voyage! Even though the mayor had heard none of the briefing and in the confusion of His Honor's late arrival Monsignor Bourget had not completed Queen Wild Rose's *in-flight* sand bag instructions – bon voyage!

The weather bureau had forecast moderate prevailing northwesterly wind for most of Dominion Day. They had been wrong. The wind *was* moderate, but it was also north*easterly*, which blew them toward the grandstand. The balloon cleared it, just, but the hoot and toot of the carnival grounds came next. Heat from the hot dog stands and the ride motors of the Red River Shows as well as that from black asphalt and almost as many milling humans below as Wellington led into the Battle of Waterloo created a strong updraft that sent the balloon soaring.

Although they were rising high Monsignor Bourget withheld the signal to deflate. To be on the safe side, he would give it to the president of the Western Stock Growers Association, who was in charge of deflation, only when they were past the carnival grounds and the city limits as well. If needed.

Probably the worst sinus attack of his life even though he'd doubled the pill dose from the bottle Win had given him. With the windows closed it must be at least a hundred and twenty above in the van. Hadn't Win ever heard of air-conditioning? How about another pill? No way. He could already feel their soporific side effect and lookouts must never sleep.

Even though he'd taken off his jacket and shirt, he was still dripping sweat in this oven. Couldn't go outside, because he'd just inhale more cottonwood fluff and really sneeze his ass off. Better get out of his pants as well. No. First get out of here and roll down Poundmaker Drive a ways with the vents open, then back to a nearby sheltered spot that wasn't surrounded by cottonwood trees and fluff drifts.

Well past the city limits, the Monsignor gave the deflation signal to the president of the Western Stock Growers Association, who gave two tugs to the valve cord. Unfortunately by now they had drifted over Loon Lake so that descent turned into plummet. It was lucky that Queen Wild Rose had not clearly understood the in-flight sand bag instruction, and instead of a couple of *handfuls* of sand she was *supposed* to drop, she dumped two *full* bags … so that the balloon basket missed the water by inches before swooping up again, leaving a startled water-skier, who had been innocently enjoying the holiday weekend, shaking his fist from the water at them, while his boat circled to pick him up.

Rising fast, the balloon also missed the power line. When he vomited, the mayor did not miss either Queen Wild Rose or the hand-tooled kangaroo leather riding boots of Maxwell Lampert.

"Where the hell is the sonovabitch!" Win turned from the window. "Stay here with the cart, Art – over by that garbage can. No, leave it and you squat down behind the can – aw, sheeyit!"

In spite of the Charolais herd of cattle below, this patch of gently rolling prairie near the foothills had seemed an ideal landing spot for the balloon. They were well away from the cattle, perhaps a hundred feet from settling gently to earth, when they heard the ten-gauge Imperial Goose Load Magnum shotgun blasts over the propane roar. Whoever it was, his target must have been the fleur-de-lis bag itself, for among the crew he got only Dean Aaron Hopper with three bee-bee pellets: one in the right ear, another in the chin, and one in the left forearm. All of them appeared to cause the dean a great deal of pain.

"That'll learn the bastards!" Jeff Ottowell said as the balloon lifted off his back twenty and he pumped six more shells into his shotgun.

Darryl had showed up at the ramp a good ten minutes late. They loaded on the art, pushed the cart into the bushes, and took off. Art mission accomplished! In spite of Darryl.

All of them had hoped that their third descent, this time onto a summer-fallowed field well west of Jeff Ottowell's Bar Jay spread, would be a final one. It was not to be, for His Honor, Harry Come-Lately, had missed the most important part of the briefing: "At the end of descent, when basket has touched earth, do *not* exit basket until pilot captain has given exit signal."

The basket was still a good two feet off the summer fallow when he scrambled over the rim to safety. Balloon lift was instant, but the mayor was still holding the basket rim so that he was carried upwards, with legs dingly-dangling, to a height of two hundred feet before the president of the Western Stock Growers Association and Maxwell Lampert were able to pull him back inside. The next time they landed in accordance with Monsignor Bourget's bellowed instructions.

End of flight.

It would be the last one for: Mayor Blakely, the minister of agriculture, the president of the Western Stock Growers Association, Maxwell Lampert, Dean Aaron Hopper, and Queen Wild Rose.

The three-decker Dairy Maid vanilla soft ice-cream cone touched down to come in first in the IAHAB race. Whopper hamburger was second, and the Great North-west Stampede stetson third; the Shell gas pump was last.

The Professor had not been at the gate to meet them, nor was he anywhere in sight after they crossed the bridge and drove up to the yard. While Darryl and Win unloaded the Dürer collection, Art headed for the house. The Professor wasn't in there either.

He took down the referee whistle from its hook by the back door. The Professor never failed to come running whenever he heard it. Not this time, though it shrilled again and again and again. Maybe he was with Charlie in the shop.

No Charlie, no Professor in there. Neither were Charlie's rod and creel. That must be it. Gone fishing with Charlie on Tongue Creek.

He went back to his studio to make sure that Darryl and Win had stacked the art in the corner behind the couch and covered it carefully with the tarp.

They had just finished toasting their art mission success with the last of Peter the goose boss's chokecherry wine when Charlie showed up. He said nothing, but the expression on his face indicated he was not the slightest bit interested in their art caper.

More importantly, he had not seen the Professor since noon.

"Don't worry, Art. He'll show up," Win said. "Sooner or later."

"Yeah," Darryl said. "He's probably off somewhere with that lady coyote been hanging around last couple of days – south side of the creek."

Not a comforting suggestion at all!

After supper they all went looking for him, searching without a trace till nightfall. Art let the others turn in, then sat out on the back stoop. As the sky lit up with the Great North-west Stampede fireworks, he punctuated their distant thunder with the referee whistle.

When Charlie came down and out onto the porch the next morning, he said, "Didn't you turn in at all last night, Art?"

"No."

"Professor hasn't showed up yet?"

"No."

"Art, something I should tell you. Yesterday just as I went out fishing – ah – I heard some shots."

"Oh no! Not rifle –!"

"Shotgun, I think. Number of them."

"From Ottowell's?"

"I'm afraid so."

"Why didn't you tell me last night?"

"I was going to, but I decided to wait till we'd searched for him. You were enough upset as it was. Where you going?"

"Where the hell do you think I'm going!"

"I'll come with you."

"No! I don't want any witnesses to what I may have to do to that –"

"It's just a possibility, Art."

"Almost as strong as what I intend to do if he's –"

"You're not going to take a gun –"

"No. A goddam branding iron!"

He found Ottowell, leaning over his tractor, and came within a hair of letting him have it with the branding iron over the back of his skull.

"All right, Ottowell! Did you shoot my dog?"

Ottowell straightened up and turned to him.

"Not yet, I ain't, Ireland."

"Come on! He's missing! Yesterday afternoon you fired off your shotgun!"

"Yep."

"At my dog!"

"Nope."

"The hell you didn't and if you've killed –"

"Nope. I had a lot bigger target than your dog."

"What!"

"One of them goddam balloons been stampedin' my cattle the last four years. Came right down on my back twenty – all covered with them floor-dee-lizzies so it must of been all the way from Quebec. Put down that goddam brandin' iron."

"You really – you didn't?"

"Yep. She's open season on the Bar Jay for dogs, hunters, coyotes, fishermen, and hot-air balloons. *All* trespassers. Includin' you *and* that yellah dog yours. Yesterday it was a balloon. Tuh-morrah if you don't keep him tied up, it could easy be him."

"If you ever do, Ottowell, I will brain you with this –"

"You're welcome to try, Ireland. Even though I got no taste for givin' a shit kickin' to senior citizens."

"Well I have, Ottowell – for good neighbor pricks like you!"

Charlie was the one who found the Professor, curled up in the fetal position in a far dark corner under the front porch. Whatever it had been roaring and hissing up there, he wanted no more to do with it than Jeff Ottowell did!

Metropolitan Tribune, Monday, July 9

Art Search Heats Up

City police, theorizing international art thieves carted off priceless Renaissance masterpieces from Livingstone University, this week continue an intensive hunt for the treasures.

Theft of the 450-year-old woodcuts and engravings by Albrecht Dürer, a painting by Monet, and others by the Group of Seven a week ago was considered by world art experts to be a major loss. Police have no suspects in the weekend break-in at Livingstone University. The artworks were on loan from the collection of Maxwell Lampert, Texas oilman, for a 20-day showing.

As investigators continue to scour the campus for clues, Detective Inspector R.S. Valentine said he believes the theft was the work of professional international thieves. "Definitely more than one," he said. "Two at least. The way the library building housing the gallery was entered and the items taken indicate professionalism."

A police source indicated that the search was concentrating on airports and border crossings. The RCMP, major metropolitan police forces, the FBI, and Interpol have been forwarded descriptions of the works, and speed is needed in tracking down the culprits before the works can be secreted in countries where they would not likely be discovered.

Point of entry to the Livingstone University Art Gallery was a basement window hidden by shrubs, which campus security found broken about 7:30 the morning of Sunday, July 1.

More than six hours later, a gallery technician

found a second broken window in a door leading to the display area.

Extremely upset, dean of the Faculty of Fine Arts, Dr. Aaron Hopper, said, "I do not know how we can possibly overestimate the damage this has inflicted on our fine university in the eyes of the world. Two months ago, I came back from art conferences in France, Italy, West Germany, and Australia, and I assure you that everywhere I went our Livingstone University arts program was held in the highest esteem."

See HEATS UP page B4

Dr. Hopper explained that the art theft was in a sense a personal outrage for him, since the collection belonged to his long-time friend, Texas oil magnate Maxwell Lampert, whom he had persuaded to lend his Albrecht Dürer collection for a 20-day showing in the Livingstone University Art Gallery. "I don't know how I'll ever be able to make it up to Max," Dr. Hopper said.

He was quite disappointed that campus police did not check the gallery as soon as they discovered the first broken window, because they thought it might be a prank-style piece of student vandalism. "Not unusual," Dean Hopper said, "at this University."

He said he was not referring to the lawn ornament thefts that swept the city last year. Those culprits, widely believed to be art students, have not yet been identified and brought to justice.

The Livingstone art gallery has no specialized burglar alarms or electronic devices, he said, though he has done his very best to have them installed for quite some time.

University vice-president in charge of security, Thomas Parsons, was not available for comment.

7

Tonight would be the finest hayloft night they'd ever had, for now it would be an art show as well. Along the loft walls they would hang the Dürer collection, the Monet water lilies, and the Group of Seven paintings. It had been at Win's suggestion.

At first Art hadn't liked it. "No way, Win."

"But why not?"

"Too risky. The last place for those paintings to be with the barn roof the shape it's in. Just think. If it rained ..."

"But if the weather's not a threat –"

"And most of those pigeons still have diarr –"

"I don't mean permanently, Art. Just for our meetings."

"Nope. We can't take any chances they might get damaged up there."

"Damn slight chance."

"However slight, we are not going to take it."

"Look. I mean just for our meetings. We hang them up just before. We take them down right after. Darryl's all for it."

"And Charlie?"

"Hell – he's still pissed off with us for doing the job. Matter of fact I'm still worried he might ..."

"Might what?"

"Oh ... no ... he wouldn't do it."

"Do what?"

"Ah ... sorry I ... he ... shouldn't have mentioned it. Charlie wouldn't squeal on us."

"You're bloody right he wouldn't. Let's have a little trust, Win!"

"Sure. About hanging them – how about just this once?"

"Mmmmh."

"To celebrate pulling it off."

"I guess so. Just once."

In the week since they'd pulled off the job, it was as though they had ceased to exist for Charlie. So sad: the end of twenty years of friendship! And in the light of this, what *had* Charlie decided to do? What *did* he have in mind? He must find out before their hayloft meeting tonight.

He found him in his studio.

"Charlie."

He remained turned away as he stooped down over whatever he was doing at that big cardboard carton in the corner. Art noticed a whole rank of others lined along the wall.

"Just talking with Florence and she said why don't she and you and I get out along the Tongue Creek and try our luck."

Charlie straightened up and turned around. He himself was his finest sculpture. He wasn't a big fellow, but there was power in that trim figure. Why not, given the years he'd worked in stone and iron.

"Too much to do here."

"Aw, come on, Charlie. Just this morning I saw a big brown hanging below the beaver dam. I bet he'd go over five pounds."

"I've more important things to do right now."

"Please. Do it for me, Charlie. We have to have a talk and doing it while we flog the water seems a nice way to do it. Please, Charlie."

For long moments, his blue eyes held Art, then released him. Thank God!

"All right."

With rod and creel and Florence grunting anticipation behind them they headed for Tongue Creek. Professor hadn't liked it at all when he'd put him in his run and closed the gate. Wasn't fair they'd take a goddam pig with them and not him! But there was no way Professor could resist the lure of water, Art had explained to him many times; he'd just plunge off the bank and into every new run or hole after a mallard or a beaver. He was good company for shotgunning, yes; angling, no.

Charlie had agreed they should head downstream as far as the beaver dam first, then work back up, and that perhaps a small gray wet nymph might work better than a black leech streamer. Maybe dap dry mayflies. As long as it was fly patterns and angling strategy, Charlie was a little more relaxed and communicative, but not very damn much so.

Before they had reached the beaver dam four bluebirds brilliant as fluttering fragments of spring sky flew by. Good for you, Charlie. You really pulled it off. Ever since he'd moved in, whenever he'd been blocked, Charlie had left his stone or wood or ceramics or metal to build bluebird houses, hundreds of them, nailing them up against fences and telephone poles almost all the way into town. The Charlie bluebird trail!

Just above the dam pond when they stopped a moment at the long gravel spit, Charlie started on downstream.

"Hold up, Charlie. Let's stick together. I have to talk with you."

"Yes. I think we should, Art."

In silence except for the creek murmur, the distant slap of a beaver tail, or Florence oinking now and again as she rooted under the wolf willow behind them, they took turns casting.

"Art."

"Mmmh."

"I have to tell you something. When you made your theft suggestion in the hayloft, my first response was that you were kidding. You couldn't be serious about it."

"Oh I was, am. Deadly so."

"My second was that you'd completely lost your wits. Just temporarily, I hoped. I didn't believe for a moment you'd really go through with the thing. I was wrong. You have." He had taken his rod down. He slung his creel over his shoulder. "I'm leaving."

"But we just got started, Charlie."

"Not Tongue Creek. Your rural round table. I'm moving out. I've found a place in town."

"Oh no!"

"Sorry, Art. There is no way you can possibly carry out your art for all mission. You haven't even set up a way to get the Dürers into a public gallery."

"Yes I have."

"Oh, you have contacts in the States? Brazil? London? In Paris? In Rome?"

"No."

"Then just how in hell can you possibly –?"

"I have it all worked out."

"Then fill me in."

"I will. At our meeting tonight."

"I don't think so, Art. If that's the meeting topic, I want no part of it. We've known each other for a long time. We needed each other when we lost Doris and Irene. Now you've turned Camelot into Scamalot, I'm saying goodbye."

"Okay, Charlie. But will you do one last thing for me?"

"Depends."

"Come to the hayloft meeting tonight? One last time."

"Aah – if you insist."

"Thanks. Oh – and another thing. For Florence and me. This is one hell of a mayfly hatch. Look how they're pocking the water under every overhang bush and tree. Put your rod back together and we'll score a Guinness Book of Records catch of browns."

"Okay."

"One other thing. After you've heard what I have to say tonight and you are convinced that I have a way to transfer art from one to all. Really –"

"No, Art."

"I'm not asking you to take an active part in it – but to change your mind about leaving us."

"I doubt it, but we'll see."

"Thanks."

Win's suggestion that they hang the paintings around the loft walls had been a fine one indeed. They made such a lovely setting for his message to them tonight. If only he could get it through to Charlie.

"Visual art has an important distinction from all other forms – music and the literary arts of poetry, novels, plays – in that it lives only in the actual presence of the painting or sculpture in plain sight of the viewer. A symphony or a play comes back to life with each performance and a novel or a poem with each reading. It's impossible to take these arts away from everyone. Hitler tried to do that, of course, with book burning; and he succeeded well in gutting many conquered nations' public art galleries. And you can hide visual art away.

"With this Dürer collection we have begun a mission to return art to all. I said 'begun,' for it is only the very beginning. I do not want this to be a one-time operation. Thanks to Win, we have proved that we can do it, and we must do it again and again and again so that our message to the world will be loud and clear.

"Now, I have given a great deal of thought to just how – once we have artwork in our possession – how we restore it to all. Liberate it. I think I've found the answer to that. I have gotten in touch with not one but three different art insurance experts, and all three of them verified a common practice. When pieces have been damaged or destroyed the insurance claim is automatically paid off. With stolen art there is the possibility of recovery, and if that should happen after the insurance claim has been paid off then the art belongs to the insurer – *not* to the original owner. If that owner returns his claim payment to the insurance company then he gets his painting back. You follow me?"

"I do," Win said.

"Me too," Darryl said.

Charlie said nothing.

"Now – here's the important part. First, the original owner is not going to try to reclaim the stolen painting unless he is told that it has been recovered. Also, he has to be fully aware that he has an option: to keep the money and leave the work in the hands of the insurance people, or return the money and get the art back. Now, invariably that option is in very fine print, or perhaps the party of the first part has not let the party of the second part know about the option at all. As in most commercial deals I'm afraid not everybody is squeaky clean."

Except for Charlie, he had their undivided attention now. Not a sneeze out of Darryl, so far.

"Given that the first owner was not aware of the option and

doesn't return the claim money, then the insurer may sell the painting to recover the money that has been paid out. Sounds fair enough, doesn't it? Not necessarily so. Not with hot items. You see, with what is happening with art today, thanks to international art auction houses, often the value that has been estimated for insurance purposes is much lower than the current market value.

"Quite understandably, then, the insurer with ownership of an internationally precious collection – like this Albrecht Dürer one – may have inadvertently not let the original owner know of the option. There's a time period during which the money may be paid back and the art returned. Just how long that might be I don't know – but I can get back to my experts and find that out."

"Wait a minute," Darryl said. "I don't see how us taking it from one rich owner and transferring it to the insurance people so they can sell it for a profit to another owner ends up as art for all, Art."

"Yeah," Win said. "Some billionaire in Hong Kong or Tokyo or Brazil or the Grand Caymans. Look at those sunflowers of Gauguin –"

"Van Gogh, Win."

"Went for millions."

"It did," Art agreed. "Once major art comes on the market, and the insurers make sure its availability is known in all the right places, public galleries and museums all over the world come down with auction fever. And here's the key: at that point few private bidders stand a chance of winning. Public galleries with government funding have an edge over private collectors. There are exceptions – win some, lose some. But the odds are probably nine-to-one the art will go public. Does that answer your concern?"

"Sure does," Win said.

"Me too," Darryl said.

Charlie said nothing.

"So I think what we do is, we keep the art for whatever the option waiting period of time may be, then we arrange for it to be found."

"How?" Darryl said.

"Aah – we'll work it out. Not too complicated. We'll just leave it –"

"Where?" Win said.

"Oh – a university Fine Arts faculty, shopping mall perhaps – carefully, then notify the police anonymously."

Charlie had gotten up, gone over to the loft ladder opening and was halfway down.

"What's wrong with him? Why is he –?"

"Didn't work, Win."

"What didn't work?"

"I had hoped he would change his mind after he'd heard what I had to say. He hasn't. Now, let's move along.

"Our city – our province – is a mother lode of classic masters' art held in private hands. I know what I'm talking about because for years galleries, insurance firms, and art collectors have come to me for evaluations. For birthday, retirement, Christmas, New Year's celebrations, for soirees and afternoon cocktail parties, I have been invited into nearly every elite home in town, to stand and to drink and to admire the owners' art in front of their friends.

"Last few years more often than not I've declined invitations to embellish collectors' egos. Not any more. In this way we can find what we want. Or, to use a Winston expression, 'case the joints.' Now let's have no misunderstanding. We must target only private collections. Public galleries are out. Aw – I didn't have to remind you of that.

"One other point. Commercial collectors aren't all that willing to acquire the work of contemporary artists; there's little opportunity for capital gain, and it's risky. Poetry is at the bottom of the bestseller list, unless the poet's safely dead for fifty years. Talented actors like you, Win, have a tough time making it up to the poverty level. Simply put: they won't take ours; we take theirs."

"With you there, Art," Win said.

"Me too," Darryl said.

"I can see that you have seldom taken your eyes from those Dürer prints, from Monet's water lilies, or Lawren Harris or Lismer. The joy of art. Nothing can equal it."

"Oh, I don't know about that, Art," Win said.

"Keep it clean," Darryl said.

"I'll try, celibate boy."

"Something just occurred to me, Darryl. In the light of what I've been explaining. When the time comes – the keep-return option has run out – we can do a first test with this art – a trial run. How old were you when you came over with your father?"

"Seven," Darryl said. "A couple of years after my mother passed away."

"Do you still have relatives in the Old Country?"

"They populate most of Yorkshire. I got them in Kent, in Sussex. There's an aunt and uncle and cousins still in Tottenham."

"I'd hoped so."

"How do you mean?"

"A possibility. After a decent interval we crate these paintings, and ship them over. Have them put them in a safety deposit box in a U.K. bank till further notice."

"Sounds great," Win said.

"If you say so, Art."

"Okay. Any questions?"

"One for Darryl," Win said. "You been in touch with all those relatives of yours over there lately?"

"Just one of them. Tottenham. My father's brother. Long as I can remember, almost every second or third year he came over to visit us. Uncle Eric. In the undertaking business."

"Great," Win said. "Forget that crate. We can use a casket."

"Another crack like that, Win," Darryl said, "and you'll end up in one."

"All right, fellows, meeting over. Win, you and Darryl get these paintings back in my studio. Under the tarp."

He found Charlie out on the porch. Full moon and the night scented with the smell of his perique and latakia pipe tobacco.

"So you haven't changed your mind, Charlie."

"'Fraid not, Art. For quite a while I've been pretty sure you weren't planning a one-shot – ah – event. I anticipated what your sermon for tonight would be. Disappointed I was right."

"Aw, well."

"But I do accept now that – for you – it's a sincere mission. You've thought it out carefully and done your homework well. Very clever, that insurance wrinkle with the conveniently obscure keep-or-return option. I can see now that you'll move one hell of a lot of art off-shore into public national galleries for all to see. I wish you luck in your theft venture."

"Thanks."

"Until you're apprehended. You know I can't be part of it, Art. I have to leave. Day after tomorrow. Sorry."

"Me too."

He had to have one last try with him after breakfast the next morning. In the shop, Charlie was wrapping what looked to be the last few of his frog sculptures and nesting them in a carton. He soon realized he was wasting his time, not Charlie's, who went right on packing.

"There. That's almost it. Truck's coming out tomorrow afternoon. Win's taking some in with his van." He straightened up and looked at him. "Tell me something, Art. What would Irene think of this matter?"

"I haven't checked it out with her yet."

"What?"

"I said I haven't –"

"I knew you talked with the Professor and Florence, and you're always muttering to yourself. But Irene?"

"Yes."

"In your dreams."

"Few times. I do most of my dreaming when I'm awake and working in my studio."

"Hmmm. Makes sense."

"I do talk to Irene. Especially the past two years or so. You find that strange, eh?"

"No. I don't. Doris keeps coming back to me. Less and less, though. You said the past two years –"

"Ever since they doubled up my medical check-ups."

"I didn't know –"

"I never told you. Anybody else. Except Irene."

"Told me what?"

"They discovered I have an abdominal aneurism."

"Oh! No, Art!"

"Doctor was reassuring. Last measurement a month ago it had moved up from two centimeters something to a high three. He said we'd just wait till it hit six, then an angioplast. My check-ups changed from every six months to three."

"Oh! Art, I wish you'd told me earlier!"

"No point. I never remind myself of it, and friends certainly aren't for worrying needlessly."

"Yes. They are."

"Then how come – after you moved out of ceramics and into iron pieces the size of the Eiffel Tower, you didn't whine once to me about your double hernia till the day before you went into St. Barnabas Hospital for surgery?"

"I get your point. Give me a hand, will you?"

"With your packing?"

"No. With my *un*packing."

"Oh, Charlie! You changed your mind about stay –"

"Yeah. Sadie and Irene told me to."

"Oh, Charlie! I love you!"

"Not easy for me – but it's mutual."

Daily Citizen, December 4
Steal To Order Suspected

July 1. The Livingstone University Art Gallery stripped of Renaissance prints on loan from Texas oil baron. Value: roughly $1,500,000.

August 26 or 27. Crown Antiques entered through an old unused door by thieves with skeleton key. Stolen: antique silver pieces dating back to the 18th century and worth about $50,000.

September 18. Three bronze sculptures from the Chinook Ranchlands Club. Value: $75,000.

October 1 or 2. The home of Real Estate C.E.O. and art collector Stanley MacIntyre entered while he was in Palm Springs. Stolen: 14 paintings including a portrait by English 18th-century painter Sir Joshua Reynolds, and two Picassos. Total approximate value: $525,000.

October 15. Old Master's Gallery. Paintings, sculptures, 10 by A.C. Leighton and other artists. Value: $50,000.

Five separate art heists. About $2,700,000 worth of works stolen in less than four months, in a city where there have been no art thefts to speak of in the previous 20 years.

"They are going in and stealing specific articles," says Detective Inspector R.S. Valentine. "It's as though somebody told them what they wanted and they broke in and stole those articles. Very selective."

In charge of the art theft investigations, Inspector Valentine is sure the five crimes are related – "and may be related to a number of similar thefts in other western cities as well, showing the same skills and apparent careful selection," he said.

And while a job is being pulled in one city, nothing happens in any of the others. In fact, between thefts there was ample time for the culprits to travel from one city to the next. In all cities investigators have been stymied in their attempts to trace the missing goods.

"None have turned up," said Inspector Valentine. "Street sources, usually valuable aids in locating stolen property, have come up with absolutely nothing.

"It would indicate to me that they are being taken right out of the city after the offences are committed," he said.

"No doubt in my mind – the stuff is stolen on order, taken out of the city, and delivered to the person who ordered it in the first place."

See STEAL TO ORDER page B2

"What that person could be doing with the artwork is anybody's guess. Resale is almost out of the question because there's been enough publicity on these articles that no one would buy them," Inspector Valentine said. "In our country, that is. They could show up on another continent, although a tourist could easily stumble on them and identify them. But if the person ordering them wants them for himself, location of the artwork will be next to impossible.

"If they are part of a private collection, the only way we'll find out is through an informant. We've been questioning everyone arrested on break-in charges that could possibly be related to the five thefts. Our pride's involved in this case. We don't want to miss any bet at all. Whoever is responsible, we're going to catch them."

Part Two

Daily Citizen, November 1

Art Thieves Raid Collector's Home

The gang of art thieves who have been selectively stripping homes of the city's elite and wealthy have struck yet again.

Latest victim is leading lawyer J.M. Donahue, who has lost pieces of art valued at $190,000.

Police report someone broke into Donahue's residence in the 2200 block Royal Way Monday.

Worried by the steep rise in art and antique thefts, city police organized a three-day seminar last week.

Detective Inspector R.S. Valentine said, "Our knowledge and expertise in this area of crime is in its infancy and therefore requires considerable sophistication as quickly as possible.

"This sophistication is essential," he added, "if we are to adequately cope with what we believe to be a complex network for the theft and disposal of stolen antiques and works of art."

Besides the 14 paintings, the haul also included three Persian rugs and a bronze sculpture of a horse and cowboy, another of a flying dolphin.

"We have no idea how thieves could ever fence articles like that, but they certainly knew exactly what to take," said police spokesman Detective Herbert Laverty.

Inspector Valentine, who is heading the Donahue investigation as well as all the others, agrees the thieves knew what to take. "They probably have had buyers set up for all pieces stolen long before they stole them. This is big league, and they have everything planned right down to the last detail."

Donahue was out of town at the time of the robbery and his loss was discovered by relatives early Tuesday morning. The collection was insured.

I

～⊃◯⊂

So – you've finally made it onto the great art scam case. Good going, Detective Kathleen Tait of the Metropolitan Police force! Been one hell of a smart move of Valentine's: holding that seminar and coming up with the idea of sending someone undercover into Fine Arts at Livingstone University so they could become better informed about what the art thieves might likely be after.

And tomorrow morning it won't be out on the beat for Detective Tait with lard-ass Laverty for a partner. For the next three months it won't be drug or hooker or traffic detail, it'll be classes in Art Appreciation and Art History. How about that!

Half past one. Better turn in. University's way out on the edge of town: it's a nine-o'clock and you mustn't be late for your first class. Those supper dishes can wait.

Who could have predicted that after five years on the force she'd be going to university. Damn! How often she and Julie had talked and dreamed about going one day. How often they had giggled and hooted themselves to sleep in their shared double bed.

Sleep wasn't going to come quickly to her tonight. It never did whenever she remembered Julie. Dear Julie! Remember. Remember. Remember.

In or out of their three-story house enclosed in caragana it had been such a loving competition. Julie was better than she was at sliding down bannisters; she did it without holding onto the rail, her legs wide apart and arms aloft. And she usually beat her at their dad's pool table up on the third floor, also on the schoolyard, shooting plunks or chase or poison for keeps. But Julie beat most of the guys, too. Out at the lake cottage Julie had managed to pull off a first jack-knife before she could. And then a somersault. So what! She had an unfair year-and-a-half edge on her.

Julie was taller. She had buttoned on the first bra, and made it to the menstrual starting line ahead of her. She thought she'd beaten Julie in that olympic event until her mother reminded her they'd had beets for supper the night before.

Julie had been cooler and quieter than she was; more inner to Julie and more outer to herself. It was as though they completed each other and made one together, yin and yang. Nostalgia could distort, of course; there had been screaming and crying sometimes, and on occasion hair pulling.

No differing opinion of their father, though. Negative. He was a well-to-do real estate accountant given to fatuous statements he thought to be of great wisdom. She and Julie had trouble deciding which one took the cake. There were so many to choose from:

"Easy always comes hard."

or

"Time will always tell on you."

He'd got off the emptiest one of all out at the lake cottage one summer as they looked down at the beach: "Footprints in the sands of time." It was repeated every time they went on the beach.

And how about the very specific homily: "Approval seldom comes to those who chew with their mouth open." They had finally with distaste voted for: "Fate decides our fate."

Julie on the left side of the bed; Katie on the right; laughter in the dark till their father stormed in. "Neither success or sleep ever comes to those who stand and giggle!" Well – he'd never used that one, but he could have. Julie had made it up for him. An untidy room drove him up the wall too. "Order is the best weapon of defense." And every case that failed to fit in with his accountant's view of the world was "the exception that proves the rule."

They promised each other they would become famous: Julie, a ballet star; Katie, a painter. Every night each had a gangplank for getting into bed, with Julie holding the brass footrail while she did dance workouts, and Katie at the dresser doing watercolors.

Julie had almost kept her promise. She had made it with the Royal Winnipeg Ballet for a year before she was raped and strangled to death in the Rue Madeleine alleyway.

To hell with canvas and paintbrush! Let's even the score in Julie's memory! Hence: Detective Kathleen Tait today. Hadn't been easy: father hurdle first. She'd cleared that one by leaving home to work as a waitress, then as a taxi driver. The day she reached twenty-one she applied to the Metropolitan Police force. She was turned down three times because she was under the height limit as well as being a woman. But she had hung in and was finally given a chance.

During her training and probation period she had two officer coaches. The first one for a three-month run was the detachment clown, Ike. She'd had lots of laughs and giggles with him. He was caring too, seemed to understand what a lovely high it had been when she was issued her uniform. When she got her gun he sensed her concern and tension.

"Just relax, Kate. I know what you're – what goes with the job. Wish I could tell you it'll ease off, but it won't. You'll always have it in your gut, and that's a good thing. Take my word for it. Keeps you on your toes.

"Been a lot of us one time or another came close to shittin' our pants. I *did* one time. Tommy has, twice. Don't you ever tell him I told you that, or I'll say you're lyin' in your teeth."

"I won't."

She hadn't been so lucky in the next three months with Herb Laverty, six-foot-four with shoulders a yard wide and a third trimester gut. Their first day when he had parked the car during a coffee and hamburger break, he quit chewing with his yap open to announce, "I'm going to level with you. I'm not looking forward to the next three months with a lady partner. We get into a jam – one-two-three time, I'd rather have a guy backing me up. Just what the hell could you do –"

"My best."

"Which won't be none too good. How tall are you, anyway?"

"Five-three."

"Uh-huh. What you weigh?"

"One-twenty."

"How come a nice little girl like you ended up in this line of work?"

"I've been asked that question a lot."

"Yeah?"

"Not as a cop, though."

"Huh!?"

"First time it was a lard-ass john like you when I was a hooker on Sixth East, then others quite a few times over the next two years."

That shut him up for a moment.

"Look, lady, let's get one thing straight. Right now! Next three months I'm stuck with you I ... am ... in ... *charge*! Understand?!"

"I believe I do."

"And no more of that kind of shit!"

"Is that a promise?"

"Huh?"

"That you are in charge and while you are you promise not to take advantage of it because I happen to be a woman five-foot-three, hundred and twenty pounds, and you will not verbally batter me the way you've been doing ever since we climbed in this car this morning?"

"Well, well, well. What have we here?"

"What you have beside you here, Laverty, is a partner still in training who, although she does squat to piss, does not intend to take any more shit from you for the next three months!"

His eyes were hard on her. She hoped hers were just as hard on him! His dropped first.

He turned on the ignition, shoved the gear shift forward. "Not surprised."

"At what?"

"You did time as a hooker before you joined up."

For the rest of their three months together and long after, she knew he told others of their exchange and passed it on as gospel truth that she'd done two years of tricks on Sixth East. Hoped they weren't going to make a practice of hiring ex-hookers like her for cops. Had she ever conned him!

In spite of him she'd made it through eighteen months' probation to graduation. As constable she'd actually gone undercover as a prostitute, at which Laverty felt she'd do very well. She had. Drug detail undercover had been a nasty one, too.

Thank God she and Julie had spent a lot of time shooting marbles and snooker balls. Her good hand-and-eye coordination learned then must explain why she had come in first of all her class during target practice on the range. It also enabled her to humiliate Laverty the time he sarcastically invited her to join the other guys at Shorty's Chalk and Cue. A few awkward decoy shots to let him win a bet, then up the ante and clear the table right down to the eight ball. As he handed over fifty bucks Laverty did not look happy.

It was after that incident that he stopped calling her by her proper name; now it was always "Ms Marble." Not all that discomforting. And taking her Art Appreciation and Art History course out at Livingstone University was going to put nice distance between her and Lard-ass Laverty for the next three months.

Boy oh boy! Like a whole semester holiday! Quarter to three! Get some shut-eye, Katie, or you'll be late for your nine-o'clock. She was still having trouble believing it was for real. She'd never forget the full detachment parade just before the morning shift called by Inspector Valentine in the Metropolitan Police boardroom. Very quickly he disposed of several minor matters, to get to the major purpose of the special gathering.

"All right, I've saved the worst for the last. I am referring to the art thefts that started on the opening day of the Great North-west Stampede last July. Almost one and a half million. Three more since then. A hundred big ones, then five hundred, then three hundred thousand for a total close to two and a half million. In *four* months!

He sighed, leaned back in his chair, running a hand through the wheat stubble of his hair and then the generous crop of blond mustache. What a hunk he was. She'd liked him from the start of her police career. "We have been bugged by the fourth estate more than I have ever been all the time I've been with the force. Isn't a day goes by there isn't a story – editorial, broadcasts, requests for interviews on news developments." He shook his head. "We don't get some sort of breakthrough on this we'll be having the *first* estate and the second and the third – whatever the hell they are – snapping at our …"

He sat up, slapped the desk. "Going to get worse! I know it. From the look of them, these are careful, complicated, well-planned jobs – right from the first one. We have uncovered not a single lead. And somehow, some way, we've got to! I'm asking you for suggestions." He waited. "Anybody got anything *creative* to suggest to get us moving on this!" He sat back in his chair.

"Sergeant."

"Detective Tait."

"Is this a one-man operation?"

"Got to be more than one. Even has a gang smell to it. The university one certainly did."

"Is it true they know what pieces to take?"

"Good question, Tait. Whoever these babies are – they know what they're doing, and what they want. They know the value of a piece of art. That's why we got to start checking with insurance companies."

"Insurance companies?" Kate said. "Why?"

"Because these operators often have a taker up front. What we hear from Interpol, it goes like this. They make a deal first with a customer. You want a Picasso? Okay. Then they go to insurance companies and find someone who works there who – for a consideration – will hand over a list of hot items, in this case Picassos, complete with the name and address of the owner. Hard to believe, but it's so. When art experts do an evaluation for a collector they warn him about this. They tell him not to let the insurer know the title of a painting or the artist who did it, like Picasso. The experts just photograph the stuff with their identification card tucked in the lower lefthand corner of the painting and tell the collector to inform the insurer they have this as evidence if it's needed. But *not* before it's gone missing."

"This – these guys aren't amateurs," Laverty said.

"They aren't! *We* are. Now, I'd like to know if there's one of you maybe paints – uh – secretly. Did when you were, say, in school? Sculpt?" He waited. "Didn't think there would be. Anybody got a wife – mother – sister that does?"

Behind her left shoulder, Kate heard Herb Laverty's grunt.

"Detective Laverty," Valentine said.

"My wife does watercolors."

"Uh-huh."

"All the time draggin' me out to art shows where everybody's standin' round hip-shot. Starin', sippin' wine, eatin' cheese and pickles and little sausages speared with toothpicks."

"Attended quite a few, have you?"

"Lost count. Long as we been hitched – even a couple years before that. Fall an' winter at least twice a month. Last year I missed the Super Bowl – year before most of the Stanley Cup final game. What's this got to do with . . . ?"

"I was wondering myself, Detective. Let's leave football and hockey for a moment. Get back to art. The idea came to me – if these jokers know all about art – what's rare – high value – so should we. If we did, too, then we could go to the insurance companies. Get a list of owners. Legally."

"Makes good sense," Laverty said.

"Your wife is an artist," the inspector said.

"She thinks she is."

"Wants you to go to all those art shows instead of hockey or football or –"

"Yeah."

"Then here's a way for you to solve that problem of yours.

We need somebody to help us find out what's on the most-wanted list. Art – that is. Now what would your wife think if you were to make a deal with her? Suppose you said to her you wanted to know more about art because she loves it and you're willing to go to great lengths so you can appreciate her work better, and you will register to take a course in Art Appreciation and Art History at Livingstone Univers –"

"Shee-yit!"

"– ity if she doesn't screw up your passion for football and hockey."

"Hell no!"

"Undercover. So we'd get a jump on those thieving bastards and then go to the insurance companies and get names and addresses of their likely next –"

"Why me, for Chri –"

"You have attended a lot of art shows. Something must have rubbed off on you."

"You aren't serious about me bein' the –?"

"Oh yes, Laverty, I am. You were the one brought up your art connection through your wife."

"That's *her* – not me!"

"Your attendance at art shows –"

"I don't know fuck-all about paintin' pictures. It's Myrtle that –"

"Your wife is not on the force, Detective, but she *can* help you. You register in the Extension Department at Livingstone – undercover, of course. Find out the list of most-wanted. You can check with your wife –"

"Look, I spend most of our marriage tryin' to keep her nose outa what I do to pay the goddam rent and grocery an' telephone bills. Sergeant – is this an order?"

"No, it isn't. But it is a chance for you to help us solve what is probably the biggest case we've got right now. You can turn it down, Detective. I promise you – I'll do my very best to forget you did."

"Thanks. A lot." Herb slumped over onto his other cheek and as he did caught sight over his left shoulder of Kate's wide grin.

"Wipe it off, Ms Marble," he muttered. "Ain't funny!"

"On the contrary," she whispered back. "It is *very* funny. You'll do a lot better job with a palette and a paintbrush than you ever did with a cue in stripes and solids."

"Fuck you!"

"Even better than you'd ever be at *that* undercover game."

"Laverty – Tait. Would you care to share with the rest of us whatever it is –"

"Nothing important, Inspector," Laverty said.

"All the same," Valentine said.

Laverty jumped in. "Oh, I was just telling Tait, it seemed more like a girl's job than a guy's – being art and taking art courses. And Tait, she said she agreed with me a hundred percent on that and she wouldn't mind taking it on herself."

"I did not!"

"Well now, why didn't I think of that?"

"Inspector – I didn't say any such –!"

"I guess that does it for this morning. Tait – see you in my office."

"But, Sergeant, I didn't –"

"Oh – and after Tait you, Seeley, on that child molester showing up right inside those North-East elementary schools. Sinclair, those three drive-by shotgun –"

"I'm trying to tell you, Sergeant –"

"Tell me in my office, Tait."

2

Metropolitan Tribune, May 1
Choosy Antique Thieves Know Their Stuff

Three weeks of intense police investigations across Canada have failed to uncover even one antique stolen in a $500,000 theft.

On April 10 thieves broke into the Poundmaker Drive S.W. residence of international developer P.T. Brockington, while he was out of town.

Brockington, head of Principal Planners Int., is past president of the Foothills Quarter Horse Association, present president of Magna Meat Packers, chairman of the Great North-west Stampede board, owner of the Northern Blades of the Patrick Division of the NHL and the Western Broncos in the CFL. He arrived home shortly before midnight to discover his house ransacked and more than $500,000 worth of jade and coral artifacts, jewelry, paintings, and tapestries gone.

A number of rooms had been entered and Inspector R.S. Valentine said Monday: "They certainly seemed to know what they were looking for. Only the best stuff was taken."

The antiques – all of which were fully insured – were carried off in a valuable tapestry, which had been ripped from a wall, and six pillowcases, which were without value.

The theft – one of the city's largest ever – was immediately tied in with a string of robberies that have hit the city during the past summer and fall.

Brockington's collection of jade, built up during a number of years, is famous throughout North America and has been exhibited in many countries.

Dogs sent into the house failed to pick up any scent, nor have various police departments from coast to coast who have been asked to help.

"Nothing has turned up yet," said Inspector R.S. Valentine, who has been in charge of the investigation ever since the art heists began almost a year ago. "We are leaving no stone unturned in this case."

Well, here we go again, Art. Start of one more academic year. Sorry, Irene. Just one more and that's it. I promise. This time I keep it. Cross my heart.

What a year it had been. Art for all had exceeded their highest hopes. So much so that his studio had no room left for all the paintings and sculptures. Win had quickly solved that problem by persuading Peter the goose boss and the preacher, who always called the final shots for the hook-and-eye colony, to let them use the broken-down shed between the edge of their acreage and his. Nice deal: a year's use in return for restoring it.

It had taken almost a month of their spare time to patch it up, insulate it, build shelving, seal and cover windows, do a new roof, and put a padlock on the door. Maybe as Win had said,

Darryl didn't know the art of theft, but he sure did know the art of carpentry. Right away he took over as straw boss. If he hadn't, it would have taken *two* months to finish the job.

He wasn't proving to be all that good as lookout, though. He'd almost blown it when Real Estate C.E.O. MacIntyre had cut short his stay in Palm Springs, but they'd made it out of there with the 14 paintings, including the Sir Joshua Reynolds portrait and two Picassos, by the skin of their teeth.

"We nearly bought it that time, Art. Darryl simply isn't cut out for the job. Sooner or later –"

"Yes, Win."

"So what do we do about it. Take him off the team?"

"How would he take that?"

"You know something? I think he'd be relieved."

"And we'd be without a lookout. We have to have two in and one out."

"Yeah, let's think about it."

Once more Win came up with the answer: two in and *two* out. Darryl would have company on lookout duty: Professor.

"Darryl thinks it's a great idea, Art. We start training Professor tomorrow. I've got a siren and flashing red light to go up on the van roof. I've picked up a 'Phantom of the Opera' mask and a dummy pistol and police uniform at the Sock and Buskin. We shock him with the siren and the light and Darryl brandishing the gun while I set off cannon fire crackers. I'll bet Professor proves to be a quick learner. Especially if Darryl uses sound poetry on him."

At first Professor had gotten the wrong message, and for days gave the van a wide berth, but with lots of treats and patting had gotten over that fearful hang-up. Now they would be a gang of four.

Professor had learned something else as well: stay clear of

Ottowell property. Last summer he had nearly bought it when Ottowell began dropping arsenic-loaded coyote bait on both sides of the dividing fence line, the sonovabitch! Correction: asshole! Ottowell would be a disgrace to the canine race! Luckily Professor had vomited up most of the poisoned bait and Art had got him into the veterinary clinic just in time.

What to do with the Professor at the beginning of fall session at Livingstone, when he'd be in town and there'd be nobody to keep an eye on him? Charlie had finally given up hope that they'd knock off *ars gratia artis* and had moved out.

"Keep in touch when you're in town, Art. Let me know when you fellows are ready to behave. I'll move back out then. But not before."

He'd explained his concern to Val in Continuing Education and Val had agreed to his bringing Professor in with him as long as he kept him on a leash and didn't let him use the classroom for a bathroom. Considerate of him, and he had also gone along with the idea that he alternate semesters of Art History and Art Appreciation with painting studio classes.

Get it, Irene? I'll have *my* easel and palette and paintbrush with them in there, too.

Even if she'd had a choice, it would have been hard to resist the inspector's generous terms: to be taken off full duty, attend university, study Art Appreciation and Art History, and, maybe, solve a major case.

Professor Ireland certainly wasn't at all what she had anticipated. Maybe professors had a higher than usual average of vandyke beards, but few of them wore a beret in their classes. Or ignored the chair to sit up on the front of the desk to lecture with legs dangling.

The class was a large one, at least fifty if you included the dog he brought with him into the lecture theater. Evidently both were popular with the students. Easy to tell why. Nobody slept in this old boy's classes. He really cared about them, eliciting and respecting their opinions instead of parroting retread lectures to be taken down in notes and regurgitated in later tests. And he sure knew his stuff, which was not surprising since he was a painter as well as a teacher. He must, she suspected, be damn good at both arts. He was informal; he was witty; he had a nice touch of vulgarity. He treated them all as equal partners. He believed in one-on-one tutorials, often over coffee in the Student Union cafeteria.

Her turn came up in the second week.

"I've noticed Professor seems to have taken a liking to you. Others, too. He loves all humans. But particularly you. Prefers to curl up by your desk in the front row instead of near me. This is his first semester in university. Because of complications I can't leave him alone at home. He's always wondered what I did when I left him to come into the university. I can tell he's decided now that higher education isn't for him, especially up front with me yapping on and on. Boring. Probably why he wants to be near you. Your first name is Kathleen. May I –?"

"My friends call me Kate."

"Well, Kate, Professor has really fallen for you."

"I have for him, sir."

"Please – don't call me sir. It gets in the way. Maybe you'd do something for me. For us. I've got a pretty full teaching plate and I've been wondering if maybe you could take him out for a run now and again. Or if, say, in the middle of a class he has to take a –"

"Oh! I would love to!"

"He's well trained. Heels beautifully. Comes to the whistle. Here. This is an extra one I happen to have picked up just in case I found someone who'd help me out. You sure you don't mind –?"

"Not at all. I always wanted a dog of my own when I was a kid. My father never let us have one, and living in an apartment in the city it's been out of the question."

"Professor will be glad to hear the news. Tell me, Kate, what led you to enter Fine Arts?"

"Oh, I've always been interested in art. Long as I can remember. Just as much as my sister was in ballet."

"Have you done any painting?"

"I did, up until some years ago. Hardly ever after – ah – after Julie died. We were pretty close. I still miss her."

"I can understand that. But let me tell you something. The practice of art can ease the pain of loss. Maybe you should start doing it again."

"That has occurred to me. Ever since I started your course."

"You still have any of the work you did?"

"Some. Mainly watercolors."

"Not surprised. I'd like to see some if you –"

"That's very kind of you."

"Not at all. Repay you for taking over Professor for me. Oh, by the way. Whenever you command him to come or heel, call him Sir. That's what he's used to. I look forward to seeing your artwork."

One of them she wanted him to see for sure, that one she did of Julie in her pink nightgown, holding onto the brass bed rail, with her leg up, toes pointed, head back, arm aloft, wrist gracefully drooped.

What an old sweetheart he was! If only she'd had a father like him! Ah well, the past can never return.

Right from the start Kate had been special. Indeed it had been he who had gotten her to change her desk in the back row for a front one. Those watercolors of hers had sent him a strong message of optimism. Good sense of colour and form. She had definite potential. She had something else too: with those same dark eyes and hair, slight and short and piquant, she was a ringer for the young Irene. Hadn't been for the three miscarriages and the final hysterectomy she could have been the daughter that might have been.

When she'd promised him she'd return to her art, she really had. With a vengeance. She must be spending every spare moment at it, judging from the stuff she brought to him. He hadn't been ready for that one last week.

"Now – this is very interesting. Has quite a flaky energy. Intentional?"

"Not sure. I just finished it over the weekend."

"My first impression is one of movement. Very strong. But it's color that's also getting to me. And I can't figure out why. You say over the weekend, yet this doesn't look like a quickie to me."

"No. This is a second run at it."

"It's a good one, Kate. You've pulled off something quite unusual. I keep coming back to color. All that white background doesn't seem to be separating your colored forms totally. Look at these street figures of almost people. That formal forest of possible sky-scraper buildings smoking up disintegrations to fill the sky – a *white* sky flaked with all those color fragments. Should be chaos but it isn't. Why not?"

"Search me."

"It's color that's doing it. Why am I having a strong feeling of déjà vu?"

"I think I know the answer to that. You see, I did this one a while back. You saw it then."

"I did?"

"I wanted to take a try at abstracts. It was before your seminar when you said the real is always under the abstract. Then I realized I didn't have any real under it. So I shoved it aside."

"Now I remember it. What was my response to it then?"

"So-so. You did say I have a good sense of color but to look closer at the effect side-by-side colors have on each other. You called it color chording."

"Yes?"

"Last week I went back to it. I laid the white background on top of the color abstract to define a figurative patterning."

"Oh, Kate!"

"Bass-ackwards, I guess."

"When it comes to creativity, Kate, anything goes. Even bass-ackwards."

"All right, Tait. Bring me up to date. How's your university career going?"

"Not bad, sir. Reading break coming up next week."

"Reading break?"

"Lectures called off so students can cram for the semester finals. I now have a list of works most likely wanted, done by noted artists dead or alive."

"That's what we're after."

"I'd like to write my final and then …"

"Yes?"

"… do another semester in Fine Arts."

"But you already have a list of –"

"Just a start, sir. You see, the quality of an artist's work isn't necessarily consistent. Prices of individual paintings can vary widely."

"So?"

"I think I should enroll again in Fine Arts. So we can narrow our focus on the hottest items."

"You think another course in Art Appreciation –?"

"Not in Art Appreciation – a course in *painting*."

"And you think that would –?"

"From Professor Ireland. He's probably one of the most expert art judges in the country. While I did the painting course under him I could in time invite his opinion on most of the works on our list. Matter of fact, the painting course was his suggestion. I've been doing watercolors and oils on the side and he likes my work."

"I don't know. Another three months seems –"

"Wouldn't have to be a *full* semester. Just until we've got a clearer idea of what those thieves might be after."

"Makes sense. I hope. Okay."

"Yes, sir."

"Good luck on your Art Appreciation and Art History exams."

Foothills Phoenix, May 5

Hefty Reward Offered For Help On Art Theft

An insurance company is hoping their largest ever reward offered will turn up leads to the second largest ever art theft in the city.

Swendler and Company, insurance adjusters, are offering a total of $50,000 for information resulting in a conviction for the theft of the antique jade and other artifacts stolen on April 10 from the home of Paul T. Brockington, president of Magna Meat Packers, owner of the Northern Blades of the NHL and the Western Broncos of the CFL.

This latest haul in the series of art thefts that have plagued the city over the past year came to a total of $500,000, second-largest in the series. The biggest was the first one last year from Livingstone University Art Gallery, estimated at $1,500,000.

"It is most unusual to have a theft claim of this value and a reward of this magnitude," Charles Swendler of Swendler and Company said Thursday.

Swendler suspects international professionals may have masterminded the operation but employed local break-and-enter talent.

"It may have been a theft-to-order situation, and that could make the stolen goods difficult to track down," he added.

But several jade chips were found at the scene and that indicates the people who did the stealing did not know the actual value of the items, and were not careful with them.

Some miscellaneous pieces of jewelry were taken, as well as carefully chosen jade antiques.

"This could indicate one of the thieves might have pocketed a few items for himself or herself, to be kept from the employers," Swindler said.

"If that's the case, it wasn't a totally professional job, because in organized crime such a thing is a no-no and the stuff can be traced."

The thieves apparently wrapped some of the loot in

a valuable Chinese tapestry they tore from a wall "and a pro wouldn't do that, either," Swindler said.

The state-of-the-art burglar alarm at the Brockington residence was turned off for a few hours April 10, the date of the robbery, on the hours the burglary must have occurred.

But this might have been "pure coincidence," Swindler said, "though I doubt that very much. Pros like these would have known there was an alarm and how to put it out of commission.

"Even if the organizer of the burglary is not attracted by our reward offer, such a large operation must have employed several people and the $50,000 reward might work with them," he said. "Either way, we hope it will bear fruit."

All the earlier robberies were apparently professional thefts of specific valuable art items as well, none of which have yet been recovered.

Foothills Phoenix, May 6

The Phoenix wishes to apologize to Charles Swendler of Swendler and Company, insurance adjusters, for any public embarrassment he may have suffered as a result of two unfortunate and quite unintentional typorgraphical earros made in our May 5 story of his most generous reward of $50,000 for information leading to the return of jade antiques stolen from the resident of Baul Prockington.

3

See, I'm keeping my promise, Irene. Sure I'm coming in here, but not just to teach; I'm going to be painting right along with them. Lawren Harris, da Vinci, Monet, brace yourselves. Here I come!

Maybe.

Been a nice ten-day break between semesters. They'd pulled off some good ones, and the Hutterite shed was filling up more and more. Now we're getting close to the next stage in the operation: drop-off time. Now that the option waiting period on many of the paintings was over, when the insurance company would be keen to cash in the art at auction – to end up, where it belonged, in public galleries.

And what a dandy coincidence: right out of the blue the invitation to do a series of visiting lectures on art history and art appreciation at the University of Turin. It had come to him via External Affairs and they'd wondered whether there might be other European universities that might like to have him visit at the same time. He'd make sure there would be: West Germany, France, Spain. *International* drop-off time!

But not till after this semester was over.

"Well, now – looks like we're going to be stuck with each other for a whole semester. We'll all be painting together. I include myself. I happen to be a painter as well as a teacher. Oh – and you have to be teachers, too. You will be teaching yourselves – by doing. And when this semester is over you will continue to teach yourself for the rest of your life. If you don't quit. And I'm afraid many of you will, because the practice of an art is the most difficult thing that humans attempt. Take my word for it.

"Do not stop trying. Every day, every week, every month, every year. Tell me – do any of you fish?"

Just a couple of them: the young man with the long dark tresses and the older fellow over by the studio door.

"You don't?" he said to the girl in front of him.

"Fishing sucks," she said.

"I respect your opinion."

"What's fishing got to do with –?"

"This. It is analogous to art in one regard. You." He pointed to the young angler. "You never go out on the river or the lake except when you know you're going to land a Guinness Book of Records trout, do you?"

"No way."

"Right. In angling or in art you cannot predict when you will score. But if you go on the creative stream every day you'll be there when good things happen for you."

"Boy," the young girl said. "You sure answered my question, Professor."

"Well, I can't really take credit for it. I was plagiarizing a literary artist, Stephen Leacock, in using that analogy. Now, let's get down to work."

Daily Citizen, January 16
Art Theft Ring Strikes Again

Police think the theft of about $60,000 worth of antique silver this week may be linked to five earlier art heists here.

More than 50 items, mostly irreplaceable family heirlooms, were stolen Sunday night from the home of Princess Natasha Koblenska, well-known member of the Russian aristocracy, who sought refuge here after the revolution.

Police said the theft included antique brass, gold, and platinum pieces. The culprit appeared to be an antique expert because less expensive items were left behind. One that was not overlooked was a gold and tortoiseshell snuff box, which Princess Koblenska says her parents obtained when she was a young girl during the family's years of exile from Moscow in Paris. It was her dearest possession, for it belonged to one of the earliest known snuff addicts, Catherine de Medici. This is the reason, the Princess says, the French phrase for Scottish or dry snuff is "tabac a reine."

The rarity of this piece has made it difficult to place an exact value on the stolen articles so that $60,000 is a conservative estimate. "We could be out a mile," said Inspector R.S. Valentine.

Princess Natasha told the Citizen that most of the valuables dated from the 18th to the 19th century, with the exception of Catherine de Medici's snuff box, which dates from the 16th century, when she was Queen of Henry II of France.

Detective Herbert Laverty, who has been investigating the art thefts under Inspector Valentine, said, "It looks like the culprits believed responsible for the other jobs have struck again."

Since the art thefts began, $2,960,000 worth of antiques, paintings, and sculptures have disappeared.

"I do hope you catch those thieving b***s!" Princess Natasha said, using a simpler name suggested by the old royal heraldic term: "bar sinister."**

"Have you noticed how hard it is to get your creative momentum going when you come into the studio for another go at it?"

Evidently most of them had noticed that.

"It's one of the reasons I start off with my tongue each time, instead of letting you get to your paintbrush right away. Or me to mine. I wish I could tell you that the longer you paint and the more skilled you become, the easier it will be for you. Sorry. It won't. I've been painting a lot of years, so I know. Ask any painter or writer or composer and they'll all tell you the same thing.

"You see, all art is one and indivisible. C.E. Montague in his book *A Writer's Notes on His Trade*, based on a series of Cambridge lectures, addresses the unusual technical literary things: point of view, theme, characterization. He illustrates the unpredictable nature of creativity in writing by moving into visual art.

"He says painters – good ones – always start with a tentative concept that motivates the first brushstroke. Lucky for the painter, what he's trying to do is *outside* himself so he can step back from his work. 'Hey! That's neat! I didn't realize that!' He changes his original concept, and the changed concept motivates the next brushstroke. And the next one and the next. It's the changed changed changed improved concept growing and becoming that results in the final work. Which, I warn you, may still turn out to be another bucket of shit."

"So, what do you do if it does?" the non-angling woman student said.

"Hang in. Paint. The longer the working gap the harder it is to get rolling again. It's called artist's block and I'm trying to break through one myself. Fear of failure sets it up, and it grows and grows if you don't keep on trying, because you know you're never going to win the Nobel prize. The answer is just do it and do it and do it. Come on – sometimes you're hot and sometimes you're cold."

"I been cold for over a week," the senior citizen student said.

"I been cold for a lot longer than that. That's why I'm painting in here with you people. Hang in, all of you. Let it happen. Let it happen. Let it happen."

"Well, well, look what's happened here. You've surprised me again, Kate. I haven't seen you working on this one."

"No. I did it at home."

"Did you have a reason for that?"

"Aah, I guess so. It was a funny thing that just happened. So damn funny I didn't know whether to let you see it."

"Mmh-hmh. Quite linear, isn't it. How did you manage that? Not with a brush. Corner point of your palette knife."

"No."

"Pen?"

"String."

"String!?"

"I don't know why the hell I did it. Put a nail in the top and fastened a string to it after I soaked it in paint and then stretched it taut and snapped it against the canvas."

"You don't happen to have a pet monkey, do you, Kate?"

"Hell no!"

"There was a New York artist who did once. He laid paper over his studio floor, then let the monkey do the painting for him."

"You're kidding!"

"No. He daubed the monkey's hands and feet with paint. Maybe its ass too. Set the little boy down on the paper and let him go to it."

"Are you trying to tell me something?"

"Yes. That New Yorker did it to make a public statement about much of today's avant-garde art. With that monkey's help he pointed out how meaningless and ridiculous much of it had become. He signed his monkey's work himself, held a showing. Got rave reviews, then went public with his angry plot."

"All right, Art. I get your message. No surprise. I'll tell you one thing though. Doing it broke the goddam block for me."

"And you won't move on to using beef stew instead of paint. You won't start doing tomato soup cans or condoms or dog turds?"

"You've made your point, Professor. Don't flog it."

As her father might have put it: "Time always decides in the end." Sad decision. She was going to miss those studio painting classes. She was going to miss both art and Art, and Professor. How she would have liked to stay with it till the end of the semester.

"I've dropped out, Inspector. Wasn't easy."

"Didn't go well?"

"Went great. It's why I dropped out. With Professor Ireland's help we've really got a list of specific possibilities now."

"You said it wasn't easy."

"Dropping out wasn't. Ireland tried to persuade me to stay in. I told him I was having financial difficulties. Had a good job offer I couldn't turn down. He said he thought he could help get me a student loan. I thanked him but said I had to take the job offer right away. He told me to keep on with my art work, and stay in touch with him. Pretty decent fellow."

"I gather that."

"I *am* going to keep in touch with him and it's going to be a lot nicer – what I mean – I really fell for the old guy and wished I wasn't there undercover. I don't like to con people I like and respect."

"Goes with the job. But not too often. Coffee?"

"Yes, thanks."

"Cream and –?"

"Black."

As he poured out for them he said, "You say it went great."

"Oh yes."

"So, what do you think we do next?"

"Just as you said during the seminar you set up last fall. Find out where the pieces might be through the art insurers. Galleries and art auction houses too, I think. It should be easier to get them to cooperate with us than with thieves."

"They'd better."

"You know, I still find it hard to believe that anyone could just walk into an insurance company and get names, addresses, phone numbers of clients."

"Nobody's squeaky clean, Tait."

"I guess not."

"Lots of people are ready to take a couple of hundred in appreciation under the table."

"Uh-huh. But how would a guy approach a possible taker?"

"Your guess would probably be as good as mine. How do you think he would?"

"Maybe he'd have an opening pitch, say he is an art representative, that he has a client interested in purchasing pieces by certain artists, that the current owners might appreciate an opportunity at today's highly inflated prices to – ah – cash in."

"Well, good for you, Tait. You sure you're in the right line of business?"

"I've wondered several times, sir."

Valentine laughed. "Haven't we all. You going to use that pitch?"

"I might. Just for curiosity's sake."

"Keep me informed."

"Yes, sir. I've gone over this list and there's one painter who stands out above all the others. He belongs to the Group of Seven."

"Didn't their work turn up in a number of heists?"

"Yes. They were all landscape artists mostly. Georgian Bay, Muskoka, Algonquin Park, and the Laurentians were their main outdoor studios. Franklin Carmichael, Arthur Lismer, Lawren Harris, A.Y. Jackson, and so on. The group formed around the early twenties and the one that looks most promising is a fellow named Tom Thomson. Large ones of his go as high as $100,000. The reason for this is that big canvases of his are in short supply. He drowned young when his canoe capsized in Algonquin Park."

"Okay, Constable. What next?"

"Insurance companies, I guess, and art shows and auctions so we can find the names and addresses of the owners of any hot local pieces."

"Then?"

"Then we get in touch with the owners. Ask them to keep an eye peeled for anything out of the ordinary."

"Such as?"

"Oh, you know, hang-up phone calls. Regular appearances of slow-moving vehicles. Strange to the district. That sort of stuff. Ask them to report in to us."

Except for having Lard-ass Laverty as a partner again, the art auction, commercial gallery and insurance company search trail had gone well. He'd turned down her suggestion that they split into separate cars, each of them with a list of art to check out, but he had agreed to stay behind and let her go in alone.

Even though it was tempting she decided not to use the art agent pitch. She found that when she simply explained her mission, she got what she wanted because everyone was aware of the rash of art thefts and was eager to help. The third day, at the Western Insurance Institute, she really scored: name, address, and phone number for the owner of one hell of a collection that included an Emily Carr and, of all things, two Tom Thomsons. Sooner or later this one had to be a target for the thieves.

Inspector Valentine agreed with her.

"Get to it right away, Detective."

"This afternoon, sir."

"And let me know how you and Laverty make out."

"The owner is a woman. A Mrs. Farnham. Laverty suggested I do her while he checked out others. Oh, by the way, guess who I ran across when I was doing the Western Insurance Institute.

Professor Ireland. When I was coming out of there. Invited me to have coffee with him but I told him I'd have to take a rain check on it and get back to work. Wish I could have."

"You'll have other chances."

"I sure hope so."

How nice it had been running across Kate this afternoon. He'd sure missed her ever since she'd dropped out of his art class, as much as he had missed any student he'd ever taught. Such promise, and he knew she'd keep her word to him, that she'd never quit trying. When she had a chance she said she'd bring new work out to the university to show him. He could hardly wait.

Now he'd finished the evaluation for Western Insurance Institute he had a really good one to show Win when he got back.

"Could be our next one, Win. Deerhaven district again. A Mrs. Farnham. Looks like the jackpot."

"How's that?"

"Quite a collection. She has an Emily Carr – a Harold Town – and not one but two Tom Thomsons. Those two alone have an insured value over three hundred thousand."

"That *would* be a jackpot. Where'd you come across this one?"

"Western Insurance Institute. Home, Contents, Fire. They've used me several times for evaluation. Matter of fact, art insurance people and owners have been coming to me much more since we started our operation. Given the inflation rate on art, collectors want to be sure they'll recover the real current value if their stuff is stolen. This looks promising, Win."

"I'll get to it right away."

There was a long wait after she rang the bell and heard the chimes within. She rang a second time and was just about to leave when the door was opened by an elderly woman.

"I'm Kathleen Tait, Mrs. Farnham. May I have a word with you."

"No solicitors, Miss."

"I'm with the Metropolitan Police Department, Mrs. Farnham."

"Your uniform away at the dry cleaners, eh?"

"No. This is my badge."

"I see. What do you think I've done wrong?"

"Nothing I know of. May I come in?"

"Sure."

Her slow progress down the hall and into the living room explained her delay in answering the door.

"It's my hip," she explained once they were seated. "Replacement surgery a month ago. Could have been worse. I'd still be frozen in a cast, only they don't use them anymore. Doctor screws you. Now – what's this all about, Miss Bates?"

"Tait. I believe you have some valuable paintings."

"I do."

"A couple of Tom Thomsons?"

"That's right."

"Are you familiar with the art thefts that have been going on?"

"I read the papers. Been quite a few of them right here in Deerhaven, haven't there?"

"Three, Mrs. Farnham."

"You figure I'm next in line?"

"I don't want to worry you, but – two paintings by Tom Thomson would look pretty attractive to most art thieves."

"And Emily Carr. And Harold Town and –"

"And quite a few others I see all around your living room."

"Oh, these are only the half of them." She grabbed the arms of her easy chair and made a couple of preparatory lunges to get to her feet. "Let's go in the family room across the hall and off the kitchen. That's where I spend most of my time with Tom and Emily and the TV. Would you like a cup of tea?"

"That would be nice."

"I'll show you where the tea bags are – the pot and kettle. You can make it."

Over their tea Kathleen explained how they hoped eventually to apprehend the art thieves.

"You mean the insurance company gave you my name and address and told you what I had?"

"Yes."

"Isn't that real nice of them! You think they might have given that information to those –"

"We don't really know that. You are just one of many art owners we're alerting. We want you all to help us."

"How?"

"Well, we think the way we can get the jump on them is to get in touch with collectors like you, get you to watch out for anything unusual that might suggest that they're – that they are what we call casing the joint for a possible break-and-enter."

"Unusual how?"

"Tell me, have you had any phone calls where when you answered the caller hung up?"

"Quite a few."

"Really?!"

"Ever since that young doctor screwed me and I'm not right next to the phone – takes me a while to answer. What else should I be looking out for?"

"Well, say you noticed a car or truck or a van making regular appearances – but for no apparent reason. It slows down or it stops nearby, but nobody gets out. Just sits in there. Then the next time. And the next and the next. If that happens then you let us know, and then *we* keep an eye on your place. What we're trying to do is make a good guess about where they may hit next when the time is right."

"Right how?"

"When they think the house is unoccupied. If the owner is away for a weekend or vacation maybe."

"Thanks to this hip that's not very likely for me. Not taking my walks in the park anymore or shopping across the bridge. My daughter does that for me. She checks me out regularly. Oh – wait a minute. Every Sunday Sadie picks me up in the morning. We go to church – Knox Presbyterian – then dinner together in her condo in Heritage Towers."

"There you are."

"You think they might – on a Sunday?"

"Most thieves don't keep the Sabbath holy, I'm afraid."

"So you think they might –?"

"Just a possibility, but I doubt it. Not too easy for them to establish a weekly routine absence with your daughter long enough to do a job. Are you willing to help us?"

"Oh yes. I am! Once it's spring I'm outside a lot. Mostly on the front porch. Or in the gazebo in the back yard. Can't stoop to do my flower beds yet. Sadie does that for me. From now on I'll make it the porch. I can see clear to both ends of the block from there." She pointed to the long side table under the window. "Open the top lefthand drawer, will you. You'll find a pair of binoculars in there. I was about to get them just before you rang. I generally take them with me when I go out to sit on the front porch so I can keep informed about what's going on in Deerhaven. Oh-oh! Don't you dare tell any of the other ones about –"

"I won't, Mrs. Farnham."

"They were Clayton's. Right up till his stroke ten years ago he used them on geese, ducks, deer, antelope. Me, I just use them on humans. But for the right reasons. When you get to be my age, Miss Tait, you'll understand better."

"I think I do now."

"And I think I'm beginning to like you. I'm guessing Sadie would, too. She's a lawyer. *Divorced* lawyer. Should I say anything about this to her?"

"Of course. Unless you think she might not –"

"Oh, she'd be all for it. This art collection, it's hers really. Just mine for a short while now. Anyway, I'm so glad you dropped by. Most exciting thing that's happened to me in a long time. By the way, I have another collection as well. All Clayton's shotguns and rifles."

"Put them under lock and key, Mrs. Farnham. You'll need only the binoculars out there on the front porch."

4

As usual Win had been quick off the mark on the Deerhaven job. Poor fellow; he hadn't had a try-out call for over a month. But this break in his theater career had certainly given him lots of time to get ready for theater of the real. Matter of fact, it was hard to tell whether or not actual break-and-enter drama wasn't his first performance choice.

"How's it coming with the Deerhaven possibility, Win?"

"Not bad. So far. The house is right next the Fourth Street Bridge and backing on Wild Rose River."

"Which side?"

"South. Near as I can tell, three times I happened by, looks like it's a single old lady living in there. Only one I've seen going in or out except for a young woman – could be a close friend or maybe a daughter checking up on her ma, couple of times carrying grocery bags to her. Sunday, when I had the place in the binoculars, about ten in the morning she picked her up and I followed them. She's evidently continuing Presbyterian. Knox on Sixth and Thirteen Avenue. I parked and waited till after the service and trailed them again to Heritage Towers. Long wait. They didn't come out again till three. Could be a weekly church visit and Sunday dinner thing. I'll wait and see what happens next Sunday."

"I'll come in with you then. How long do you think the house was empty?"

"Oh – four, maybe five hours."

"Not a very large window for us."

"Large enough."

"We'll see."

"Looking good, Inspector. Remember that Deerhaven one with the two Tom Thomsons among others?"

"Yes."

"Mrs. Farnham was very cooperative. She just got back in touch with me. Says there's been a van showing up all last week. Stops, stays quite a while on the opposite side of the street nearby. Nobody gets out. Looks interesting."

"Possibility."

"Pretty strong one, I think. At first there was just one fellow. Then there were two. That time one of them got out and crossed the street to go between two houses up the street. To the river, she thinks. She went out back of her place to see if he might be coming down the riverbank path in her direction. No show."

"Maybe casing another place up the block."

"Not necessarily. Mrs. Farnham had a hip operation. Took her a long time to get up off her deck chair, make it through the house and out back. He could have been there, she thinks, because he had plenty of time to go under cover in the bushes that fill the space between the river and the jogging trail. She stayed in her gazebo for a half hour or more. No sign of him in her binoculars."

"Binoculars? Did you give her a pair of –?"

"Her own. Told me she always takes them with her when she goes out on the porch or in her back yard."

"Birdwatching."

"She's well on in years and alone. *Human* watching for

clearer company. Gave me a detailed description of the two guys."

"Well – nice to have *her* on the force."

"She's a good one. When she got back out to the front porch the van was gone. Gave me a good description of that too."

"Licence plate number?"

"No. She said it was smeared. I'm seeing her after lunch."

As she left Kate turned back at the door. "By the way, Inspector, I don't think I mentioned that those guys had binoculars too."

"Well, now, you certainly do save the best for the last, Detective. Or the worst."

"Sir?"

"If she could see that they were using binoculars, strikes me they could notice she was using them, too."

"God! I should have thought of that! I'll tell her to leave them behind when she goes out on the porch."

"And we'll hope those boys figured she was birdwatching, too."

"Let's not rush it, Win."

"Hell! Been over two weeks now. Only time the old girl's going to be out of there is for those Sunday church and daughter visits. Been three in a row. Any one of those times we could have scored."

"Patience pays off, Win."

"This is one hell of a big one!"

"All the more reason to take our time."

"How long do we do that?"

"Till we – I don't know. I just don't like a few hours' absence. Too risky."

"Okay. You call the shots. But don't wait too long."

"I won't."

"Like till the old girl dies. She'll be absent a good long time then."

"Win, I would appreciate it very much if you never ever again made a nasty comment like that one."

"Sorry, Art."

"To me."

"Nothing stirring so far, Inspector. They must be waiting till she leaves that house, maybe leaves the city for a spring holiday. That's not likely to happen the way it is with that hip of hers."

"Hip?"

"She had surgery on it. The doctor screwed her."

"What!"

"Her words. Doctors don't use casts anymore. She said they just screw you. She's a pretty witty girl."

"Evidently. So what do we do about it?"

"I think I have the answer to it. With her daughter's help, let's make it look like she's leaving for a long spell. Taking a vacation trip. Her daughter picks her up with a lot of luggage and they take a trip to the airport, but they don't fly away on holiday. She moves in quietly with her daughter for two, three days. Makes sure newspapers and junk mail pile up on her front porch. Nobody answers her phone. And then we set up surveillance."

"Sounds good to me."

"I'm heading over there now."

"The fact that they're showing up is a good sign, and as I explained, this fake trip of yours might do the trick for us. Get luggage together and ready. A lot of it."

"I will."

"Mother generally takes a lot with her when she travels," Sadie said.

"That was before the doctor –"

"That was funny the first time, Mother."

"No, it wasn't. Just you wait till you have to have hip surgery. Anything else, Miss Tait?"

"Just keep up your surveillance on the front porch – but no binoculars – and the next time they show you get in touch with ... Sadie and tell her you're all set to take off on your pretended airline trip."

"To the airport?" Sadie said.

"Yes. If you think you're being followed, you'll even have to get your mother in and wait till you think the coast is clear. Then back to your place."

"And how long is this trip I'm not taking supposed to be for?"

"Just as long as it takes for them to make their move."

"Or as long as I can stand living with Sadie."

"Oh for heaven's sake, Mother. She's being funny, Detective. Again."

"You're dead right, Sadie. I'm looking forward to seeing more of you than I generally do."

"Wouldn't be surprised if it happens pretty quick," Kate said. "Inside a day or so, if they establish that you don't have anybody moving in to house-sit for you. Might even be that same night. We'll see."

"About those binoculars."

"No way, Mrs. Farnham."

"I know that, but I got a dinky pair of opera glasses. You know. With a handle –"

"I don't think so."

"Always used them when I went to the theater last few years – before the doctor – you really think they're going to – ?"

"Yes."

"Okay. You're the boss. This is some drama. Better than *Otello* ever was. You like opera, Kate?"

"In my work I get enough in real life, Mrs. Farnham. Well, that's about it. Soon as you take off and the van leaves we're setting up our stake-out. Thanks to both of you for your cooperation. We appreciate it."

"Pleasure's all mine, Kate."

"They'll probably come over the bridge, Inspector, so we have somebody to spot them there. We'll have another on Royal Way. Her side of the river – along the bank there's a cycling and jogging trail that goes down to the park at the end of the block then around the foot of the escarpment with Holy Cross Cemetery up above. Lots of bushes between the path and the riverbank."

"I'm getting you."

"We go under cover there."

"Sounds good to me. Let's set it up. Anybody you'd like to see on the detail with you?"

"Oh, Tommy for one and Ike for sure."

"And Laverty."

"Well …"

"He's been on the case with you from the beginning."

"Yes. He has. I – ah – I have to tell you I'm not all that comfortable working with him."

"No time for personal differences, Constable."

"Sorry, sir. Oh – oh yes, just came to me. Besides the riverbank bush babies, might be a good idea to have somebody going up and down that recreation path."

"Uh-huh."

"How about Laverty for that?"

"In a jogging outfit?"

"Or on a bicycle."

The inspector considered that for a moment. "I'm for jogging. He can use the exercise."

"One more thing, sir. Who calls the shots?"

"Who's your choice?"

"Ike."

"I don't think so. *You*."

"You're back early, Win."

"Like always. You were right, Art. At noon that daughter of hers picked her up – all her bags – headed for the airport. I followed them out there and watched them turn off to go in. I just kept right on coming out here. Boy oh boy – couldn't be better! What do you say? Tonight's the night?"

"Tomorrow night, I think."

"Like you said. Patience pays off. Sure did."

"And what's our plan of action?"

"Had that all worked out a week ago. Way I see it, we park the van right across the river from her place. On Marlborough Drive. Darryl stays in the van. You and I walk across the bridge. Take Professor with us and we go along the jog and cycle path to her back yard. We go in. We do it. We come out and take that path again."

"Back over the bridge. With those paintings in plain sight?"

"Nope. On down the path toward Jumping Pound Park."

"Doesn't make sense if the van's on the other side of the river."

"Yes, it does. Look. Here's a sketch I made. Van here. House here. When we come out with the Tom Thomsons we head east down the path to Jumping Pound Park, then up the park escarpment where the Blackfoot used to run the buffalo over in the olden days. On top we'll be in Holy Cross Cemetery."

"Of course we will. But the van will be on the other side of Wild Rose River."

"Right. When we come out of the house we signal across to Darryl. Three with the flashlight. Short-long-short. He heads for the cemetery and picks us up. What you think?"

"Now it makes great sense, Win. Just one thing, though. Last couple of days I haven't been feeling up to scratch. I may be coming down with what looks like a vicious bout of flu. Could you go this one alone?"

"Well . . . except for not having you tell me the right choices to make."

"I don't think it's a problem. Keep it simple. You won't have trouble identifying the Tom Thomsons or Emily Carr's Indian totem poles in the Queen Charlottes. As for Harold Town, if it's one of his Hollywood film star series or the mythical heroes, leave them. If it's his rocking horse period, take."

"Okay."

"I'm sorry."

"Not to worry, Art. I'll take Professor in with me."

"Good. He's a pretty fine judge of art."

"Hell of a lot better than I am."

It had gone off without a hitch. The next time the van showed had been close to noon. Mrs. Farnham phoned her, then Sadie, who picked up her mom and the luggage and took off. The van followed them. The squad moved in to prepare for stake-out. With Ike and Laverty she'd picked the right look-out spot behind the jogging path and riverbank bushes.

"Now what we do," Ike said. "We dig the pit in here. Shallow. You, Laverty, get going with the spade. Kate, come with me to my car."

"What for?"

"You'll see."

"I thought I was supposed to be calling the –"

"You are. You don't like what I got in mind, okay."

What he had in mind was a rod-framed hemisphere covered with chicken wire. The thing was split in two equal parts.

"Goose pit cover," he explained. "We weave sprigs and branches in that chicken wire for camouflage. You like?"

"It's great, Ike."

"You see how it's split in two. That's so when you're under it and a flight comes over low you just got to jump up and the halves roll off each side."

"May not be open season on Canada honkers, but it sure is on art thieves, Ike."

"Damn rights, Kate."

"Evening flight."

"And we're going to take our limit."

They were agreed that there were three entry possibilities: the very back of the house with its double plate glass doors or one or the other of the side basement windows. More likely the latter, with the back door saved for exit after the job. Usual break-and-enter procedure.

Even though the heist wouldn't probably happen till well

after dark, just to be on the safe side all positions were taken up about four in the afternoon: one man across the river on Marlborough Drive by the bridge, another on Royal Way, she and Ike in the goose pit, and Laverty loping resentfully now and then up and down the jogging path.

The rest of the day and through till dawn the thieves never took off from their home slough.

"Ten to one they'll show tomorrow," Ike said, stretching and red-eyed.

"Let's hope so. I think joggy boy's getting a little pooped."

The next day they set up their positions again in mid-afternoon and settled down for the long wait. A really long one.

Twelve hours later she whispered: "What time you got, Ike?"

"Three-twenty."

"Quite a while since we've seen Laverty's lard ass come bobbing by," she said.

"Yeah – lot longer between times."

"And I can't get him on the motorola. He hasn't answered for over an hour."

"His last run was toward the park. Maybe he stopped there, and he could be round the foot of the escarpment so transmission's blocked."

"Or else he's taking a snooze."

"Don't be too hard on him, Kate."

"With him that wouldn't be possible."

"What you got now, Ike?"

"Four-thirty."

"Hey! See that?"

"Yeah! *Yeah!*"

"Coming down the jogging path from the bridge!"

"He's got a dog with him! Lay low, Kate!"

"This is it, Ike!"

"Maybe. That dog. Could be just out walking him."

"At four-thirty A.M.? No way. You don't generally carry along a duffel tool bag that big when you walk your dog."

So far so good. That goddam yard light on the peak of the neighboring house had looked like it might be a problem at first, but a good half of this back yard from the gazebo over was in nice deep shadow.

Professor was heeling well. Leave him behind and head for the basement window. In then out the back door and up the trail to Jumping Pound Park and Holy Cross with Emily Carr and Tom Thomson.

"All right, Sir. Down. All the way down! Stay!"

"Can you see two of them, Kate? Who's he talking to?"

"The dog. Laverty – come in, come in. Over. Aach! Still not answering!"

"He's going in! Get ready – oh shit! Goddam dog's headed our way!"

Professor's spotted something! Barking and raising hell over there by that clump of buck brush. Get your ass out of here, Forsythe! Round the house and out to Royal Way. No! This looks like a stake-out and they'll have somebody out there, too, so head over to the neighbor yard then cut down onto the jogging trail, then on to Jumping Pound Park and up to Holy Cross!

How in hell could they have known ahead of time? Hadn't been for Professor he'd have had it!

"Push! Harder! Push, Kate!"

"I am! Damn it! That dog on top of us – got us locked – there!"

They made it out and up.

"He's headed for the house with the yard light!" Ike said.

"I saw him. I think he'll hit the jogging path and head for Jumping Pound. Down!"

"Aaaaargh-aah – yuh-duh – aaaghuh!"

"Bugger off, you waggy-tail sonovabitch!"

Professor did that and took off down the jogging trail.

"Great!" said Ike. "He'll take us right to him."

"Laverty! Laverty! Come in, Laverty!"

"Laverty here. Over."

"Brace yourself. Break-and-enter guy coming your way! Nail him!"

"Atta boy, Professor! Saved my bacon. So far. Now – out! Get out! Somebody may be waiting for us up ahead. Smell him out just like you did back there."

Professor took off down the jogging path full steam ahead.

Keep going, Win. Keep on going till he – oh no! He's onto something! Oh shit! They got you trapped. Fore and aft! What now?

The river! You didn't signal with the flashlight, so the van's still there.

"Hup! Hup! Come, Sir! Come! Got to take a swim now! Come on, boy!"

"I tell you. Nobody showed. Just a dog."

"Okay. He's still got to be close by. Laverty, you get out onto Royal Drive – Ike and I will beat the bushes along –"

"I'd think maybe we should –"

"Do as I say, dammit!"

"Hey! Look!" Ike was pointing out to the river. "Him and the dog! They're over halfway across."

"Put it away, Laverty! Put it away! They're out of pistol range. Marlborough Drive, come in. Come in. Over. Over."

No answer.

Kate lowered the motorola. "Looks like this thief hunt is all over, boys."

They'd made it across and up the riverbank and into the waiting van, both of them dripping. Professor's teeth weren't chattering but his were.

Darryl met them halfway. "Shee-yit!" Professor had given him a cold shower welcome. "What happened?"

"Get your ass back to the van and start the goddam motor!"

"What went –?"

"Move it! I'll tell you on the way home. If we make it!"

Darryl raced the old van through the quiet streets and out of the city, while Art watched the road behind. Nobody followed them.

Well before they had reached home he had told them all there was to tell. "What gets me is – how did they get the jump on us? How did they know we were going to make a Deerhaven hit? The exact house? I can't figure it out!"

"However they did, Win, they did."

"Thank God for Professor."

"Hadn't been for him we'd all be facing a stretch in prison," Darryl said. "Art – shouldn't we knock it off?"

"Yes. For now."

"For good," Darryl said.

"We'll see," Art said.

"Oh, Ike! So close! I thought we had it made!"

"So did I."

"I keep asking myself over and over and over. What did I do wrong?"

"You didn't. We didn't. Way it goes sometimes."

"Ike. Whose idea was it to dig that pit on the riverbank back of the house? I was the one suggested that angle."

"And when you did you were reading my mind."

"If we hadn't been back there –"

"– we wouldn't have spotted the guy coming down the jogging trail. We had no other way to go, Kate."

"But –"

"I'll tell you where it went wrong. That dog. We had no way of knowing he'd be bringing one along with him. Win some, lose some, Kate."

"Yeah – but ... then he got away and over the river."

"That was the dog again. Raised hell when he spotted us and then when he saw Laverty. Quit blaming yourself, Kate. Oh, about Laverty. Some good news for you."

"He isn't good –"

"Yesterday Valentine decided Laverty isn't going to be going jogging on this case anymore."

"You're kidding!"

"Nope."

"Well, who's going to?"

"Me. Some reason he thinks you and I might make a better team."

"That's great, Ike. I asked for you to be on it with me –"

"He did happen to mention that. Look, Kate, in a way it's just as well we didn't grab that guy."

"Now you *are* kidding."

"If we had, what could we have charged him with?"

"Art theft."

"Hardly. He hadn't gone inside. He didn't have any paintings on him. All we could charge him with would be trespass, which isn't all that high on the crime list."

"But if we questioned him then we could have found out –"

"Probably diddly-squat. He'd just clam up. We're going to get these babies dead to rights in time. You and I. Then it'll be *after* a break-and-enter and they'll have high-priced artwork clutched in their hot little hands."

"Oh, I'm glad we're partners now, Ike!"

"Me too."

She dropped Ike off at his place.

"See you in the morning, Kate."

"Yeah. Be nice to have you with me when we explain to Valentine how I blew it."

"You didn't. We didn't. Go get some sleep."

"If I can. I know one thing. After Valentine I'm going to get in touch with Mrs. Farnham. Tell her the coast is clear for her to move back in. When she does I think I'll pay her a visit."

There was a car parked in front of Mrs. Farnham's, somebody up on the front porch with her.

"Well if it isn't Miss Craig! How nice of you to drop by. Two visitors at the same time and I owe the both of you. Dr. Taylor, meet –"

"Kate Tait, Doctor."

"– he's the doctor who screwed me, did my hip. Doctor, Kate is a detective and she saved my art collection for me and you –"

"– to meet you, Miss Tait."

"Sit down. Sit down. First time in a long time these deck chairs have ever been loaded."

"'Fraid I can't, Mrs. Farnham. Just took my noon break to check up on how you're doing. I have to get back to the hospital."

"Do it whenever you can, Doctor. I mean drop *by* whenever you ..."

"I will. Good day, Miss Tait. Nice meeting you."

"Same here, Doctor."

He headed down the porch steps.

"Mrs. Farnham, I can use your help again."

"Those thieves are going to –?"

"No. They'll never come near your place again. Relax. Remember you told me that one of the times they were casing your place there were two of them?"

"Yes."

"One young. One old."

"That's right."

"Let's just go over your description of them again." She opened her notebook. "You said one of them – the one that went through to the jogging path, you thought, was young. What age would you say?"

"Like I told you before. I think. Young ones all look the same age to me."

"What about the other one?"

"Lot older fellow. Still quite a ways till he catches up to me. You know something, Kate. Besides these" – she lifted the binoculars hanging from the deck chair arm – "too bad I didn't have a camera with me out here at the time."

"Only if it didn't spook them. What else, Mrs. Farnham?"

"That's about it. Sorry I haven't got anything new for you. Oh! There is one thing I didn't mention to you. The dog."

"There was a dog?"

"With the old boy. When the young one went back the old one got out with this dog on a leash. Call of nature. The dog's. Lifted his leg against the weeping birch out there."

"Can you describe the dog?"

"Shaggy. Yellow."

"The breed?"

"Golden retriever."

"You're sure of that?"

"I sure am. God knows how many of them there are in Deerhaven. Now why didn't I tell you about that before?"

"Important thing is you have now, Mrs. Farnham."

"That dog being with him is important?"

"It is. You see, the fellow who got away on us had a golden retriever with him. Minor. But another piece in the puzzle."

Ever since Deerhaven the night before last he'd thought it over. In the hayloft tonight Darryl would be relieved to hear they would be doing no more heists for a while.

"We've come to a new stage now. For the next month or so certainly. The Hutterite shed is bulging and it's time we moved on to getting all that art into public galleries and museums, where it belongs. I've just heard finally from External Affairs.

They're willing to fund me – all expenses paid – as a traveling artist-in-residence in Europe. For six weeks. The Extension Department has granted me leave of absence."

"Congratulations, Art. Drop-off time."

"That's right, Win. First stop is Turin University, then in turn Rouen and Strasbourg, then West Germany doing lectures in art appreciation and art history at universities in Bonn, Munich, Heidelberg, Kiel, and Berlin. Tour winds up in Paris. At the Sorbonne."

"Wow!" Win said. "Have we ever gone international!"

"First thing we have to do," Art said, "is get all that art off-shore."

"Yeah. Wouldn't fit into your personal luggage."

"That's where Darryl comes in."

"Me? How?"

"Way we did with the Dürer collection. We crate and ship most of the art to your Tottenham relatives to go into safety deposit boxes there. London will be the center of the whole operation as needed pieces go out from there to me at my hotels on the other side of the Channel. Darryl, when were you last over in the land of your birth?"

"I never been back since I was eight and we came over here."

"You think you'd like to handle the London end?"

"Oh Art! Would I ever!"

"Think you can get leave from your Sears job?"

"I'll see. Probably. If I can't they can go look for somebody else."

"Okay. That's it, then. No more art jobs for the next six weeks or so. We've got a lot to do between now and take-off."

"Sure you don't need another helping hand over there, Art."

"'Fraid not, Win."

"Well, bon voyage, you lucky bastards."

This would be the most complicated part of their art for all enterprise. Step by step he carefully went over the procedure with Darryl.

"We drop them off where they will be found, recognized as lost or stolen, and handed over to the police, who will return them to their insurance companies to be auctioned off to the highest bidders."

"Public galleries and museums."

"We hope."

"How do we know a finder won't keep them or cash them in himself?"

"Pretty hard for him to do that. Been a lot of publicity, and if he went to commercial galleries he'd have to answer embarrassing questions about how he came by them."

"From the gallery owners."

"Or maybe the police. I don't think we have to worry about that possibility, because we're going to leave them in both public and commercial galleries and university Fine Arts departments."

"Well, just how can we walk around with big paintings or sculptures under our arms without attracting attention from –?"

"I think I've figured that out. They'll be packaged. We'll each be carrying one. You've noticed I have a beard and I wear a beret."

"Yeah. I have noticed that, Art."

"What do they say?"

"Huh?"

"That I am an artist carrying some of my own work. You're my young helper. Before we're approached by anybody, I give you my package and you drift off to another part of the gallery to leave them in some inconspicuous spot while I talk with the owner or a staff member."

"But – how do you explain why we came in carrying ...?"

"That I'm sorry to have bothered them. My memory isn't what it used to be and I've got the wrong gallery. Something like that. Now – our first stop is going to be Toronto, and I have a list of galleries there. Wasn't easy to come by, because several of them in the distant past have handled my work and there'd be risk of recognition. Europe will be a different matter in that regard."

He could tell that Darryl was enthusiastic about being involved in this part of *ars gratia artis*. Instead of shipping the Dürer collection over to Berlin, why not just get it out of safety deposit, where his uncle had stored it, and then leave it at the National Gallery? Same thing for the Joshua Reynolds portrait and selected others. They'd work London together. As for the other artworks, maybe he could arrange for them to be stored in his uncle Eric's Tottenham undertaking parlor?

"Would your uncle buy that?"

"I think he would. You see, when we shipped the Dürer collection over to him I ... ah ... led him to believe that besides being a noted poet, I was also a major dealer in Canadian art."

"Good for you."

"Well, not entirely. It was Win's suggestion."

It would have been nice if they could have done a trial run right here in the city before they took off, but he was too well known for that.

Darryl got in touch with Uncle Eric, who was delighted that he would be seeing his favorite nephew after all these years. Darryl was quite welcome to use the basement casket room of his undertaking establishment for storage of artwork. Uncle Eric also had room for Darryl and his famous painter friend, Arthur Ireland, to use as long as they needed in London.

Darryl got right down to preparing the art for travel overseas. He was as good at this job as he had been in fixing up the

Hutterite shed, carefully removing from their frames those paintings that could be rolled up and enclosed in cardboard cylinders. Those that couldn't be removed from their frames without risk of damage, and all the sculptures, went into crates he constructed.

Just as he had done with the earlier Albrecht Dürer shipment to Uncle Eric, he handled all the customs red tape and sent them on their way a good week before he and Art were to take off.

First part of the art mission, thanks to Darryl, accomplished.

5

It had been a lovely homecoming, with Win picking them up at the international airport. Professor came inside with him. What a welcome he gave them! As soon as he caught sight of them through the reception area glass he tore free from Win and with long leash snaking behind ran in high gear to the automatic doors, mistook exit for entrance, knocked back an outgoing passenger to go inside the baggage collection area and set a fifty-meter slalom record winding past travelers, jumping carts and luggage, and rising on his hind legs to embrace and to kiss the beloved two he'd lost for a whole six weeks.

"Aaaaaaaaaaaaaaugh-ughaaaaaahr ... aaaaw-aaaah ... whaaaa-ay-urrrhyuh faaaahr-tuhrrrrds! Why-eye-duh-yuh ... leeeeeve ... mmeeee-uhaaaay – low-soooooo-looooong! Eye-eee-yigh-ah-yigh-yaaaah-raaaaw-rawton-taaw-wah-tawrick!"

He sat in the front with Win driving, Darryl and Professor behind them. Actually he was halfway into the front with his head shoved through the seat gap so that he could snug his chin against his master's elbow and forearm the whole way out to the farm.

No doubt about it after six weeks away, this was his favorite part of the earth's skin. What a record bluebird crop this year, thanks to Charlie's fencepost houses. Look at all those tiger lilies blow-torching on the foothills slopes. How about that wild perfume of wolf willow as they crossed Tongue Creek. Welcome home to the new world where he belonged.

And surprise surprise! Charlie was there for the first time since he'd moved out. God, how he had missed his company with just the odd visit in town without the chance to respond to each other's art. What a supper he had prepared! If he hadn't before, he sure as hell did qualify now for the cuisine cordon bleu with this one: brown trout amandine, saskatoon pie, chokecherry wine. They toasted and they talked and they remembered, but halfway through the meal Charlie fell silent. He was the first to leave the table. And the room.

He left Win and Darryl to do the dishes, and joined Charlie and his pipe out on the front deck.

"Nice homecoming supper, Charlie."

"Mmmph."

"Wish you could have been over there with Darryl and me. You'd have loved it."

"I doubt it."

"Something's bothering you."

"Of course."

"What is it?"

"You know, Art. What's been bothering me for over a year. Dammit!"

"I see."

"That Deerhaven caper, when you guys nearly bought it. I thought to myself maybe it would smarten you up. Looked like I might be right, the way there were no new jobs to be done while you and Darryl were doing your drop-offs all over England and France and God knows where else in Europe. So – wait and see. But from the tone of the conversation at supper, I realized I was optimistically wrong. God, how I've prayed you idiots would knock it off before you got busted to enjoy your just deserts. It's been over a year, Art! Been hard, but I never gave up hope. Tonight, listening to you guys congratulating yourselves, I ran out of hope."

"Don't"

"No more false hope left."

"Don't run out of hope, Charlie."

"That's what I'm telling you. I have. What?"

"You do not have to run out of hope."

"Am I hearing you right?"

"You are."

"You really mean it?"

"Yes."

"What brought you to your senses?"

"I never intended it to go on forever, Charlie. We did knock off doing any new ones until most of the pieces were safely on their way into public galleries. That whole month in Europe I gave it a lot of thought. In London, where we picked up the Dürer collection, and in Heidelberg, where we left it to be found, in Amsterdam and Turin and Rome. In Paris, where we left Sir Joshua Reynolds, I decided it was time to wind it up. Louis convinced me."

"Louis?"

"You know. My dear old mentor during my student days in the Sorbonne."

"Mmmh."

"In a way it was Louis got me into the thing. Preached again and again that art was for all. He would not sell his work to private owners."

"Isn't that stretching the blame a little too far?"

"Whatever. Maybe it was just reliving my young days over there, seeing the same old napkin tuckers in sidewalk cafés. When I dropped by for old time's sake, l'Hôtel du Nord was still in business. I was going to forget some pieces in the lobby, but the film crew shooting that day wouldn't let me."

"What do you mean, film crew?"

"L'Hôtel du Nord, it seems, is the main venue for many, many award-winning hardcore porn movies. Plus ça change. The lady by the lamp would have approved."

"What's all this got to –?"

"Made up my mind. Mission accomplished."

"You really mean –?"

"I do."

"I've waited a long time for this, Art."

"I know, Charlie. I appreciate your patience."

"Wasn't easy. So – what next?"

"You know. Studio time. As Louis told us: every day – every week – every month. His voice has echoed for me all down the years. Hey! Maybe that's what I meant. Louis got me into it. Remembering him in Paris, Louis got me out of it."

"Good for him."

"So – how's your art been going for you?"

"Like always. Up and down. I'm on a real roll now. Ever since I won the one to go in Sherwood Park. Just before you guys left. Floating."

"What?"

"On the duck pond."

"You haven't gone back to frogs, have you?!"

"Nope. Been doing fourteen hours a day on it. Abstract. Hints at dolphin – fifteen foot – maybe killer whale. Couple weeks ago had a great breakthrough. Just came to me out of the blue. Water's blue, right?"

"More or less."

"Reflects?"

"I agree."

"So, I invented an all-weather and splash-proof fluorescent paint. Blue. To reflect the duck pond the thing will float on."

"Sounds great. You invented the paint."

"I did. Tried and tested all sorts of ingredients till I found the right recipe."

"You're really something, Charlie."

"So are you. Oh, Art! This leaves me no choice but to move back out here with you guys. Not right away. After I finish the Sherwood Park piece and install it. You really mean – of course you do. No more knights of the round hayloft! God save King Arthur!"

"This meeting is a special one. Since we made our decision to launch our campaign to return art to all, we have taken paintings, drawings, woodcuts, and sculptures out of private possession to end up in public museums and galleries here in our own country and throughout the world – London, Turin, Berlin, Munich, Paris, Barcelona, and New York to name a few.

"It has been a dangerous venture and I want to thank you for undergoing the high risk involved. Together we've done what we set out to do. While I was overseas – indeed ever since the Deerhaven event, I've been doing quite a bit of second-thought thinking and I've come to a conclusion. The time has come for us to call a halt."

"Thank God!" Darryl said.

"Win?"

"Ah, I guess – if you say so, Art."

"You disagree?"

"Well, no."

"I don't hear enthusiasm in your response."

"Maybe not."

"Care to explain why not?"

"Just that, well, in a way I do agree with you. We have done – pulled off what we started out to – almost."

"Almost?"

"It's just that ... I got this feeling. Like – ah – like ..."

"Go on."

"Well – shouldn't we end it with a real bang? We quit now we'd be missing one last one that would win us an Oscar."

"I see."

"In the art section of this Saturday's *Globe and Mail* there's an interesting announcement. Lilian Milne Art Gallery. Picasso, Matisse, de Kooning, Dubuffet, other big twentieth-century babies on loan from all over the world. Show opens in Toronto July twenty-fifth. Ends August sixteenth. Estimated value, over two million. That's in U.S. dollars. Wouldn't that give us one hell of a curtain call?"

"It would."

"Wait a minute! Art just said we ought to call it off."

"Yes, Darryl. Enough is enough."

"If you say so, Art," Win said.

"I say so too!"

"You been saying that the whole past year."

"And now Art's saying it too. Aren't you, Art."

"Yes."

"Over two million dollars!" Win said.

"Count me out!"

"All right," Art said. "Let's drop it for now. Think about it."

"Sure," Win said.

Darryl sneezed.

"Two million is nothing to sneeze at," Win said.

"We've still got a few pieces left in the Hutterite shed, Win."

"Yeah."

"I'm going to need your help dropping them off."

"Uh-huh."

"Tell me if I'm wrong. You still have a problem?"

"Sort of."

"You want us to –"

"Like I said – that Lilian Milne Gallery big one."

"I see."

"Damn nice surprise in my mail last week. The big manila one was a play script and a letter. I been tapped for a try-out."

"Congratulations."

"If I make it."

"You will. All the more reason for us to end the –"

"It's Theatre Sagittarius, one of the finest equity companies going. One sweetheart of a script too."

"All the more reason for us to –"

"– took the Playwright Pulitzer with the Louisville, Kentucky, production year ago."

"What has this to do with –?"

"Theatre Sagittarius is in Toronto."

"Yes?"

"So is the Lilian Milne Art Gallery."

"I still don't see what –"

"I get return airfare, hotel, and meals. I'd be right down there Johnnie-on-the-spot at no cost."

"Win, I have promised Darryl and Charlie – no more."

"I know. You're probably right."

"I am. We've done what we set out to do."

"Sure."

"When are you supposed to be there?"

"Next week. The ticket was in the envelope."

"Well, that means we put off the final drop-off. When you

get back we can do it. I thought we'd wind it up in Vancouver and Seattle."

"Whatever you say, Art."

"Tell me. What's this play about?"

"Oh – it's a dandy! Called *Scam and Be Damned*."

"Interesting title."

"Topical as hell. All the media fuss there's been about those televangelists. I want that triple lead in the first act, the second, and the third. There's a sideshow barker – Barker Billy Barker – then a medicine man." He laughed. "He peddles a tonic that's good for man or beast. If he's got a lot of old suckers listening to his pitch on the carnival grounds he has another set of bottles. LALS Formula Four. Hey – maybe you oughta give it a try, Art."

"What's LALS Form –?"

"Lactic Acid Longevity Stimulator."

"Maybe I will."

"Guy in the third act is a faith healer. You want to, you can read the script."

"I can hardly wait. Now about –"

"Forget it, Art. I guess you're right. Time to behave."

First chance in big time! For three days he'd gone over and over the script, chicken-tracked it with blip and stress marks to get his timing just right. Darryl had read cue lines with him for Barker Billy Barker and the medicine man and the faith healer. Just for insurance sake he'd also gone through the old-time Scottish preacher in the first act in a barley stubble field with a Presbyterian dirt mound for his pulpit. Not a lead part but a damn good one with him slapping and slapping at his arse and delivering his tag line when he realized he was standing on a fire-ant pile: "I've got the spirit of God in ma soul, but I've got Auld Clootie in ma breeks!"

No way. His Scottish accent wasn't too bad, but they'd probably cast an actor the like of Douglas Campbell, who as a Lowland child might have had fire-ants up his breeks. Correction – in Glasgow he might have had safety razor blades neatly tucked under the bill of his cap.

The play looked like a winner, probably a sell-out for the Theatre Sagittarius six-week run then off-Broadway, then the main ring of the drama circus: *on* Broadway.

During most of the four-hour flight he took another run at the script, added a few good business notes in the margins, then put it back in the attache case when the hostess made the prepare-for-landing announcement. Why didn't they teach in-flight attendants to project and articulate more clearly!

As usual his ears plugged up as they lowered altitude. A baby up front began to cry. Probably because of the same discomfort he was experiencing. Poor little thing!

Pinching his nose and pushing his breath, then releasing and yawning and swallowing didn't help a bloody bit. Something must be wrong with the cabin pressure. This was worse than any of the landings he'd ever made. Way worse! Especially the right ear. Hell! It wasn't pressure block. It wasn't the *ear*! It was that upper right molar the filling had dropped out of last week. Should have got to the dentist right away. Come on, come on – cool down!

It didn't. The pulsing pain got worse and worse right through baggage pick-up and the taxi ride to the hotel. The message at the desk said he'd be picked up at ten the next morning for the try-out. Oh God!

He left his bags at the reception counter and headed for the drug store they said was down the block and just round the corner.

He made it to the back of the drug store and the prescription counter.

"What you got for a toothache?"

"A moment, sir. Soon as I finish this." He had his head down as he worked on whatever it was. Made a final jot, straightened up, then left through the door behind him.

Moments later he came back.

"Now then. May I assist you."

"You sure can. One of my upper molars just blew up and I need something to ease the pain."

"Your dentist –"

"I just flew in. It's way after dentist hours. Isn't there something you've got that you can –"

"Perhaps." He turned and moved along to come out of the gate. From the long shelf-rows of non-prescription panaceas for all human allergies and aches he made a selection. Two of them. A bottle of pills and a tube of ointment.

"These will give you some temporary relief. Pay at the check-out counter at the front."

He made it back to the hotel and up to his room. The pills were codeine and aspirin, the tube an analgesic ointment to be rubbed on the gums.

Here's hoping!

He looked up the Theatre Sagittarius number but got only a recorded track on all the shows they'd be doing from now till the New Year.

God knew how much sleep he managed that night, with only intermittent relief till pain would wake him up to rub more numbing salve on his gum. No way he could manage breakfast. He did go with the driver to the theatre instead of to a dentist's office, explained his problem to the director, who shoved his try-out ahead two days.

Diagnosis: major pulp decay, with root canal work inevitable. The dentist's analgesic prescription did quell the pain enough that he could eat, but there was no way he could do lines in two days' time.

Try-out: out!

Well, there was one way Win could win. Goddamit!

Gonna be hot-wire time in the old town tonight! This Rose Buddy blooms again! Lilian Milne, here I come!

The Globe and Mail, August 5

Gallery Show Will Go On
Despite $1-million Theft

The Lilian Milne Art Gallery will continue its show of drawings and sculptures by 20th-century masters despite a theft of drawings worth over $1-million from the gallery early Monday morning.

The drawings, part of a collection called human form, were on display as part of an art show that began on July 25 and ends on August 16.

Detective Sergeant Paul Bradley of the Toronto Metropolitan Police said yesterday entrance to the gallery was gained by breaking a window.

"We have B&E's (break in and entry) like this all the time. This is a popular way of breaking into places. They just took out the whole window and went in and out," he said.

Bradley does not think there is a market for the

paintings unless they are sold to private collectors who can afford them. "No way they could be purchased by another gallery and if they fall into the hands of a private collector they could not possibly be displayed," he said.

A total of seven drawings were stolen from the gallery, including two which were on loan to the gallery. One entitled *Head* by Picasso was on loan from the Thalia Deitrich Gallery in New York. A spokesman for the gallery who refused to be named said they were very upset when they learned about the theft. "It was a beautiful Picasso which was on consignment at a net value of $60,000 U.S.," he said.

Another drawing by Picasso called *Femme Assise dans un Fauteuil,* valued at $80,000 U.S., was on loan from Les Arts International in South Africa.

Five other paintings stolen were an untitled one by Willem de Kooning valued at $160,000 U.S.; *Tête de Femme* by Henri Matisse valued at $200,000 U.S.; three drawings by Jean Dubuffet, *Avec Quatre Personnages* ($250,000 U.S.), *Hommes aux Cheveux Longs dans un Parc* ($70,000 U.S.), and another untitled valued at $65,000 U.S.

Harold Knowlton, director of the Lilian Milne Art Gallery, said the pieces stolen could all be seen from a window outside the gallery. "They are not all properly lit, but they are all discernible from the outside," he said.

"The theft was a professional job," he said. "They (the thieves) knew what they were after and they took what they wanted in order of priority."

6

Oh no! No! No! It couldn't be! Simply couldn't!

Inspector Valentine had dropped the bomb first thing in yesterday's morning meeting.

"This is going to be the most important announcement of my career. We have had a breakthrough in the art scam case. Out of the blue we have an informant, who showed up here armed with detailed information on three likely suspects, their names, their addresses on the west edge of town. They are neighbors of his."

The inspector consulted the sheet on his desktop.

"Informant's name, Jeff Ottowell, farmer. His neighbors do not farm, he says, 'Just a bunch of lazy goddam artists' to quote his exact words, 'been a pain in the ass ever since they moved in next to me.'

"He said he should have come in to us long before now, but held off till he could be sure it wasn't just wishful thinking. It sure isn't now. He says he has wondered what they were up to with all their visits to a shed on the edge of another neighbor's property. Storing stuff in there. What looked like it might be artwork. Couple of days ago he saw one of them ..."

He checked his sheet again. "'... Winston Forsythe, an actor, carrying in a number of large, skinny cartons.' ... 'Had to be more of them goddam paintin's,' he said.

"After Forsythe left he decided to go inside and see what all was in there. The place was sealed tight, but he did a break-and-enter himself with the help of a handy rock.

"What he saw confirmed his suspicion. '... No way one fellow done all them pitchers. Just one of them is a painter. Fellow that left a while back whangs out statues. Forsythe, he's an actor. Looks like he's a bad one. The others, too.'"

"Just a minute," Kate said. "Isn't this just – ah – guessing ...?"

"*Good* guessing. I went over with him all the items in that Toronto heist a week ago. The one over a million. Detailed descriptions of the paintings lifted from the Lilian Milne gallery. Nearly as he could tell they fitted what he saw in the shed.

"Now then. I have gotten a search warrant. We get to it. Right now. The place is off RR3 and third west on the north side of Wild Horse Road."

"What name on the mailbox?" Laverty said.

"You'll have that. Tait, see you in my office."

She'd known what he had to tell her. As soon as he'd given that address on Wild Horse Road!

"I'm sorry it's turned out this way, Kate."

"I still can't believe it! Not Ireland!"

"Looks that way. We'll see."

"It's his place, but that doesn't necessarily mean he was part of –"

"We'll see."

"Sergeant. I – do I have to – I don't think I could – can I be excused from the ...?"

"Of course. I understand. We can handle it without you. Take the rest of the day off. Or whatever you think you might need."

Foothills Phoenix, October 7
Art Theft Hearing Opens

The preliminary hearing began yesterday of three men arrested after police discovered more than $1 million worth of art treasures. The artworks were stolen from the Lilian Milne Art Gallery in Toronto and other galleries and private homes in a two-year series of art thefts from coast to coast.

Livingstone University professor Arthur Ireland, 69, Winston Forsythe, 29, and Darryl Duckworth, 27, face joint charges; Forsythe, breaking and entering, Ireland, possession of stolen property, and Duckworth, accessory. The three men sat in the prisoner's dock yesterday as the pretrial hearing began.

Crown prosecutor Herbert Martin opened the proceedings by telling Judge H.L. Fouckes, Q.C., that he expects the preliminary to last at least a week.

"There'll be in excess of 100 witnesses," reported Martin. Up to seven witnesses, he added, are not available this week, and will have to be called at a future date. People scheduled to give evidence come from a coast to coast range of cities.

Ireland, Forsythe, and Duckworth, who wore prison khaki uniform, have been in custody since the raid made on Wild Horse Road 18 kilometers west of the city, beside the Tongue Creek Hutterite colony. The Lilian Milne Art Gallery collection of missing works was uncovered along with other stolen artwork in a shed just inside the colony property.

Crown prosecutor Martin has opposed bail, arguing the case was complex and widespread, and he was worried if Ireland, Forsythe, and Duckworth were released it might interfere with much more police investigation yet to be done.

"Our investigation is far from over," Inspector R.S. Valentine said. "Except for the Lilian Milne Art Gallery collection we found intact and some other stuff along with it, only about ten percent of the treasures stolen were seized in the foothills raid," he said.

"In time, though, we'll hit the mother lode."

At first bail for the three totaled $950,000. That figure was later cut to $98,000.

The reduction was accompanied by strict terms laid down by Judge Fouckes, Q.C.

He ruled that the defendants must have no communication with any of the Crown witnesses, deposit their passports with the court, and notify the police of any change of address or employment.

Ireland, Forsythe, and Duckworth are represented by Hugh Archibald, Q.C.

The month in remand jail was a foretaste of penitentiary time. All three of them were held from Labour Day to the hearing. They'd been cell days of regret and self-questioning and apology to Darryl and Win.

Darryl was taking it the hardest. He simply wanted distance from both of them, from all other human beings for that matter.

"Don't worry about him, Art."

"I have to! He's in awful shape."

"For now. He's been there before. I've known him a long time. He'll pull out of it."

"I hope so! I'm sorry I got you fellows into it!"

"The hell you did. Both of us went into it of our own free

will. You let me handle Darryl. Sooner or later he's going to realize he's lucky."

"Lucky?"

"Sure. Only charged as an accessory – with parole he's probably just facing months in the bucket."

"I hope you're right."

"You'll see. You know something? I'm kind of looking forward to the trial."

"Oh, Win!"

"Sure am. I got the lead. You guys just got bit parts. Haven't you read the papers lately?"

"Of course."

"Didn't you notice the great advance reviews I'm getting? 'Winston Forsythe a.k.a Raffles pulls off one-million U.S. art heist.'"

"You – you're – Aw, Win – I'm sorry! I really am!"

"I already told you, Art. You don't have to be. Could be a hell of a lot worse."

"It couldn't!"

"Take my word for it. I know. You never did commercials or Uncle Ben on a bucking horse with Aunt Martha and those fucking rabbits."

Along with the others, Kate had testified against them in the hearing. What a surprise witness she was! He had never dreamed her to be more than one of the most promising art students he'd ever had. Maybe if he'd known she was undercover he'd have called the art caper off before he got himself into this mess. Too late now for maybe! Sorry, Katie! Sorry, Irene!

The day after the hearing ended she came to see him in the remand center. She wasted no time in explaining her visit.

"I've put it off and I've put it off, but I can't anymore. I want you to explain to me just how in hell – at your age – you decided to change from artist to thief!" Her dark eyes were hard and direct. "Look, I've been a cop for over five years now, and you pulled the biggest con job on me that anyone probably ever will in my whole lifetime career!"

"I'm sorry, Kate."

"Sorry! Apology isn't an explanation!"

"I know. Believe me, the worst thing about it is –"

"I fell for you and you have hurt me –"

"The worst thing about it is hurting you."

"You want to know something? My father was one boring and fatuous sonovabitch and right from the very first time I met you I wished I'd had a father like you!"

"And I wished I'd had a daughter like you."

"Oh sure you did! What a hell of a fine way you took to prove it!"

"Kate, please!"

"Don't you ever use my given name again!"

"You asked for an explanation. Let me give you one."

"I'm waiting."

"That art was not taken for personal gain. It was done to make a public statement."

"I'm asking you for an explanation. Not bullshit!"

"I'm trying to give you an explanation. We have not sold one single piece of the art."

"Where is it?"

"Let me rephrase your question. Where *will* it be."

"All right. Where will it be?"

"Eventually, mostly in public galleries and museums here, and in the States and Europe. In just a matter of time it'll start showing up, and keep surfacing for the next six months or so."

"Now let's just get this straight. You bastards haven't sold this missing art?"

"No."

"Just stashed it away. Too bad you're going to have to delay cashing it in till after you get out of the pen."

"Please, Kate –"

"I warned you!"

"All right. Do you remember my opening lecture in the Art Appreciation and Art History seminar?"

"Vaguely."

"When I told you that ever since the industrial revolution the patrons of art had changed and art stopped being art for all – had turned into art for the wealthy elite? Capital gain art?"

"Go on."

"My purpose in doing – what we – I figured out a way to return art to where it rightfully belongs. By taking the art, we planned to transfer ownership to the insurance companies who after recovery, because they'd paid the insured's claim, then owned the pieces. Usually there's an option waiting period in the contract: return the insurance money and keep the work or keep the money and – are you following me?"

"With difficulty."

"After the option waiting period is over then the new owners – the insurance owners – can put the art up for auction. Now in spite of public belief that the highest bidders are billionaires in Tokyo or Hong Kong or wherever, actually nine times out of ten the winners are public galleries and museums. Not just on our continent but all over the world. That is why we did six weeks of dropping off, with another month in Europe."

"And you're telling me you guys don't have them."

"That's right."

"That they'll start showing up."

"In a short time."

She was slowly shaking her head. "Incredible."

"Which means you don't believe me."

"Not yet I don't. I'll have to wait and see."

"Do that. And do something else for me. Give *me* an explanation just who conned whom?"

"Huh?"

"I had no idea at any time when you were in my class that you were an undercover policewoman. I'd say you're pretty good at the con game."

"I didn't know … I just thought you were my art teacher."

"Another question."

"Shoot."

"Incredible or not. Have I given you an explanation?"

"A weird one. I'll have to wait and see. Have you been in the wood shed with your lawyer on this?"

"Pardon?"

"Has your counsel rehearsed you?"

"I have told him."

"Does he think a judge or jury would buy it?"

"He's not optimistic, though he does think it might soften my sentence some."

Slowly, slowly she was shaking her head again. "You sure are an original." She got up. "I have to go now. I'll be seeing you."

"Really?"

"Mmh-hmh. I'll drop by here in remand and then when I testify in your trial and …"

"And?"

"Oh – down the road a ways. I guess you are my favorite felon, Art. One thing: you *can* call me Kate again."

"I'll think about it."

For a change, good news for you, Irene. Charlie's moved back to the place to look after it and Professor for us while I'm in here till the trial. Maybe sooner, if he can raise bail by putting the ranch up for security. It's high, but he thinks he can get enough for my release. And in spite of this mess we've got Katie back with us again. She's been dropping by regularly, has almost forgiven me. Last visit she was on a real high.

"Well … one good thing about it; I'm out of the trenches. No more night or day shifts, patrol duty."

"Sounds nice, Kate."

"Damn rights it is. From now on office hours, eight to three. Special commendation from the chief himself."

"Great!"

"Let's give credit where credit is due. Thanks to you and the great art scam case I've been promoted to Special Constable to enforce the identification of criminals' act. Supervisor for the AFIS computer."

"Whatever that is."

"I'm in charge of the Automated Fingerprint Identification System, one of only three in North America hooked up to Interpol. As supervisor I run the fingerprint/latent search unit."

"Congratulations."

"God, eight to three, weekends free. I could go back to university – part-time."

"I have a better idea. Forget more classes. Now you've got a chance to do painting. Consistently."

"University affords me a free studio to –"

"Distracted by unnecessary classes. I know what I'm talking about, Kate. I'm optimistic about you. As much as I've ever been of any student I've ever had. I have a suggestion."

"What?"

"Well ... within the next week or so, Win and Darryl and I probably are on our way to Moose Mountain Penitentiary. Leaves Charlie alone on the place."

"Yes?"

"It also leaves my half of our studio space available. From there into the city is about twenty minutes' commuting distance. While I'm doing my time how about you moving out there?"

"Oh, Art!"

"Well?"

"I'll – I'll think about it."

Daily Citizen, October 9

University Suspends Ireland

Arthur Ireland, artist and university professor facing trial in a multi-million-dollar art theft, has been suspended without pay from part-time teaching duties by the board of governors of Livingstone University.

William McLeod, the board's secretary, told the Daily Citizen Thursday that governors had suspended Ireland for failure to fulfill his university duties. Ireland has been in jail since August 21 and was recently committed to stand trial.

Daily Citizen, November 6
Artistic "Robbing Hoods" Trade Sherwood Forest For Moose Mountain Penitentiary

Supreme Court Justice Aeneas Molinaro Wednesday would not accept "by any stretch of the imagination" the "Robin Hood" defense of Professor Arthur Ireland, Winston Forsythe, and Darryl Duckworth on charges arising from a Labour Day raid on Ireland's foothills home southwest of the city.

For them there would be no storybook ending.

Justice Molinaro after hearing them plead guilty in connection with a series of art thefts totaling about $7 million handed Winston Forsythe six years for 30 charges of break-and-enter, Arthur Ireland four years on 8 counts of possession of stolen property, and Darryl Duckworth two years as an accessory.

Justice Molinaro pointed out that they occupied a position of responsibility in the art community, Professor Ireland in academe as well, and they had used this fact to conceal their crimes.

Apparently no one who knew Ireland even considered the noted teacher-painter capable of cheating on his income tax, never mind organizing a wave of art thefts.

The judge noted that Ireland, Forsythe, and Duckworth got tips on which places to "hit" from a variety of sources. They visited art shows, galleries, and auctions, and went to parties of the elite, who welcomed their artistic judgment. In this fashion they would learn who had what, where they kept it, and when they'd be away.

"Those boys never stopped thinking," Detective Inspector R.S Valentine said. "Upstairs they were working all the time."

Their methods of breaking in were basic in the extreme, either smashing a basement window or breaking the back door glass and reaching in to undo the lock.

"It was this crude approach which for many months led us to believe the masterminds behind the art heists were not doing the break-ins themselves but were employing local amateur talent," said Valentine.

"Lion's share of the credit for solving this case must go to Detective Kathleen Tait," Valentine said. "Had it not been for her long and tireless efforts the 'culture caper' would still be going on."

Constable Tait, who testified earlier in the trial, did not choose to expand on her role in the case.

In his summing up, Justice Molinaro said that he found the defense of an altruistic return of stolen art to public galleries and museums for all to see and appreciate to be incredible. It had to be a "deliberate and calculated and outrageous scheme" motivated by "avarice and greed."

He commended local police "for their perseverance and competence in handling this extraordinary case."

"Well, Art – last day for you fellows in here. They're moving you out tomorrow." She shook her head. "Oh, Art, I wish you hadn't –"

"Me too, Kate."

"You're going to find it tough – two years' hard time in Moose Mountain."

"Four."

"Closer to two with likely early parole for you. Short time for Duckworth. Forsythe the longest. Dammit all, Art, I still can't … Surely there must have been some other way for you to –"

"There wasn't. I'm sorry you agree with the judge that we did it for –"

"I don't! I believe you did it for your noble reason, but ends never justify thieving means!"

"Maybe you're right. Anyway – you've had time to think over my suggestion that you move out to my place."

"Yes. I went out there – met your sculptor friend, Charlie. He showed me round."

"And?"

"That's one lovely place you have, Art."

"And?"

"How many artists have a studio like yours?!"

"And?"

"And I started packing the day before yesterday."

"Aww – that's what I hoped for!"

"So I'll be out there till you get out."

"No, you won't."

"Huh?"

"You are going to be out there long after I'm out of Moose Mountain!"

"We'll see."

"Do something for me. When you get there give Professor a hug for me."

"I will."

Part Three

I

There had been eight of them cuffed and on the long benches of the van, facing each other on their way to Moose Mountain Penitentiary. It would be a two-hour trip, mostly in silence. They made two stops, the first one so the driver and his partner could pick up hamburgers and coffee. Just for themselves. The second one was made at the request of the middle-aged, portly, bearded prisoner, who called through the barred opening to the guards.

"I have an urgent call of nature!"

It had got more urgent until his third request was granted and the van came to an unscheduled stop.

"Holy water time, eh, Reverend," the guard said as he opened the rear door and came in.

Art had wondered who this fellow was. Now he knew; during waiting time in jail till trial they had been permitted to keep up with the news. This had to be the Reverend Elijah Matthews, starting a four-year sentence for child abuse. Judging from the expressions on most of the other faces, it was evident they had twigged to the reverend identity as well. Bugger you too, Elijah!

Unloaded from van. Into Moose Mountain Penitentiary. Gray concrete cocoon.

Halt. Wait.

Receiving area.

Halt. Wait.

New guards.

Halt. Wait.

Through a kinking maze of passageways, iron doors clanging open, clanging shut.

Halt. Wait.

Into shower room to be lined up against wall.

Enter head guard.

No more waiting. For now.

"All right! Our new school! Of fish! Strip! Including socks and gaunches. Right down to the buff. Now!"

He had some kind of short club stick in his right hand, with which he slapped his palm for rhythmic emphasis.

"Clothes onto the floor in front of you." Slap. "Then into the showers." Slap. "When you're clean and dry, your stripe and cap uniforms of the day will be waiting for you." Slap – slap – *SLAAAAP!*

When they got out of the showers and lined up against the wall again their remand khaki had been replaced by penitentiary uniforms in eight neat piles.

"Hey! No hard-ons allowed!" SLAAP!

Bull's eye right on the glans of the devout child molester. Uncircumcised. End of erection. Orgasm denied.

"From now on you keep your fucking Good Shepherd's crook in your pants!"

As they climbed into penitentiary gear the head guard briefed them.

"We have already tagged you fish with your numbers, allotted each his cell in the fish tank." Slap. "Where" – slap – "you will spend the next month. You will not set fin out of those aforementioned cells" – slap – "you will eat in there" – slap – "sleep in there and, except for you" – with his stick he pointed out the Reverend Elijah clothed again and holding his crotch with both hands – "jerk off in there." Slap – slap – *SLAP* – *SLAP* – *SLAAAP!*

They would be given medical examinations, he told them. These would include "piles and scabies and search for lice. Head" – slap – "armpit" – slap – "and crotch." *SLAP!*

After tank month, if they had followed all rules and regulations to the letter they would be moved into term cells, where they would be allowed during set periods out into the exercise yard, use of the library, and shop hours in work of their choice: plumbing, upholstery and carpentry, janitorial clean-up, shoe repair, auto licences, elementary, junior, senior high school, perhaps even in the odd case university correspondence courses.

Briefing over.

No. 1205

So, in here for the next two or three years of any remaining life the aneurism might grant you. Years without sight of land or sky, leaf or blade, all living shape and color denied. With four raw walls of concrete it's narrower than your university office was – perhaps by five feet but just as long. That little barred window does give you a niggardly glimpse of guard or inmate life out there. There'd been no window at all in your university cell. All those years in Academe and until this moment you never recognized the fitting irony of the university's name: *Living*stone. What an oxymoron!

One cell on the eleventh floor of the Fine Arts building now traded for this one in Moose Mountain Penitentiary, gray as the filing cabinets in your university cell. Now you are *truly* filed away!

You aren't the first and you won't be the last artist punished for the crime of non-conformity. John Bunyan was found guilty of heresy in the first degree and wrote *Pilgrim's Progress* during his term in Bedford jail. William S. Porter did penitentiary time for till theft. Ironic he should choose to use a pen name: O. Henry. Daniel Defoe was another one; hadn't helped his case that he'd invented the novel with his quill pen. Could have been worse for all of us during the Spanish Inquisition or more recently when Stalin or Hitler were calling the firing squad shots: capital punishment. You and Darryl and Win not sentenced to death of course, just to a term of allegorical life in Moose Mountain Penitentiary.

But I can still talk to you, my dear Irene. Can't I? Even more often, you say. Tell me something. That Great Justice in the sky – does He agree with the verdict? Haven't asked Him? Don't intend to? *You* do not find me guilty as charged? Aw – I love you, Irene! *And* the Professor and all the protégés I ever had. But I shouldn't have pulled Win and Darryl into it? I agree! Do I ever!

Tell me – has He ever mentioned John Bunyan to you? You don't think so. Do something for me. Ask Him what His judgment in that case was – is. Better still, if you run across the Reverend Johnnie up there, find out what he thinks of this mess I've gotten myself into. Thanks, dear.

No. 1206

He'd really blown it! Exceeded his old man's worst expectations. First time in the big time: Theatre Sagittarius, *Scam and Be Damned*. Not just the lead: *triple* lead. Would have played Barker Billy Barker in the first act; Dr. Cureall, the medicine man, in the second, and Orville Joyfull, the televangelist called home by God, in the third, saved in the Lord's Holy Broadcast tower by the Atlantic City Strip Club owner's $2,000,000 donation, only to rise to Heaven then descend to Hell when the uncertified cheque bounced.

If only he'd listened to Art and Darryl and not made that last heist! Since opening, what rave notices the play had received! It was moving on at the end of the run to off-Broadway. No-win Win!

That head guard was no amateur at slapstick. He'd got his broad message across to them: no improv in here.

Well, costume fitting was over. From remand khaki into stripes and engineer's cap. No make-up. First time on or off he'd ever played this role, and this was a three- to six-year run. For real. Wouldn't have to project to the last seat in the house, remember to turn always *through* the audience, pick up cues three beats ahead. No missing fourth wall in here.

Aw well, at least they don't do pig shaves on inmates anymore. Wassermann negative, ditto for scabies and crabs. And you'll do your best to follow the head guard's directions. Didn't he have one hell of a good sense of timing though!

Wasn't that a lovely bit of business he'd used on the born-again bugger!

No. 1207

Bang – clang – bang … click – clack – bang …

Surrounded by sound.

Buzz – buzz … whir – whirrrrrrrrh …

Imprisoned by sound.

Clang – cluck – clang … bug – bang – dang

Loud and ceaseless martial and mechanical sound.

Clang – guh – bang – gang … cluck – a – tuck – clack …

Unending.

… clack – a – tuck – clack … click – click – tuck …

Punitive sound.

Clack – tack … clack – a – tack – tack …

In this surfing sound sea what could be factual – what could be actual, real or unreal, make sense or make nonsense, be precise or concise.

I hear, therefore I am not!

Never had he dreamed it would be like this! Never had he – What's that? Listen, Darryl! You *are* hearing that! You really truly are! Above – above – above! Live and untidy lyric sound. Must be hundreds of them up there! Dear God, never let those little sparrows fall!

At first he had thought it was the dawn howl of a coyote but it was the wake-up siren. No use trying to get back to sleep, because it would ululate for the next five minutes. He threw back the covers. As he sat up, stood, the whole cell shifted, swung, and drifted and he almost keeled over. Forgotten again to take it carefully. He waited till the world had steadied and gained back uncertain balance.

"All right! Daylight in the swamp."

That was Bert out there, the only guard who seemed to know that speech with inmates didn't have to be limited to shouted orders. The first morning, through the mean little barrel window, he had taken the trouble to introduce himself.

"My name's Bert. You'll be seein' me regular whilst you're in here." He explained that he was on the morning shift, or as he put it: "I'm your morning shit guard. You'll be moved out in a month, but I'm servin' a lot longer term in the fish tank than you are. Damn it!"

Now Bert stopped outside his cell. "Your last day in the fish tank. Ten A.M. you got a date with the warden. Along with your two buddies. Tidy up for it."

It would be the first time he'd be in touch with Win and Darryl for a whole month. Strange that this would be his first meeting with the warden.

"What sort of fellow is he, Bert?"

"Just a warden."

"I've never had a glimpse of him."

"He don't slum with us scum. Sort of a figurehead, you might say."

He'd finished shaving when Bert showed up again with the breakfast cart and slid the porridge bowl through the food slot to him. "Bun appletit."

"I'll miss you."

"Same here." Bert rolled on down the passageway.

Not even warm! He hated it now as much as he had when he was a complaining child and his mother had told him that it was good for him, that little starving Armenian children had only cakes made out of mud and grass for *their* breakfast and he had said then to let *them* have his oatmeal. He lifted the lid on the toilet, dumped out the porridge, and flushed. Worst fodder prepared since man's discovery of fire!

Well, at least a solitary month, with all of the outer world denied, was over now. The next stage of incarceration could only be an improvement over this past one. Good God! December seventh. His birthday! December 7, 1912. Happy seventieth, Art. Another year closer to the Last Supper. Welcome to the penitentiary of old age, handcuffed by sixty-five years; before he got out of here old age would be a real ball and chain. Settle just for remembered life until memory fails and past loved and hated delights and sorrows refuse to return. Final sentence for all those found guilty of mortality: Capital Punishment!

Come on! Knock off the self-pity! You've had a good life. And you know it. You had Irene and those teaching years you bonded with the young. Your dedication to art reprieved you all your life. Together with Win and Darryl you pulled off one dandy international statement: "*Ars gratia artis!*"

And don't forget Professor. Oh dear! How he missed him now! His hands yearned the most for the patting and hugging, for the living warmth, the moist surprise of the ice-cube nose.

Do you miss me, Professor? Miss me, damn it! Don't touch your food. Whimper at the door. Ask Charlie a thousand times where I am. When am I coming back? Why have I rejected you?

He did that when we lost you, Irene, sorrowed for days and days. He really loved you, Irene. Almost as much as I did. Do.

Tell me something. Are there any dogs up there, Irene?

Irene?

No answer.

I'll get back to you, darling. After I've been to the warden.

Not feeling so low now. Hey! Just maybe – just maybe. I'll ask the warden if Moose Mountain allows dog visitor privileges!

Any guesses he'd made about the warden were contradicted the moment he and Win and Darryl were led into the office. As the two guards stepped smartly back to take up position on either side of the door, the man at the desk rose to his feet. He bowed. If, as Bert had said, wardens were just figureheads, this fellow was a most formal one, "Gentlemen. Please be seated."

They did that on the chairs before the desk.

Oxford gray three-piece suit. Had to be tailor-made. Bank manager or C.E.O. quality and (fittingly enough for a penitentiary warden) pin-striped. That maroon handkerchief with teepee tips peeking from the breast pocket color-echoed the tie perfectly snugged in the white collar.

He sat down, leaned back in his chair, brought his palms together and lifted contemplative fingertips to his lips.

"For the first time we seem to have in Moose Mountain Penitentiary three artist inmates. An actor, a poet, a painter. Or" – he looked at Art – "an academician?"

"Both," Art said.

"Three *thieving* artists." He leaned forward, spread out sheets on his desk. He picked up one, consulted it, looked up to Art. "Twelve-oh-five. A.k.a. Arthur Ireland. Four years – possession of stolen property."

He picked up the next sheet. His eyes flicked to Win. "Twelve-oh-six. Winston Forsythe – breaking and entering. *True* theft. Six years. And finally. Twelve-oh-seven – Darryl Duckworth – two years. Accessory."

Darryl sneezed.

"Bless you. Bless you all – if you behave. Good conduct has its reward in early parole so that six years could possibly equal three perhaps even two. Four could equal two or one and a half."

He looked over to Darryl. "Twelve-oh-seven, you could be on your merry way in a matter of months."

Darryl sneezed again.

"Please cover your mouth when you – such remission is not a matter of automatic arithmetic. Parole is entirely up to you. Oh – I see here reference to a dog involved in this two-year string of art thefts."

"Mine," Art said.

"Doberman? German shepherd? Pit bull?"

"Golden retriever."

"Never charged. Plea bargain, I suppose. Well now –"

"Professor would never testify against us," Art said.

"Come again."

"That's his name. Professor."

"Oh." He gathered up the sheets, shoved them aside. "Now then, I believe you've already been briefed on Moose Mountain rules and regulations to be followed by you during the remainder of your term with us. Any questions? Twelve-oh-five or twelve-oh-six or twelve-oh-seven?"

"No, sir," Win said.

"No, sir," Darryl said.

"I have one," Art said. "I understand we will be having – able to have visitors now."

"Weekends."

"I was wondering. Are there visiting privileges allowed for dogs?"

"Not in this penitentiary – or to my knowledge any other in North America. Kittens, yes. Canaries, budgies, yes ... no canine visitors. Well now ..." He leaned over, drew out the top lefthand drawer of the desk. He brought out a revolver, laid it down before himself on the desktop. Carefully.

"I have to tell you one last and important thing. This forty-four Smith and Wesson is loaded at all times. Has been so for the past six months. Sad necessity." He swung around in his chair to face the office window. "From this vantage point I have within view a large portion of the exercise yard below. If at any time I see ..." He swung back round. "... any one of you facing an outside wall ..." He picked up the revolver and swung back round. "I shall have no choice." He raised his arm and took careful aim. Art heard the click of the safety catch. "But to drill you right between your shoulder blades!"

He swung back to them, leaned over, put the gun back into its drawer. "Have I made myself perfectly clear?"

"Yes," Art said without adding: "Mr. President."

"Twelve-oh-six?"

"Yes," Win said, "sir."

"Uh ..." Darryl said.

"We do now have you artists with us. We will have no *escape* artists. That's all."

Three down. Three more to go: the devout child molester – the sex slayer of the twenty-year-old nurse's aide – and the seven-count forgery and fraud lawyer ... Just how in hell had he ended up in this line of business?

He looked up to the framed parchment on the wall:

Whitby University
On the recommendation of the Senate has conferred on
Charles Lansing Pepper
Who has completed the required studies and has completed a satisfactory thesis embodying the results of independent investigation of primary sources, the master's degree ...

Thirty years ago he had never dreamed what a difficult balancing act he would be letting himself in for. Rewarding or punishing. Soft or hard ...

"... *of social welfare with all the rights and privileges thereto appertaining* ..."

Way back then he hadn't realized what an empathy handicap he would have to work with, what an optimistic sucker he was. He should never have pulled that Smith and Wesson on those three first-timers, though. Maybe first and *last*.

"... *in testimony whereof Whitby University has caused its seal to be affixed hereto attested by the proper officers in that behalf* ..."

Count them: two riots in three years, five escapes in two years. But worst of all his recommendation to the National Parole Board for the release of Claude Lefarge ...

"... *on this twenty-second day of May one thousand nine hundred and fifty-nine*."

So, five rape and murders to follow in six months' time. They have to go on *my* C.V. as well as yours, Claudey boy. If only I had you back in Moose Mountain now and if only *you* faced an outside wall in that exercise yard ... just once!

He pulled out the desk drawer and looked down at the revolver in its paper nest. Oh, no. You couldn't pull that trigger. On him. On yourself. However!

He took the gun out, lifted it, and took careful aim on the framed parchment on the wall. He snicked off the safety. How about one for the chancellor – one for the chairman of the Board of Governors – one for the president – one for the registrar, and one for the director of the School of Social Welfare!

OOPS!

Thank God, it was *not* loaded!

2

Oh what a relief now he was out of solitary so that he was back in touch with Win and Darryl and with Kate and Charlie on alternating weekly visits. Such an improvement over the ones they'd made in the remand center jail; no glass separated them here in the large visitors' room loaded with tables and chairs.

Each time he showed up, Charlie told him Professor still missed him.

"Reminds me, Charlie. Hunting season began last week."

"Bang bang opening from daylight to dark. Just for migratory birds. But after the ducks and geese, at the end of the month prairie chicken and partridge and grouse and pheasant and any other upland game will have to head for cover."

"Professor, too."

"Don't worry, Art. Kate and I are keeping an eye on Ottowell."

"If you don't he'll get him. Keep him as far away as you can from Ottowell's –"

"We're doing that. He's sure fallen for Kate. Follows her wherever she goes. Meets her out at the gate every day when she comes home. God, he must have a bloody stop-watch in his gut. Does a lot of studio time with her, too."

"How's her work going?"

"Not bad. She has a nice sense of form as well as color.

Several happy accidents have happened for her. Besides busting you guys."

"Same sweet old Charlie, aren't you?"

"I try to be. By the way – she's pretty good with a fly rod, too. She sure likes to score. I wish she'd do it more on the creek and less in my kitchen. How's it going for you?"

"Some better now."

"Win seems to be taking it in his stride."

"Yes."

"Not Darryl, though."

"'Fraid not. I'm worried about him."

"I'm worried about all of you guys."

"We're going to make it, Charlie."

"I hope so. How's that aneurism of yours?"

"So far so good. I mentioned it to the doctor when they gave us our medical check-up. He explained that they don't give out warning signals. Comforting bastard. Told me not to worry, that it wasn't likely a bursting bubble would end my days, given my advanced years."

"Ah-huh."

"More importantly, you and Kate keep a sharp eye on Professor for me."

"We're doing that. Ottowell really has to behave now."

"How's that?"

"Kate."

"Yeah?"

"I told her how Ottowell nearly got Professor twice, and ever since then whenever she's outside – chopping wood, fishing Tongue Creek – besides the axe or the rod she's got her handgun."

"You're kidding."

"Nope. She's sure nice stacked with it in the shoulder holster under her blouse."

"Do you think she'd really –?"

"I'd say fifty-fifty."

"Well, Mr. Ireland. We meet again."

Considerate change of pace, addressing him by name and not by number.

"And how is prison life treating you these days?"

What the hell kind of answer could you give to a question like that?

"I trust that you find your new quarters meet with more approval than your old ones did now you are enjoying a modicum more of freedom within Moose Mountain."

Anything would be better than the fish tank.

"I suppose you have taken advantage of library use, visitor, and telephone privileges now granted."

"Yes."

"And the exercise yard, of course, though I don't suppose you are a volleyball addict."

No more than you are, Warden!

"You *are* still alive, so it would seem to me that you took seriously the escape warning I gave during our first meeting. As did your cronies involved with you in the art – ah – enterprise that ended all of you up here in Moose Mountain Penitentiary for some time to come." He glanced down at the sheets on his desk. "Duckworth, Forsythe, and Ireland." He looked up. "Sounds like the title of a top legal firm, don't you think?"

Just when in hell was he going to get to the point of this meeting?

"Celebrated specialists in the practice of felony." He leaned forward over the notepad on his desk, picked the pen out of its holder. "By my calculations one month is one twelfth of a year."

"By mine too." Watch it, Art. This is the warden!

"So we're both agreed on that. If you serve – given early parole, say, two years – twenty-four months – you will have done to date one twenty-fourth or four percent roughly speaking of your likely remaining time." He looked up. He waited. Expectantly. "Any comment, Mr. Ireland?"

"Yes. What's the point of this meeting?"

"It's routine for me when an inmate has moved from the initial phase of his term and into the one you are beginning. Not with *all* inmates. Just those I might be optimistic about or that I find interesting. Like Duckworth, Forsythe, and Ireland, Q.C."

"I find you interesting. Perhaps that's not the right word. I've come to an early conclusion about you."

"Have you."

"Yes."

"And what might your conclusion be?"

"You're quite a witty fellow. Is this a common quality in prison wardens?"

"I doubt it."

"I should explain something to you. There is an important distinction between true humor and sarcasm. Derision does not amuse; it hurts. Let me put it this way to you, Pepper: there is too much fucking pepper in your fucking humor!"

"Well, well, well. What have we here?"

"I'll tell you what we have here – one inmate who does not care to be the target of your goddam sarcasm! Any more!"

"I see."

"Even if it lands me back in the fucking fish tank!"

"It won't. You aren't the first to point this out to me."

"Or probably the last."

"You could be right. You've given me fair warning and I'll keep it in mind. That's a promise I'll try to keep."

"Thank you."

"One I made often to someone else. While I could." He

sighed. "Now – the purpose of this meeting. You are an artist. Because you are serving time in Moose Mountain it doesn't mean you have to cease being an artist. During our first meeting do you recall you asked if you could have your dog visit you?"

"Yes."

"I wish I could have said yes to that, but prison rules would not allow me to. What I *can* do is permit you to practice your art."

Good God! He hadn't been ready for this!

"If you choose to paint –"

"I do! I do!"

"You may do so in your cell – or perhaps we may be able to find you studio space –"

"Thank you! Thank –"

"– somewhere in the shops area. You will have to supply your own materials – paint – canvas – brushes – easel – whatever you feel you –"

"Of course!"

"I look forward to seeing your work."

"You will. You will!"

"Landscapes excepted, of course. Oops! Now then. I will be seeing Duckworth and Forsythe today. Have you any suggestions that might help me with them?"

Had it coming to me, Ireland. If she'd been here she'd have congratulated you. Verbal battering, she called it. How many times he'd promised her, no more taunting, no more gibes. Sorry, dear. I guess it goes with the job and I won't bring it home with me anymore. Promises, promises. So many broken promises. No more to be made, thanks to that drunken driving bastard five years ago!

I'll do my best to keep mine to you, Ireland. I will.

Now then. Elijah Matthews next. Three years' penitentiary penance for seven counts of child pederasty and buggery in the first degree. Bless you, Elijah! No. *Curse* you!

Katie always brought good news with her when she came to visit him. He'd never forget that early December afternoon when she showed up in the visiting area, excitement all over her face.

"You don't have to worry any more about a certain neighbor of yours."

"Ottowell?!"

"I sure as hell don't mean Peter the goose boss. Brace yourself, because yesterday I dropped Ottowell off in the remand center."

"What?"

"Just overnight probably till he's charged, then released on his own recognizance until his hearing and trial."

"What for?"

"Dangerous weapon charge. Firing on a police officer with a ten-gauge magnum shotgun. Three times and with buckshot lethal against bird or beast. Also resisting arrest to the point that the officer had to draw her forty-four Smith and Wesson and cuff the bastard."

"Good God! How did that happen?"

"You know that wooden bridge over Tongue Creek. Not the entrance one – the other downstream and a ways over that makes a gap in the barbed wire separating your property from his?"

"Of course."

"Professor and I were fishing there this morning. My Saturday off. Oh, by the way, I've got him trained now so he doesn't plunge in except to retrieve."

"Don't tell me you're hunting."

"Not ducks or geese. With Charlie's help I've taught him whenever we hook a trout to retrieve it for us."

"You're kidding."

"Honest. Don't carry a net anymore. When we've played the fish and worked it close to shore we yell 'Fetch,' and that's what he does. Right in, grabs it just back of the gills, carries it up and out, and drops it to flop at our feet."

"That's great! But what about Otto –"

"Did I ever hook that two-hundred-pound brown trout this morning! I was casting from that bridge – your side of it –"

"*Our* side."

"Just got started and he shows up. Armed as usual with his full-choke shotgun and he yelled at Professor and me to get our asses the hell off of his property. I yelled right back at him we weren't on his fucking property. Sorry – that's the only kind of language he understands. He said we were so, and then he stepped back and lifted that shotgun and said if we didn't fuck off he'd blow us off. We stayed and he tried to keep his promise."

"Holy –"

"I pulled the Smith and Wesson and told him I was a police officer and to drop his gun. He didn't, so I had to let him have a one-two-three –"

"One-two-three?"

"What we call it. In a bind you never fire single shots. I missed him – deliberately. He dropped the shotgun. I cuffed him – read him his rights – brought him in."

"Wow!"

"Trespass defense won't work for him when he comes up before the beak. He'll probably get a suspended sentence – and no firearm possession for a couple of years. I think he's learned a nice hard lesson and will have to change his style considerably from now on. Or else."

"Or else what?"

"Or else I'm going to have to drill the sonovabitch next time. Self-defense of course."

"Kate, please – for Charlie's and Professor's sake – clean up your goddam language."

"I'll try, Artie. I'll try my fucking best."

Another nice thing had happened on his next trip to the warden's office. Nice for him and nice for the warden too.

"Well now. How's it going for you, Ireland?"

"Can't tell yet. I've just gotten – I'm trying to get started. Got my stuff together and – Oh, thanks for the studio space in upholstery and refinishing. I think it'll work. In time."

"In time?"

"When you haven't been doing it for a long while there's what we call artist's block."

"I believe I've heard of it."

"Main thing is just *do* it – get rolling and hope for the best."

"Do you have – are you married?"

"Not any more."

"Children?"

"No. Why do you ask?"

"That regular young woman visitor you've had – she isn't your daughter?"

"I only wish she were. She's a detective. The one who lowered the boom on me. Us."

"Really!"

"I came to know her when she enrolled in my Art Appreciation and Art History class to do undercover work on the case."

"Mr. Ireland, I don't think painting's the only art you practice."

"What do you mean?"

"Sounds like fiction to me."

"It's non-fiction. She's very talented."

"Evidently she is. She did solve the case."

"I meant as a painter. I've persuaded her to move out to the place with Charlie, use my studio – look after Professor, and keep an eye on a neighbor for me. We've become very close. She's the daughter I never had."

"That's a happy ending."

"You have children?" Art said.

"No. You said you weren't married any more."

"My wife died seven years ago."

"So did mine. Makes two sad coincidences for us." He leaned down to pull out the top lefthand desk drawer. This time he brought out a photograph. "Used to keep this out on my desk, but I – past year decided it would be better to – ah – see her just once in a while."

Thirties maybe. Early forties at the most. "She's lovely," Art said.

"She was."

"So was mine."

"Did she paint?"

"No. But she was my creative partner. Always saw my work first of anybody."

"You were lucky. No such sharing for us." He picked up the photograph, looked at it. "My line of business." He laid the photo down. "Tell me. Just what school – style of painting do you do?"

"Oh, over the years, decades, everything from representational – figurative through impressionist – expressionist."

"How the hell did you ever end up in here, Ireland?"

"How did you?"

"I'll tell you when I know the answer." He looked down at the photo. "Would doing a portrait help break your painter's block?"

"Any sort of brush work can. You know, it's damn considerate of you to take such interest in –"

"I'm afraid I have a selfish reason for it."

"Selfish? How?"

He pointed to the photograph. "My dear departed."

Wow!

"I don't want to take unfair –"

"Unfair! Jesus! It would give me a lovely chance to repay you – show my gratitude for what you've done for me! I'll do you a portrait of her!"

"Thank you."

"This looks like it's going to be one tough block, so I might have to do half a dozen of her. Tell you something. Let me have a full-figure photograph – you must have a favorite one – just of her. No posed wedding photo. I'll do you a big four-by-four that would make Titian proud!"

"I do have one. Taken in Banff when –"

"There's a condition to this, though. You hang it up and you look at it every goddam day, Pepper."

"I will, Ireland. I'll bring the photograph in with me tomorrow. By the way. My friends call me Pep."

"And mine call me Art, Pep."

Even though it had copy birth in a photograph, a process he had again and again warned his students to be a no-no, he had pulled off one damn fine painting with her long and slender figure in blue, dramatically graceful against the froth-white flow of the Cascade Falls, Rocky Mountain jagged majesty in the upper background.

By mutual consent the warden was not to see it until he had finished. When he was done he got a frame made for it in carpentry, wrapped and carried it into Pep's office. There he set it against the wall and unveiled it.

For long long moments the warden stared. He reached for his breast pocket handkerchief.

"Banff."

He swallowed, coughed a couple of times. He blew his nose.

"Our honeymoon there."

Remember ours, Irene? In that Stoney Lake one-roomer the old girl rented us for a week?

He'd never forget it. Their wedding night bed was a plural one, for it was or were two hospital beds, high on casters, twinned together to make a double. In the middle of consummation it swiveled apart and they ended up on the floor between.

Just a momentary interruption. But there were more to come after he had wired the bed back together.

A four-year-old boy seemed to find them interesting and kept them under surveillance, either out in the privy or more often with his nose pressed up against the screen door. Again and again he would repeat the same question: "Wha' chew doin'?"

3

More than twenty had showed for his first drama class. The next time at least ten more joined them in the library. It shouldn't have been all that surprising given that a pretense talent must be a prime requirement for a successful career in crime.

He started them off with a pantomime. "Make all movements clear and precise. Overdo it with your hands, arms, legs, your eyes, your mouth – your ears if you can wiggle them. Charlie Chaplin it – Red Skelton it – Marcel Marceau it. Take a few minutes to think of a possibility. Then, come up here – in turn – and do it for the rest of us."

No takers.

"All right. Here's one for you. Ever sewed your fingers together?"

Evidently none of them had.

"Watch this."

They did and laughed when he stabbed his thumb with the needle. He followed that with a trip and pratfall, which they took for real until he said it had been deliberate. Now he had 'em! Didn't have to do the stepladder number.

The shoplifting mime was a good one. The next up, although he was only doing life, had obviously given the gallows a lot of serious thought. After the hanging had gone off well, he wanted to do a cop shooting for an encore, but settled for a Las Vegas crap shooter and black-jack dealer.

Best of them all, though, was young Rolly Duncan, in for robbery with arson. His bowlegged cowboy established thirty feet of lasso rope, did a meticulous running noose knot in one end of it, then halter-trained a library chair, which he saddled and mounted, being thrown three times before he had broken it. One of its legs actually. Sad but imaginative ending, having to put the chair out of its misery with his imaginary six-shooter.

Two weeks of this sort of pantomime had been fun for all, and he sensed that it had softened some prison stress for them. It sure as hell had for him.

"Now we move on to voice. I've had copies made for all of you of Ecclesiastes and the Song of Solomon – Sunday School time."

"What?!"

"Back to the Bible hour will teach you cadence and timing. Couple of weeks ought to do that."

"Holy sheeyit!"

"You're right, Rolly. It is holy."

Less than half showed up the next time, and those who did were less than enthusiastic about Ecclesiastes. The wise but sexy bits of the Song of Solomon did loosen them up some.

When they moved on to doing reading scenes from plays, class size returned almost to normal. *The Devil and Daniel Webster* was a hit. So were *Death of a Salesman* and the Hades scene from Shaw's *Man and Superman*.

Only half a dozen had showed up for his opening class in the library. First and last.

He had worked so hard at preparing his first lecture. They had just groaned when he announced that to begin with they would be doing poetry.

"Pomes is for wimmen," the manslaughter two fellow said.

"Sex gender is irrelevant in poetry," Darryl said.

"At least they're a hell of a lot shorter'n a story or a book."

"They are, but length does not mean that they're easier to write. Indeed poetry is the most difficult form of literary art. Now – more than any other mode, poetry is an oral art. There are many styles: blank verse, classical, with traditional rhyme and assonance and alliteration, sprung rhythm. Perhaps it's closer to singing than it is to writing."

"Music's mostly for wimmen too."

"The hell it is," serial bank robbery beside him said.

"Maybe – if you're loose in the wrist."

Heads turned meaningfully toward Elijah Matthews, with black beard and shoulder-long hair. "My understanding was that we're here for a course in creative writing," Elijah said, "not coarse badinage."

"Whatever the hell that is," manslaughter two said.

"It's certainly not poetry," Elijah said.

"Up yours," manslaughter shot back. "But not mine."

"Come on, you fellows. Cool it." That was the lawyer doing five for fraud.

"Thank you," Darryl said. At least he had two of them on his side. "To continue. Poetry has gone through many stages. Historically speaking. Classical, patterned with rhyme and assonance and alliteration. Some may seem strange to you: sprung rhythm, for instance, or concrete poetry, in which the poet shapes words and lines in the form of the subject of the poem. Then there is sound poetry ..."

Oh God, he could tell he wasn't getting through to them. Maybe he could wake them up with one of his sound poems for illustration.

He had picked what he hoped was his best one to do for

them, but from the head shakes and expressions of all except for the reverend he could see that they just weren't buying sound poetry.

Aw well, carry on, Darryl. "The human voice has such a wonderful variety of sounds. You have glottal and labial and lingual –"

"And anal and gastric." It seemed that he had lost five-for-fraud.

"They are not the human *voice*."

"Human sounds, though," the former lawyer said.

"There are sibilant consonants: *s* and *sh* and –"

"Last century there was a Parisian able to crepitate his whole way through the Marseillaise. Made a pretty good living at it in the Folies-Bergère."

"What's crapitate?" asked manslaughter two.

"Fart," fraud said.

"I knew a kid in Grade Four," bank robber said. "He could belch 'yes' and 'no'. One time he burped 'Go to the cloakroom' before he got sent to the cloakroom."

"Now look," Darryl said, "this is a writing class. I would appreciate it if you would make sensible and relevant comments and responses –"

He was interrupted by a long and resonant fart from manslaughter two. This was followed by a belch from fraud, and a cacophony of hiccups, sneezes, belches, and farts from the entire class.

End of writing lecture.

No one showed up for the next class.

The following week, at his request, the warden shifted him to library duty.

It was a happy coincidence that the only one in the class who had taken poetry seriously should be working in the library with him: Elijah Matthews. It was hard to believe that this well-read man of the cloth deserved to be doing penitentiary time. Certainly not on charges of child abuse.

He had devoted all his ministerial life to the little ones, he explained to Darryl, just as Jesus had. One time when he was with the Ebenezer Victory Temple in Long Beach, California, he had even risked his life to save a child. He had thrown himself in the path of a Budweiser truck to rescue a little golden-haired three-year-old girl, who had run out into the middle of Ocean Boulevard to retrieve her red balloon. He had snatched her from the very jaws of death, but a truck wheel had rolled over his stomach.

He still suffered acute spasms of pain from that old abdominal injury. The pain was why he was in Moose Mountain Penitentiary today.

"The only way to relieve the pain is to put pressure on my lower abdomen," he explained. "That was the only reason I would from time to time take a child into my lap, then hug close to ease the pain."

Win didn't buy that. "Sounds like bullshit to me, Darryl."

"No, I believe him. A couple of the deacons in his church had it in for him. They framed him. He's in here because of a gross miscarriage of justice."

"Darryl. Do something for me. While you're in that library with him you keep your distance from him, and keep you know what covered at all times."

It was to be the first show ever before an audience for the Moose Mountain Penitentiary Repertory Company. Not just a reading performance either, but one with props, set, costumes. The audience was not limited to inmates only, but would include caring friends and relatives as well. Damn decent of the warden to give them the go-ahead.

All of them had agreed that *Scam and Be Damned* was the play they ought to do. Liked it almost as much as he did. Charlie had mailed him the script; the warden had read it and granted permission to do it. He'd got copies made and after a reading try-out with them he had a promising cast.

Besides directing, in each act he would be playing the lead himself: Barker Billy Barker, the sideshow shill, Dr. Hepner Cureall, famous for his Cleopatra Remedy, panacea for all ills of man or beast. It was quite a fitting name for a snake oil; though it might not cure all ailments as claimed, it would not actually kill its users, as the original asp formula did the Queen of Egypt. In the third act he would also play the televangelist faith healer, the Reverend Orville Joyfull. No doubt about who should play the woman evangelist, Amy Temple Ferguson; had to be Rolly Duncan, doing six for robbery and arson. In drag with long tresses and soprano voice, he'd bring down the house.

There was a staging problem, though; the play had not been written for prison theater-in-the-round, so faith healer Orville Joyfull's ascent to Heaven after God had called him home, and then down in a CO_2 cloud to Hell after the Atlanta strip club owner's uncertified $2,000,000 U.S. cheque bounced, presented a considerable problem. Rolly came up with the solution; have carpentry and upholstery make a carnival canopy to cover the performance area, with a cable and pulley device framed by the tent poles to handle the ascent-descent business. Then have a five-by-five-by-eight box for the Lord's Holy Broadcast tower in the third act, with a trap door to welcome the scam character of the evangelist down and into the furnace of Hell.

One thing about penitentiary life, it made you appreciate the past, because the present was such lonely hell. Night after night as soon as the cell door slammed shut the only thing you could do was to lie down on the bunk and remember yourself to sleep. Sometimes it worked.

Tomorrow would be his first Christmas in here. Joy to the world, but just to the one outside Moose Mountain Penitentiary.

Of his childhood Christmases the best one of all had been almost sixty years ago. He could almost see again the tinseled tree in front of their fireplace, with spiral-ribbed candles clutched upright in those little tin claws on the tips of the branches. There had been a blizzard blowing in off the prairies; it hummed and thrummed through the felt and brass weather-stripping on the living room windows like a dirging mouth organ. At eleven he'd been too young to understand its sad message of mortality for all.

Especially at Christmas, he suspected, his mother mourned the loss of his father, who had died in the 1918 flu epidemic. He had almost no father memory at all, only dim fragments of recall: being pulled in a wagon, being found by him when he'd got lost in Ashford's Grove at the end of their street. Crossing streams in the toilet room was the clearest memory of all, especially the time he'd missed the bowl and got his father's ankle instead.

His mother had moved right in to run the jewelry store, taking him downtown with her every morning. She must have been good at it, for by the time he started school, she could afford to hire Olga, a live-in maid, and in later years she had managed to finance his trip to study art at the Sorbonne.

She'd been a fine mother with no overindulgence, putting up with his frequent impatience and annoyance just as much as he did with hers. When he was eight she set down a new rule in the Christmas ritual: he was not to know what his main Christmas present would be till the afternoon when Uncle Len and Auntie Betty and Cousin Marion would come over for Christmas dinner. Indeed three years before, when he had pleaded with her to let him know what it was, and she had held her ground, he had thrown himself on the breakfast room floor and kicked and screamed. It didn't work.

When Auntie Betty and Uncle Len and Marion came over, Marion always brought all her Christmas presents with her. She also ate turkey with her mouth open.

Come to think of it, sex reared its ugly head much higher at Christmas time. It was hard to understand Marion's delight over handkerchieves or another bottle of perfume. Even with stocking gifts, how could anybody settle for a set of jacks instead of a net bag of agates with fire in their hearts? A skipping rope couldn't possibly match a hockey stick. Same went for a doll's baby carriage instead of a toboggan, or a sleigh that could be steered. Who needed a stove that couldn't cook anything in place of an Erector set for constructing London Bridge or the Eiffel Tower? Did she really prefer a nurse uniform to a cowboy or an Indian or a sailor suit?

How he had looked forward to another Horatio Alger Junior or better still *Boys' Own Annual* with its cigarette paper thin pages outnumbering both the Old and New Testaments. Marion got *Chatterbox*, with its cloying stories about rabbits or chickadees at the bottom of gardens. In *Boys' Own Annual* young heroes stained their faces with walnut juice to fool thugs (who practiced thuggee) and waded rivers infested with crocodiles displaying sharp uppers and lowers. Probably explained why there were few women orthodontists to this day. The heterosexual dice were loaded in male favor from birth.

For days he had wondered what his mother was giving him for Christmas this year. A magic lantern would be great, or a Daisy air rifle, or a chemistry set. No way she would ever get him a bicycle, even though he'd pleaded for one for two years in a row.

Other kids in their neighborhood, in the whole town, had gotten their two-wheelers way before he had; Archie Taft when he was only eight and had to lean it against a fence so he could climb into the saddle and push off. Archie was first in everything; by the age of ten he was already chewing tobacco. One morning recess he invited Art to take a try at it, but when he accepted the offer his head went into a tail-spin and he must have swallowed some of it because he vomited up all of his breakfast porridge. By the time the bell rang he had recovered.

Each Christmas and each birthday he'd asked his mother to get him a bicycle and each time she'd said, "Yes, son, when you're old enough."

"I'm way past old enough!"

"We'll see, when the time comes."

For a good two years now the time had not come. God only knew when it would. Maybe when he reached fourteen or fifteen!

That Christmas, when he had just about given up all hope, the time came.

With Uncle Len's help his mother pulled off a beautiful surprise by storing it over at their place. After dinner Uncle Len went outside to his Ford sedan, one of several he owned, for he ran a taxi business and did not drain the radiators, take off the tires, and put his cars up on blocks for winter. He came back in with the bike.

It was a red twenty-one-incher with a bell to be thumbed

and a coal oil lamp mounted in the center of the handle bars. When Uncle Len held it so he could mount it in the living room, his toe tip could just reach the down pedal.

With that blizzard wind howling there was no way he could ride it outside, but he could in the basement. For the next three and a half months. Only once down there had he wobbled into Olga coming out of the pantry.

What a tardy spring it had been, that year he was eleven.

He'd done fifteen of his daily thirty round the exercise yard when Win caught up and fell in step beside him.

"Three days no see, Art. Where you been hiding out?"

"Studio."

"So it's going good for you."

"Not really."

"When the going gets tough the tough get painting?"

"Yeah. Been two whole months now. Not much to show for it."

"Hang in."

"Of course. How about you?"

"Moving right along. Sanscript time."

"Sanskrit?"

"San*script*."

"Ah – clever pun. Extinct Indo-European language."

"You say so."

"From 'samskrita' meaning prepared."

"Pun's all yours. Prepared, eh? Damn fine pun. Most of them got their lines nailed down starting with Angus playing the Scotch field preacher. Did the try-out reading without a script – which was pretty impressive."

"How's that, Win?"

"He's illiterate."

"How did he –?"

"Rolly read for him so he could memorize his lines. He's great."

"Rolly's great?"

"Both of them are."

"Hold up, Win. Aaaah – get my wind back."

"You all right?"

"Sure. Let's sit down for a minute. Just age."

"Hell – you aren't old. Tell me something. When a person gets older – artists – does their art slow down too?"

"I don't think so. Same for all creative energy. Sex or art."

"Huh?!"

"Downstairs – upstairs. Still do it, but longer between times."

"Jeez, Art. You sure are something."

"So are you, Win."

"I try to be."

"I've noticed that. You're always on. How's Darryl doing?"

Win got to his feet. "Let's do a couple more rounds."

"Wait a minute. I asked you –"

"Not all that great now he's doing janitor work."

"You mean he's not in the library? Why would they shift him from there to clean-up?"

"They didn't. It was at his request. Day before yesterday."

"Because his poetry class didn't work out?"

"I think he had another reason."

"What other reason?" Art said.

Win looked off and up to the guard towers. "He wouldn't tell me. Whatever it was he didn't want to talk about it. I know it wasn't just blowing his writing class."

"What else could it be?"

"I have a hunch."

"Yes?"

"All this past month he's been getting lower and lower. I've known him a long time, Art, and I don't think I've ever seen him so down. On himself. Couple of weeks ago I suggested maybe he ought to ask for counseling. Shit! Shouldn't have done it."

"Why not?"

"Goddam theraping counselor just knocked him down lower. He diagnosed him manic-depressive. Close to psychotic."

"No!"

"I'm breaking my promise to Darryl not to tell anybody else. I'm afraid he bought the diagnosis, said he wasn't surprised, that there were a couple of Old Country Duckworths did time, too. In mental institutions."

"Oh dear!"

"That sneezing gramma was one of them. Look, Art. Let's just hold back for now and give him a chance to come to grips with whatever it is on his own. I think that's what he wants."

"Okay, Win."

Oh God! Oh God! Why hadn't he listened to Win? There must have been all kinds of signals that should have warned him. Elijah Matthews was not the victim of a miscarriage of justice. No way he had devoted his life to preaching and healing the sick and the deaf and the halt and the blind. Suffer no little ones to come unto him, ever.

Quite likely in Long Beach there *had* been a little golden-haired three-year-old girl who *had* lost her red balloon on

Ocean Boulevard, but he had *not* risked his life to save her. Probably he had bought her a new balloon as well as candy and ice-cream cones, then taken her to the Pike to ride the merry-go-round and after that, under the horseshoe pier, where he could ride *her*. His trial had not been a miscarriage; he should have been sentenced to *life*, not four years!

Oh, how I wish I'd listened to you, Win! Too late now, after what he tried to pull off on me in the library washroom. I wasn't able to give him the shit-kicking he deserved, but at least I won't be doing library duty anymore now I've been moved down to janitorial work. Could have been worse: plumbing, like my old man.

"Win, I haven't seen Darryl for days. There's somebody else in his cell and I haven't run across him working – "

"Don't you know?"

"Know what?"

"He's back in the fish tank."

"How come?"

"Last week doing his clean-up he made a bad mistake. Slopping out his suds bucket, he soaked a guard from head to boots. Also got him with his mop right in the chops."

"Aw no!"

"I got it from Bert. He said the guard was always riding Darryl. 'Steve's a mean sonovabitch,' Bert told me. 'Too bad he didn't get him good with a push broom in the knackers.' "

"We've got to go visit him!"

"Not permitted, Art."

"We'll see the warden and – "

"Nope. *Darryl* won't permit it. I tried. He doesn't want to see anybody."

Tooooo – whooooo
Mmmmmmm – muhmmmmmmit
Maaaay
Cuh – hnnnnnnnnnnh
Sssssssss ... errrrrrh
Nnnnnnnnnnnnnh.
Eye – yigh – eye – eeeeeee
Daw duh aaaaarh
Illlllllllllll
Duuh – uh – ku – fuhk – wuuuuuuurh
Whaaaar ... wurrrrr
Thhhhhlessssss.
Laaaaaa
St
Willlllllll
Ah
Nnnnnnnnh
Duh
Tess ... tuh
Men – men – men
Tuh!

"Oh God! Oh God, Win! What have I done!"

"Not you, Art. Darryl."

"My fault! Hadn't been for me he wouldn't have ended up in here. He wouldn't have –!"

"Hold it, Art. Let me explain Darryl to you. When you saved my bacon on the campus that day I wasn't worried just about myself. Darryl, too, even though I hadn't touched base with him for a year. Always worried about him right from when we were in Chinook College together.

"When I asked you if Darryl could move in with us there was something about him I almost told you then, but I didn't." He stopped, swallowed a couple of times. "Art, forget blaming yourself for this. I'm the one to blame."

"Oh no, Win!"

"Oh yes. I was way better informed about him than you. Most people listening in on us would think Darryl and I weren't too fussy about each other. They'd be wrong. All that wrangling we did was initiated by me most of the time. For his sake."

"I don't understand."

"Counter-irritation. He needed it. The poor guy – probably from birth – never figured he was worth a pinch of gopher shit and I always let him win the verbal wrist-twisting. Gave him a lift every time. I know how you feel, Art. Me too. Worse because I'm the one let him down."

"I don't see how you –"

"I should have talked to the warden, got him to break the one-to-a-cell rule and moved me into the fish tank with him so I could keep an eye on him. Right after what happened with Elijah in the library."

"What happened in the –"

"He made a pass at Darryl."

"I didn't know that!"

"I did, though. Darryl didn't tell me, but he didn't have to. It was the last straw. Been a lot of them for Darryl. Remember I told you his sneezing granny ended up in a Jolly Old asylum?"

"Yes."

"She died in there. Suicide. And ... well ... this wasn't Darryl's first attempt. When we were roomies together in our basement suite I pulled him out of the bathtub where he'd slit his wrists. It is not *your* fault, Art. Mine. I knew the hand he was dealt at birth. He was allergic to life all his life."

"Poor Darryl."

"He left a note addressed to me but saying goodbye to all of us. On toilet paper squares – penciled. Bert gave it to me. Should have been kept for evidence after Bert came on his morning shift and found him hanging from the sheet noose. But that's Bert for you. Darryl has asked to be cremated and for his ashes to be floated down Tongue Creek."

"Thanks for telling me all this, Win."

"You feel some easier about –"

"Not one goddam bit!"

"Oh shit, Art. Here's a kleenex!"

He guessed he wasn't the only one in here marking off on a calendar the weeks and days and the months till release from concrete. Wasn't time supposed to speed up, not slow down to snail pace? Eleven long months and twenty-one days left of penitentiary time, given the warden's promise of early parole.

And art could not conquer all; nothing was happening for him in his plumbing and upholstery studio. In his cell sleep was more and more reluctant. Night after lone night repeated the ones that had followed Irene's …

Goddamit, I miss you as much as I ever have, Irene! And now Darryl, too. You say the Great Painter in the Sky is giving me His Last Warning: Blaspheme no more! Sorry, Irene. Sorry, Lord God Almighty.

Yes, I'll knock off the self-pity and the whining, bless our good times together. I will get into the studio as soon as it's daylight in the swamp. Every day, every week, every month. Until I join you and Darryl up there.

There had been such good times for them, best of all that twenty-fourth of May, the Queen's birthday; you don't give us a holiday we'll all run away. The day they moved on to the place she had suggested they mark the occasion by going skinny dipping in the beaver pond. To begin with, anyway. How often after she had … he had returned there to remember.

And now in his cell he was again with Florence and Professor, making it through the barbed-wire fence and into the thin clump of birch and cottonwood, where the morning sun streamed down to them in quivering bars almost intense enough to filter *green* light through the leaves.

He was feeling again leaf tickle and the scratch of a branch across his mouth and cheek. How she had loved this glade, its edges choked with wild cherry and saskatoon and alder. He could smell that live scent of moisture and the honey perfume of wolf willow predicting the beaver dam pond ahead.

Once more he was looking down on water mirror, reflecting wolf willow silver along its edge. Over there the spear green of bull rushes. The pond's mud margin held deep hoof pocks where Hutterian cattle had come down to drink.

He was startled by a frog plop. The water surface was creased with the lilliputian wake of a waterbug moving in minute epilepsy. Stopped. Held still. Twitched on again over pure surface.

He knelt and began to unlace his shoes. Perhaps the pond could wash sorrow away. With mild chill it embraced him; he pulled himself down and through the cool underwater murk, then arching broke the surface to expel pent breath and spray. He lay floating with the sting of pond water in his nostrils, the flat earth taste of it at the back of his mouth and throat. As though not part of him his hands fluttered at his side; his knees moved lazily and unbidden as he stared up to sky and still cloud.

Diluted by cool and fluid intimacy of water on nakedness, the tension flowed slowly from him.

The clouds were moving now, faster and faster. He rolled over, and realized he was caught in the spring race that would spill with fury over the beaver dam. He almost made it to the riverbank by grabbing at the muskrat house, but with record spring water high there wasn't enough of it in the clear to give him a decent grip and he was on his way again to the dam, then through and down in froth and flow to the rocks below.

He missed most of the rocks by inches till he reached the back eddy, and then came the brutal shock of head pain and the twenty-fourth of May rocket explosion of starring light.

Here I come, Irene.

Almost.

How white she was against the silver of willow over there, pale and lithely naked with her arms up and her head tilted forward as she tied up her hair. He saw clearly the shallow bend of her back, the soft curve and thrust of her breasts – Gone! The eddy had sucked him down and into underwater darkness, then total black-out!

Well up on the bank he came to, Professor at his side. What a retrieve he had pulled off! A breeze set the willow leaves above into paper frenzy. He rolled over. As he did, round a rock up the bank there slipped a blunted arrow head, slightly raised in whip-stick tracing glide. Professor bounded from his side to pull off another master rescue.

The bull snake grinned, jaws open to say "suh – sssssss" pinkly, and to flame red-forked thread again and again. Professor realized he had made a wrong decision and returned to Art.

The willow leaves had ceased their gentle tapping; he lay in silence, with just the pulse of crickets in the grass.

He had seen her so clearly that time. Not only had he seen her, but he had heard her voice, too. In the years to come they would talk with each other whenever he needed her.

Especially here in Moose Mountain Pen. Now that he had seen her again, maybe she would return to him often during the eleven months and twenty-one days he had left to serve. Could this dream image be some sort of creative promise? Could visual remembrance be translated into paint?

Let's see. Let's see!

Every night as he lay on his bunk and waited for sleep that would not come he closed his eyes and tried to project past pictures against the screen of his closed eyelids. At first there was just a dark curtain that persisted against his will until thousands of light dots declared themselves, winking and blinking so that he was looking at vibrant tweed. In time clouds began to form and drift and fade to reappear with light that limned their outer edges, still holding darkness within themselves as they grew new shape after shape.

There was color for the first time between those two; just a hint of blue. It's gone. It's back again. Maybe I imagined it. No. Over there. And there's faint red.

He knew it was silly of him, but night after night he did it and did it and did it until he dropped off to sleep. Before long he was seeing not just dark sky and cloud but the long roll of surf and the snow-capped geometry of mountains. A bloody dumbbell kept coming back. So did a large and formal key hole followed by a vagina and then a penis. Maybe he was ready for the counselor's couch.

Instead he managed to get one from upholstery for his studio space, to lie on it with his eyes closed before the beginning of each run on the canvas, then get up and try to realize in paint what he had just watched.

You've done it again, Irene, just as you always have. The five-year art block is over. We're off to the races!

Win agreed with him, had seen the first one he'd finished with the new approach. He'd just put the last touch on it when Win showed up.

"Hey, that's a nice one, Art!" He took a couple of steps toward the easel. "I really like it! What the hell is it?"

"You tell me."

"Ahh – you joined the surrealist –"

"Not quite. I hope."

Win moved closer, stepped back. "Lots of white shapes. What are they? Mountains?"

"If you wish."

"Nah – too soft. They curve too much for mountain peaks. Clouds? Those ones remind me of – uh – a woman's breasts. Nope. No nipples. Clouds maybe. Or snowdrifts. No way. All that center of red would melt them."

He ran his finger from one side to the other. "Suggests horizon to me. Am I right?"

"Possibly."

"This one's got my standing ovation, Art." He pointed again. "There and there and over here – kind of like black filigree. How'd you do –?"

"Draft pen point…"

"Nice doodling. Down here suggests an eye, doesn't it? What gets me, though, is that red explosion in the center. Well, not explosion exactly, more like fire *glow*." He straightened up and turned back to Art. "Watercolor?"

"Diluted oil."

"Does it bother you when art idiots like me –"

"Not at all, Win. I welcome it. The viewer's right to discover."

"That's a dandy one. The viewer's right to discover. Goes for what I do too, my audience's right to feel. Hope I can pull it off as well as you have with this one. When I get up on stage again."

"You will when *Scam and Be Damned* opens."

"We'll see … Tell me – this painting of yours – what school of art is it? Suggests mountains and snowdrifts and cloud and fire, but it sure isn't landscape."

"No, Win. It's inscape."

"Oh boy, you've pulled off another good one. I like it."

"It's yours."

"Huh?"

"The painting, Win. Hang it up in your –"

"Will I ever! Thanks, Art!"

The five-year block is broken, Irene. Thanks to you. Darryl, too. Take the poor boy under your wing up there. Introduce him to Horace and Ovid, to Keats and Blake and Milton and Poe – no – Edgar Allan isn't likely to be up there. E.J. Pratt probably is. Don't bother with Wordsworth.

As for me, I really believe I've finally broken through the art block. Tell Darryl for me that I owe it to him. No. I'll tell him myself. Darryl, I've had little sleep since you left us. Hardly a wink, I miss you so. Hour after hour you've been with me in the dark, and because you have been, I'm painting up a storm now. Your tragic end did it. I really owe you, Darryl.

Daily Times, September 15

Dramatic He She Escape From Moose Mountain Penitentiary

The drama was not over when the curtain closed Saturday night on the play *Scam and Be Damned.* Performed by the Moose Mountain Penitentiary Repertory Company under the direction of Winston Forsythe who also played triple lead roles, the play received well-deserved standing ovations.

All parts were acted by Moose Mountain inmates, especially well done by Forsythe, a television and stage actor before his conviction a year ago for his break-and-enter role in a worldwide series of art thefts that ended with a $1,000,000 U.S. Toronto heist last year from the Lilian Milne Art Gallery.

Thematically and ironically *Scam and Be Damned* deals with a highly popular form of crime today: religious fraud by confidence experts milking money from the vulnerable trusting of whom there seems to be a growing supply.

In a stirring climax a televangelist receives Divine and dramatic punishment for his scam crimes. Eternity in Hell.

See DRAMATIC HE SHE page B3

There was more well-rehearsed action to come after curtain call, however. Rolland Duncan, who played the evangelist Amy Temple Ferguson, made his escape from Moose Mountain Penitentiary where he was serving the second year of a six-year term for robbery and arson.

RCMP Constable George Rogers said, "It's pretty

clear to us that sometime after the play he went through the stage platform trap door instead of into his cell." Evidently guards did not check out his cell, the constable said, and with the help of a rope cable which had been used in the play and left hanging from the peak of a side-show canopy, he made it over the wall.

This clever escape is the latest one in a long series made from Moose Mountain Penitentiary over the past few years, Constable Rogers said. "He is a skinny young fellow with long dark hair and if he's still wearing his play dress and make-up, could easily be passing for a woman."

Warden Charles Pepper was not available for comment.

4

Goodbye, Pep. Goodbye, Bert. Goodbye, Moose Mountain Penitentiary. Prison days are over and freedom days are here again. Let us sing a song of cheer again! He'd made it! Finally!

Charlie and Kate would pick him up. Ironically this last confinement year had been the most productive of all his painting life; the cell that was no longer his was stacked with cartons of the creative result; they'd fill that van to the roof.

Bert helped him and Charlie move the whole works out of his cell to fill the van. He shook hands goodbye. "See you next time."

"Won't be a next time."

"Only kiddin'."

"Tell me, Bert. Do you fish?"

"Sure do. Here in the fish tank and outside whenever I'm off shift. Trout's a lot more fun."

"Drop by if you ever get down my way. Finest brown trout fishing in North America."

"Might just take you up on that, Art."

He'd said his sad goodbye to Win and, as always, Win had a surprise for him.

"I want you to do something for me, Art. I can't be there with you when you float Darryl down Tongue Creek, but in a way I can if you look in Darryl's and my bedroom. Used to be. Inside the front lefthand tube leg of my brass bed you'll find – I got to make a confession to you, Art. Remember on a few of our jobs some jewelry went missing. Couple of the jade pieces in the Brockington one got smashed?"

"Yes."

"When we hit Princess Koblenska, Catherine de Medici's gold and tortoiseshell snuff box went missing?"

"I wondered about that."

"Well, wonder no more. Couple of times I relapsed to my light-fingered Rose Buddy days. That snuff box is tucked up inside the brass bed leg. One day I'd hoped to give it to Darryl. Would have meant a lot to him. That granny of his was a heavy user. You know how he loved to sneeze?"

"Of course."

"So what I want you to do is get that snuff box, fill it with snuff, and each of you snort a pinch to say farewell to him."

"We'll do it! We will, Win! I wish you could be with us when we do!"

"No way. I'm doing six, remember, so I don't qualify for day leave yet. Oh – after you've sneezed goodbye, toss out the snuff box to follow him downstream."

And what a homecoming it was. Professor met them at the gate and followed the van all the way to the house. When his long-lost master got out, he lifted to his hind legs to hug him and to slobber kiss him again and again. He quit only to run off Florence when she showed up to oink her welcome.

As well as Kate's car there was a truck in the yard; Art recognized it as one from the hook-and-eye colony. Decades ago they had switched from team and buggy. They all belonged to the gentle *practical* persuasion, which probably explained the survival in the Russian holocaust of the fifteen souls from whom they were descended.

"Is it Peter the goose boss?"

"Him and the preacher and the bone-setter," Charlie said. "Last week I told Peter you were coming home. They've donated two jugs of chokecherry wine and three geese for your homecoming. They showed up just before we left to get you. They're the ones preparing your celebration banquet and they're staying for dinner. Preacher will ask the blessing."

"What a lovely good neighbor welcome, Charlie."

"Yeah. Hope they can cook as well as they can farm and well witch."

They could. The goose was done to a turn. Kate had second slice of saskatoon pie. He'd have to warn her against sneaking food slivers down to Professor.

There had been much laughter and many toasts as they brought each other up to date. Kate had very good news to share.

"Art, you remember you had a tough time persuading me to believe your reason for doing what you did that landed you in Moose Mountain?"

"Yes?"

"And I told you that the end cannot justify thieving means?"

"Uh-huh."

"Seems I was wrong. Most of that artwork has ended up in public galleries and museums. When I was promoted to Special Constable to enforce the identification of criminals' act, the hook-up with Interpol gave me a chance to keep in touch with the art case. You were right, Art. I have a complete list now of where those paintings are. Here – in the States – Europe.

"The really surprising one is the Dürer collection. It's ended up in Kiel."

"What's surprising about that?" Art said. "Dürer was a German artist."

"Yes. But I had trouble trying to figure out why a smart oil billionaire like Lampert, who likely had the best legal advice going, would ever let his insurance company get their hands on his paintings and put them up for auction. In this case Sotheby's. I found out something very interesting. He didn't mind losing that collection and keeping the cash. In fact, he had a very good reason for sending Dürer to shows all over the world. Each time he would up their insured value a notch higher, so that down the road he could make a generously inflated donation to a public gallery and pocket a tax credit way, way over what he had paid for them originally. This way he got cash with just capital gain nicked off."

"Mammon always pays best," Charlie said.

"Sure as hell does," Kate said.

They toasted Lampert along with the Hutterian brothers, who did not join the toast to Mammon that Charlie proposed.

Art saved his good news for the last.

"I have an announcement to make. Charlie, I had a very good reason for telling you to wait to unload these paintings and transfer them to the studio this afternoon. The reason was that they have to go into town tomorrow. To the Queen's Gallery for a show opening next Friday."

"Really!" Charlie said.

"Really."

"How in hell did you pull that off?" Katie said.

"I did have some help from the owner, Jim Osler. A month ago, just for the hell of it, I gave him a call and explained to him how I'd been permitted to paint in Moose Mountain and that it had gone well for the whole past year. I asked him if he might be interested in doing a show in Queen's.

"Was he ever. He made two trips out to Moose Mountain and really liked what he saw. He didn't like it so much when I made it clear to him that the paintings could be sold only to public galleries and museums, but he finally gave in."

"Good going, Art!" Charlie said.

"Hurray for you!" Kate lifted her glass. "I propose a toast. Here's to Art having one gang buster of a show at Queen's Gallery."

They all drank to that, including Peter the goose boss and the bone-setter and the preacher.

"It is to happen on what day?" Peter said.

"Next Friday."

"The Monday which follows that – it is not Thanksgiving Day?"

"That's right," Charlie said. "'Specially for Art."

Peter leaned over to the preacher, murmured something to him. The preacher nodded his head.

"To the opening we would like to come also," Peter said.

"Of course," Art said.

"Bring the whole colony," Charlie said.

"No," the preacher said. "Several of us just."

As he had promised Win, they held the sad sad ritual for all of them. Professor included. He sneezed too after Kate held Catherine de Medici's snuff box under his nose. He watched with them as it floated off downstream on Tongue Creek, to follow Darryl's ashes.

Daily Citizen, October 8
Landscape Of The Mind

A Queen's Gallery showing of paintings by artist and teacher Arthur Ireland opened last Friday simply entitled: *INSCAPE.* "A record turn-out," said James Osler, the owner.

"People were lined up in spite of the pouring rain with their umbrellas for over two blocks. I have never seen anything to touch it in the eight years since I opened Queen's."

The reason for this, he said, had little to do with the fact that Ireland had recently been released from Moose Mountain Penitentiary after winning early parole from his four-year sentence for the series of art thefts that started out with the disappearance of the Albrecht Dürer collection from the Livingstone University Art Gallery four years ago on July 1, the opening of that year's Great North-west Stampede.

The art theft string unraveled from coast to coast and ended with the theft of $1,000,000 U.S. from the Lilian Milne Gallery in Toronto.

All of the paintings in the show were done while Ireland served his prison term.

"People may have turned up for that reason," Osler admitted, "but they stayed because of the fine quality of the work."

Quite possibly Osler was right. The show is scheduled for a tour of seven galleries, including the National Art Gallery in Ottawa, which has taken five for their permanent collection to be hung in the Prime Minister's Office, that of the Senate head, and of prominent caucus members.

Ireland explained that he called the paintings inscapes because they had an inner genesis, growing for him out of memory after-images of land and sea and leaf and blade, which had been denied him during his term in Moose Mountain Penitentiary.

"They are intended to celebrate the human interior," he said.

And indeed they do.

This is truly a unique show. Ireland may have created an entirely new school of painting.

Among those attending the *INSCAPE* showing were many of Ireland's former art students.

NADINE TOWNSLEY

He supposed Nadine Townsley, the *Daily Citizen* art critic, had no choice but to remind one and all of her readers of his art crime past. He'd probably have to live with the likelihood that the same biographical information about him would keep hitting the press for some time to come, whenever he had an art show. Were there ever going to be a lot of them now that with Irene and Darryl's help he had broken the five-year block.

It had been quite decent of Nadine to omit mention of the Hutterite involvement in the show. He had expected Peter the goose boss and the preacher, but he had been as surprised as anybody there when at least a dozen showed up in the gallery: the horse boss, the cattle boss, the wheat, oats, and barley boss, the well witcher boss, and of course the preacher and Peter the goose boss. All were in colony garb of clerical black and were bearded since it was a mortal sin to touch the skin with razor steel. They had given permission to their wives, in bonnets and polka-dotted pinafores, to come too, possibly for practical reasons, for it doubled the number of burlap sacks and cartons they could carry into Queen's Gallery with them.

The show was well under way with the gallery crowded when they made their entrance; their timing couldn't have been better. All eyes turned from the paintings to follow the Hutterites as Peter the goose boss led the congregation to the archway dividing the gallery. There they lowered sacks and cartons, then one after the other lifted nude geese and turkeys out by the neck.

Jim Osler made it over to them on the double. "What the hell's going on here?"

"Thanksgiving," the goose boss said. "In three days it will happen."

"For those gathered here," the preacher said, "we bring these geese and turkeys for their table."

"Five dollars the turkey," the oats and barley boss said. "Four dollars the goose."

"This is an art show! Not a goddam poultry market! Jesus Christ!"

"Bless His holy name," said the bone-setter.

"Amen," chorused the others.

"Peter." Art had joined them.

"Ireland," the goose boss said. "We have come as you wished us to do it."

"You invited them!" Osler said.

"Yes. But, Peter, you never said anything about bringing in a load of –"

"That thought came later to us and we wished to –"

"Take your bloody geese and –"

"Wait a minute, Jim. These people are my friends and neighbors."

"Well they aren't mine. They'll have to leave."

"No, Jim. They're staying."

"It's my gallery."

"It's my show and they're my invited guests."

"Look. I went along with your terms for the show, but you never said anything about a goose and turkey sale."

"I didn't expect them to bring in –"

"Okay, Ireland." Osler sighed defeat. He turned away, then back again. "But I'm telling you this: first one of those women strips naked in here, they're out!"

"You've got the wrong religious sect, Jim. They're Hutterites. Not Doukhobors."

But Osler was already off greeting customers coming into the gallery.

The poultry was going well as other Osler clients lined up in front of the bosses.

"Give me a goose," one tanned woman said to the well witcher boss. He obliged her.

"Do you take cheques or credit cards?" another said to the preacher.

"Cash just," the preacher said.

"I'd like a goose and a turkey ..."

"Have you got any chickens ...?"

Three days before Thanksgiving. They had timed it right. It was a sell-out.

Osler had cooled down by the time the show opening closed. He even staked him and Charlie to a fine supper.

"I think we've got a winner, Art. In spite of these goddam geese and turkeys."

"Did you charge them your usual commission, Jim?"

"I sure would have if you'd suggested that to me earlier, Charlie."

"I'll do that the next time."

"Thanks a lot."

As they drove out to the ranch Art said, "I guess when it comes to art shows that was an unpredictable first."

"Oh, I don't know," Charlie said. "Probably a Hutterite first."

"And a goose and turkey –"

"Yeah, but don't knock it, Art. You've just had a show to be long remembered. Along with one of mine when an old fellow got down on his knees and leaned under a twelve-foot abstract that collapsed on top of him."

"No!"

"Godwin Gallery in Toronto, year before I moved west. Paramedics freed him and he came to again on their way to the Wellesley Emergency. Slight concussion and a minor shoulder injury." He laughed.

"What's so –?"

"After I welded it back together, it sold. Stands still at the entrance to the Lister Luxford Building on the corner of Gervais and Carpenter Avenue." He laughed again.

"Concussions aren't all that funny, Charlie."

"His name was Lister Luxford, Art."

It was Art's turn to laugh.

"The one that beats them all, though, was the New York Museum show."

"I didn't know you had a show at –"

"Not yet. This was a classical sculpture show from the Vatican. Before it opened a vandal knocked off all the statue pricks. Castration catastrophe. The woman curator had to make an emergency return flight to Rome and get casts made in time for the opening. Damn near didn't make it, because they opened her luggage at Kennedy Airport and held her till they established why she had them in her luggage, and whether or not there was a cross-border penis embargo."

Both of them were laughing now.

When Charlie had managed to regain control he said, "I think they had a difficult title decision to make: whether to call it a show of work from the classical or from the restoration period."

All of them spoken for before the coast-to-coast tour was even started! How about that! And then another surprise. He'd been with Professor working in his studio when a whole delegation of Hutterite neighbors showed up: the same ones as for the art show opening. Along with Peter the goose boss and the bone-setter, there had been the cattle boss, the horse boss, the wheat, oats, and barley boss, the preacher, and the well witching boss.

They had a problem: for the past two decades the childbirth crop had been high and now their acreage was overcrowded. It was an election year and the provincial government had put a hold on the creation of any new colonies for the next five.

This would not apply to expanding the acreage of already existing colonies, they explained. All the years they'd been neighbors it was evident to them that Art and his brothers were not farmers. He held eighty acres they had fenced and summer fallowed and sown and thrashed for him, using hay crop for *their* horses and cattle. Would he be willing to sell them part of the land so that the hook-and-eye colony could solve their problem?

They had approached Ottowell for his half section first. He had turned them down.

Art had checked it out with Irene first. She had agreed, but not the forty acres he had suggested: fifty. She had also made the suggestion that he seriously consider joining the hook-and-eye Hutterian Brotherhood.

"Ticket – ah – roo. Ticket – ah – roo." After slapping their way out of the loft, the pigeon choir had settled on the barn ridge to hiccup and croon and mourn. Time to lie back against the hay drifts and savor sage and sweetgrass once more.

How he had missed these let-it-happen sessions while he was in Moose Mountain, and now he would miss Darryl, never to be up here with them again. Win, too, until he'd finished his term. But now they had Katie.

Tonight he would tell them about his deal with the hook-and-eye colony, and how he had already made arrangements with the Wild Horse community council for the subdivision of the acreage.

"For now we are three again since Katie has joined us. In time we will be four as we once were before we launched a certain art enterprise, to Charlie's justified dismay.

"I want to tell you tonight my plan for the future. Money paid by the Hutterites for fifty acres comes to roughly $40,000. As well I have almost as much more from the sale of the entire collection in my show tour. I intend that the $80,000 will be spent to create a summer art center with single dormitory and studio accommodation available to one and all. Amateurs excepted.

"Katie, you've said to me that thieving means do not justify the finest ends. Does this meet with your approval?"

"It sure as hell does!"

"Me too!" Charlie said. "This time."

"I think once we get it started – maybe before – there will be provincial funding granted to us."

"Yeah," Charlie said. "Livingstone Faculty of Fine Arts and The Banff Centre – tighten up your budgets!"

"One other thing. Our arts center is to be called the Duckworth Summer Art Haven."

Daily Citizen, November 30
Newsy Note From Academe

William McLeod, secretary to Livingstone University's Board of Governors, has told the Daily Citizen that they wish Arthur Ireland, artist and teacher, well with his Duckworth Summer Art Haven.

However, he said with deep regret that Ireland, recently released from Moose Mountain Penitentiary, will not be reinstated in the Faculty of Fine Arts to carry on university teaching duties.

"He is well past retirement age," McLeod said.

Good night for now, Irene and Darryl.

BACK TALK: A Book for Bad Back Sufferers and Those Who Put Up With Them *by* Eric Nicol *illustrated by* Graham Pilsworth
At last, a funny book about bad backs, the prestige disease of the Nineties. Follow a layman (sitting or standing is hard) through denial, diagnosis, and The Hospital Experience and laugh your way to verticality.
Humour, 5½ × 8½, 136 pages, illustrations, trade paperback

FRIEND OF MY YOUTH *by* Alice Munro
"I want to list every story in this collection as my favourite ... Ms. Munro is a writer of extraordinary richness and texture." Bharati Mukherjee, *The New York Times*
Fiction, 6 × 9, 288 pages, hardcover

THE PRIVATE VOICE: A Journal of Reflections *by* Peter Gzowski
"A fascinating book that is cheerfully anecdotal, painfully honest, agonizingly self-doubting and compulsively readable." *Toronto Sun*
Autobiography, 5½ × 8½, 320 pages, photos, trade paperback

AT THE COTTAGE: A Fearless Look at Canada's Summer Obsession *by* Charles Gordon
"A delightful reminder of why none of us addicted to cottage life will ever give it up." *Hamilton Spectator* *Humour, 5⅜ × 8¾, 224 pages, illustrations, trade paperback*

THE ASTOUNDING LONG-LOST LETTERS OF DICKENS OF THE MOUNTED *edited by* Eric Nicol
These "letters" from Charles Dickens's son, a Mountie from 1874 to 1886, are "a glorious hoax ... so cleverly crafted, so subtly hilarious." *Vancouver Sun*
Fiction, 4¼ × 7, 296 pages, paperback

INNOCENT CITIES: A novel *by* Jack Hodgins
Victorian in time and place, this delightful new novel by the author of *The Invention of the World* proves once again that "as a writer, Hodgins is unique among his Canadian contemporaries." *Globe and Mail* *Fiction, 4¼ × 7, 416 pages, paperback*

WELCOME TO FLANDERS FIELDS: The First Canadian Battle of the Great War – Ypres, 1915 *by* Daniel G. Dancocks
"A magnificent chronicle of a terrible battle ... Daniel Dancocks is spellbinding throughout." *Globe and Mail*
Military/History, 4¼ × 7, 304 pages, photos, maps, paperback

THE RADIANT WAY *by* Margaret Drabble
"*The Radiant Way* does for Thatcher's England what *Middlemarch* did for Victorian England ... Essential reading!" *Margaret Atwood*
Fiction, 6 × 9, 400 pages, hardcover

THE HONORARY PATRON *by* Jack Hodgins

The Governor General's Award-winner's thoughtful and satisfying third novel mixes comedy and wisdom "and it's magic." *Ottawa Citizen*

Fiction, 4¼ × 7, 336 pages, paperback

NEXT-YEAR COUNTRY: Voices of Prairie People *by* Barry Broadfoot

"There's something mesmerizing about these authentic Canadian voices ... a three-generation rural history of the prairie provinces, with a brief glimpse of the bleak future." *Globe and Mail* *Oral history, 5⅜ × 8¾, 400 pages, trade paperback*

DANCING ON THE SHORE: A Celebration of Life at Annapolis Basin *by* Harold Horwood, *Foreword by* Farley Mowat

"A Canadian *Walden*" (*Windsor Star*) that "will reward, provoke, challenge and enchant its readers." (*Books in Canada*)

Nature/Ecology, 5⅛ × 8¼, 224 pages, 16 wood engravings, trade paperback

THE PROGRESS OF LOVE *by* Alice Munro

"Probably the best collection of stories – the most confident and, at the same time, the most adventurous – ever written by a Canadian." *Saturday Night*

Fiction, 6 × 9, 320 pages, hardcover

PADDLE TO THE AMAZON: The Ultimate 12,000-Mile Canoe Adventure *by* Don Starkell *edited by* Charles Wilkins

"This real-life adventure book ... must be ranked among the classics of the literature of survival." *Montreal Gazette*

Adventure, 4¼ × 7, 320 pages, maps, photos, paperback

UNDERCOVER AGENT: How One Honest Man Took On the Drug Mob ... And Then the Mounties *by* Leonard Mitchell and Peter Rehak

"It's the stuff of spy novels – only for real ... how a family man in a tiny fishing community helped make what at the time was North America's biggest drug bust." Saint John *Telegraph-Journal* *Non-fiction/Criminology, 4¼ × 7, 176 pages, paperback*

ALL IN THE SAME BOAT: Family Cruising Around the Atlantic *by* Fiona McCall and Paul Howard

"A lovely adventure that is a modern-day Swiss Family Robinson story ... a winner." *Toronto Sun* *Travel/Adventure, 5¾ × 8¾, 256 pages, maps, trade paperback*